IF

MOON

HAD

WILLOW

T
R
E
E
S

Dear Kette
Thank you so much
for stopping by today—
So appreciate you
And your kind words,
Kathleen

KATHLEEN HALL

Published by Collaborative Options, LLC, Austin, Texas. Inquiries should be emailed to info@collaborativeoptions.com

ISBN: eBook: 978-0990390435
ISBN: Paperback: 978-0990390428

Cover Design: Kenneth C. Benson, Pegasus Type
Interior/Print Design: Kenneth C. Benson, Pegasus Type
Typography: Electra, designed by William Addison Dwiggins in 1935, and Futura, designed by Paul Renner in 1927. Either typeface might have been used in this book had it been published in the sixties.

DEDICATED TO THE PEOPLE OF DETROIT

For their work and sacrifices to achieve civil rights then and now

Also by Kathleen Hall

NONFICTION

The Otherness Factor: Co-Creating and Sustaining Intentional Relationships

Oh yes, truth is stranger. That's why we wrap it in fiction.

Like holding a conch shell to our ear and listening to the sea.

Do you hear it?

Contents

1

The Riots

By noon, more than fifty sniper attacks had targeted police and firemen, making it impossible to fight the flames. Chants of 'burn baby burn' were heard as buildings along Grand River Avenue, Linwood and Twelfth Street raged out of control. Operating under orders of restraint, Michigan's State Troopers and National Guard could not subdue the rioting. President Johnson authorized the deployment of the 82nd and 101st Airborne Divisions to restore order. At 2:30 p.m. today, 4700 Regular Army will arrive at Selfridge Air Force Base; 1800 will muster at the State Fair Grounds.

—Teletype Tuesday, July 25, 1967 1:00 p.m.

JULY 1967—Who knew a race riot would rival the Super Bowl for pizza deliveries? Angelo Ciccarelli had owned and operated Angelo's Restaurant & Pizzeria in Detroit for more than twenty years and had never seen anything like it. To his staff he said, "Go figure. People binging on pizza like there's no fucking tomorrow." To his customers he said, "A bunch of know-nothing baby thugs aren't going to shut down this Dago." In private, Angelo danced the

Watusi through the kitchen, faked Alley Oop passes with the pepperoni and prayed the riot would last until football season.

Marguerite Soulier, Maggie to her friends, had worked part-time for Angelo almost five years, earning enough scratch to get through her undergrad and first year of an MA at Wayne State. Covering absences, Maggie waited tables, delivered pizza, cooked, cleaned and washed dishes. She thought people were so freaked out by the riots that the simple act of *ordering pizza* was a way to escape the madness and mayhem. Her killer tips seemed like acts of contrition to avoid the heavy hand of god, juju sticks to keep death and destruction away from the few square blocks of their neighborhood.

Exhausted, Maggie planned to hang loose on her day off—read, write and cop some zees. But that wasn't going to happen. On the radio that morning the disc jockey said police had nothing to drink because all city water had been diverted to fight fires. With Detroit on the brink of civil war, Maggie decided she couldn't take a nap knowing cops with guns were tired, hot and thirsty. She slipped on a pair of cutoffs, a white eyelet sleeveless blouse and her white beaded moccasins from Mackinaw Island.

Her wheels were parked in the backyard behind a cyclone fence at her Aunt Jo's house. When Maggie started college, Aunt Jo rented her a dormer bedroom in the converted attic of her bungalow a few blocks from Angelo's. The car was a college graduation gift from her umpteen French-Canadian relatives who started a fund in the 1940's to boost their tribe's interest in higher education. Maggie, her sister Isabel and their cousins had years to plan and pick the perfect car. For Maggie, there was no contest. It was love at first sight. Although she openly harangued her adopted countrymen for conspicuous consumption, Maggie decided a red Triumph convertible, the TR4, would be the one deliberate, ostentatious, materialistic and pretentious possession she'd own.

In addition to Maggie's car, the backyard hosted a rusted swing-less swing set, two overgrown crabapple trees, a cracked concrete pad for the garage-that-never-was and an untamed crop of rhubarb. Up close it was a mess. From a distance, the crabapples filled the yard with pink in the spring, promised shade in the summer and architectural interest in the winter. On the ground, fermenting apples seemed to stunt the germination of most grasses and weeds, but not rhubarb. During the third weekend each May, neighbor-hood rhubarb lovers showed up in rubber boots for the annual har-vest then returned pints and quarts of canned rhubarb to Aunt Jo's pantry. Aunt Jo called it the perfect economic model.

Top down, Maggie drove to the nearest Kroger store. Stock was low but she snagged four cases of Coke and four cheap church keys. A security guard, whose uniform still held the folds from its original package, offered to help load the pop in the cubby-sized back seat.

"Party?" he asked.

"No party. I'm delivering this to the police station. They're out of water."

"Be careful," he warned. "It's a bad scene out there, snipers all over. Wouldn't want a pretty little girl like you gettin' shot at." He jiggled a large set of keys attached to his belt. Maggie noticed a wedding band.

"No sweat. Once I drop this off, I'll be heading home. I'm cool."

"I'd say you're hot" he laughed, licked his lips and started to rub his crotch. Maggie ignored him, gunned her engine and thought *dickhead*.

The streets were as quiet as a Super Bowl Sunday, intermittent cars and bikes, a few random pedestrians. Anyone who could find a way out of Detroit had.

For the rank and file, this wasn't an option. Maggie had one more year at Wayne State to finish her MA. She was a working stiff who lived from paycheck to paycheck.

The heat would have been oppressive on its own, but with the heat from the fires, it was an inferno. Hell had erupted on the north side of the Detroit River. On the south side, Canadians picnicked along a grassy shore and watched dark smoke dominate the horizon, turning Detroit's skyline from Kodachrome to black and white. The wailing sirens and erratic gunfire reminded Maggie of World War II films she'd seen in grade school. It was surreal. *Music*, she thought, and flipped on the radio to Simon and Garfunkel singing The Sound of Silence. Maggie sang along, "Hello darkness my old friend." She didn't miss the irony.

Like an apparition rising up through the haze, Maggie saw a cop standing in front of the Fort and Green Street police station. As she pulled into the parking lot, the young cop raised his gun and pointed it at her car. He looked about sixteen with a crew cut and pants two inches too short, like he'd just gone through a growth spurt.

"Whoa girlie. Where do you think you're going?" His voice was deeper and more commanding than she expected.

"On the radio they said you were out of water and had nothing to drink, so I decided to drop off some pop."

Lowering his gun he bent down and squinted against the light. "You brought pop?"

"Yes, four cases of Coke."

"Unbelievable. You just made my day! I can't take four cases because I'm the only one on duty, but I'll take a can. The guys at the barricades along Fort Street, in the middle of nowhere, are frying on the pavement. Head downtown. You'll see them."

Maggie picked up a rubber band from the ashtray, pulled her hair in a ponytail and headed toward the turbulence downtown. In her rearview mirror, the boy cop was tipping up his can of Coke as debris skittered across the concrete.

Ahead was a scene from some post-apocalyptic movie. The highway was littered with wind-blown paper—banks, stores and gas stations abandoned. A lone man with a Detroit Tiger's cap was sitting on a bench at a deserted bus stop, his feet tapping and head shaking to some James Brown kind of beat. *Papa's Got A Brand New Bag?*

"Jesus, fucking Christ lady, what the hell are you doing here?" shouted the cop at the first barricade. His uniform was wrinkled and soaked with perspiration, his thinning hair plastered to his head. Maggie wondered if she'd ever seen anyone who looked so spent.

"Heard you were out of water and needed something to drink. I brought pop."

"Did you say pop?"

"Yes, four cases of Coke."

"Lady, you gotta be kidding me. Hey guys, we've got someone delivering Coke. Can you give us four cans?"

"I can leave four cases!"

"No, the guys at the next barricade need something to drink. Take the rest to them. They can get it to headquarters."

Maggie handed the weary cop four cans of Coke and said, "Stay safe."

He said, "lady, that's what I'm trying to do. I've got two kids and a wife. I have to stay safe."

This time, Maggie turned the radio off, fought back tears and didn't look in the rearview mirror.

Up the almost desolate road, Maggie saw an old two-tone pink and brown Edsel make a slow turn onto Fort Street. Curious, she sped up and saw a middle-aged white woman in a nurse's uniform with a starched white cap buoyed by ratted hair. The woman's left hand was on the steering wheel. In her right hand a small black revolver swept back and forth as if looking for a threat or a target. Maggie whispered, "holy crap," as she gunned the engine and put as much distance as she could between her and Annie Oakley.

Three miles closer to the next barricade, three miles closer to the fires, the air was heavier and Maggie felt the heat and acrid taste of smoke in her throat. Sirens no longer wailed, they shrieked. What was left of the blue sky had turned gunmetal gray, a grim artificial dusk. When Maggie stopped at the makeshift barricade, another disheveled guy in a uniform approached her with his gun drawn. He said, "turn off the car and don't move a single bone in your body. Got that?"

"Yes, sir."

"Now tell me why you're driving around in a red convertible in a war zone? Are you freaking crazy?"

"I'm delivering pop. The police at the last barricade asked me to bring you some Coke."

The cop's laughter sounded maniacal. He dropped the gun to his side and doubled over in laughter. Maggie couldn't help herself. She started to laugh. The sound of their shared laughter echoed in the smoky air, ricocheting against the shrieking sirens and darkening sky. Shaking, released from the tension of her absurd mission, Maggie wanted to hold onto this moment, turn it into a poem, an ode, a prayer.

When the laughter ended, the cop looked at Maggie and said, "Unreal. I'm not sure what I needed more, the Coke or a wicked laugh. Both. Both remind me I'm here, in my body. We'll take a few Cokes, but you need to head into town and drop the rest off at headquarters. They're getting nailed."

Maggie looked into another pair of tired eyes, the color of an ocean filled with phosphorescent light. His badge read Sam Tervo. "Why don't you take what's left of the open case and I'll bring the rest to headquarters. That way you'll have some extras if you need them."

"Deal," said Sam. "Do I by any chance know you from Wayne State?"

"Maybe. I'm finishing up an MA program. You?"

"MBA. I thought you looked familiar. I'll look for you in September. Buy you a Coke?"

"Deal," laughed Maggie. As Sam pulled the open case out of the car, Maggie saw the stretch of muscles in his neck and a sweet hollow under the open collar of his shirt.

"What's your name?" Sam asked.

"Maggie."

Tapping his badge, Sam grinned and said, "I'm Sam."

This time Maggie smiled when she looked in the rearview mirror and saw Sam smiling back. He was holding up a can of Coke, as if making a toast.

Before Maggie made her turn off Fort Street into the downtown area, two military transport vehicles filled with khaki-uniformed troops passed her. The boys sitting at the back of the truck looked at her with blank stares, confusion, fear, disbelief, she couldn't tell. But to her they were—boys, just boys—who had parked their ten-speed bikes in their parents' garage to put on a uniform and load a rifle. This was not Vietnam, not a jungle in some god-forsaken outpost. This was Motown, home to the Lions, Tigers, Red Wings and The Big Three. An American city under siege. A civil conflict with faceless, nameless enemies. Maggie imagined the sweltering heat in the canvas-topped truck. Hands sweating around the barrels of guns as these boys thought about Detroiters—about men, women and children who looked like their neighbors.

The area surrounding the downtown Police Headquarters, between Beaubien and Brush Streets, was dicey in the best of times.

Nearby, St. Andrew's Benevolent Society provided services to the indigent and unfortunate. Almost any time of day you'd find men on the steps drinking hooch from paper bags and entertaining one another by making lewd comments to women and girls of all ages, shapes and sizes. The game was all about getting a reaction, any reaction.

Ten years ago, Maggie spent a week of her summer vacation with Aunt Jo who just started her career at J. L. Hudson's. With twenty-five floors, Hudson's was the tallest department store in the world. Maggie spent her days wandering up and down the elevators and escalators, trying on everything from bikinis to formals, and checking out her image in three-way mirrors. After work, Aunt Jo would meet her in one of Hudson's five restaurants for a snack and they'd talk about their day. Maggie hit pay dirt on the last day of her vacation when Aunt Jo finally gave into her pleas to check out the city on her own. After three hours of hard sidewalks and no shade, Maggie headed away from Woodward Avenue. With temperatures topping ninety degrees, Maggie was relieved to find a street named Beaubien, where she thought she'd find shade and a park bench to finish reading *The Ugly American*. As Maggie passed St. Andrews, one of the porch-sitters yelled, "Look at them sweet little titties!" Unsure of herself, Maggie flipped him the bird. She could still feel the humiliating blush of that moment, smell the urine soaked ground and hear the cackle of laughter.

Beaubien Street, with its unfortunates, had always been a strange place, but it never looked like this. Armored cars barricaded the far end of the block. A cop with a sawhorse stood guard at the entrance. The weathered three-story building across the street looked like a scene from a B-grade movie. Four rifles sticking out of every window, on every floor, two soldiers kneeling and two standing. Maggie's heart seemed to be pumping fire and then, to her surprise, fear as she pulled up to the cop beside the sawhorse.

Older than the others, he looked at her like a parking attendant ready to guide her to the next open space. Maggie thought he seemed unhinged, unfocused. Who wouldn't with sixty-four rifles aimed at you all day? Maggie wanted to say *what the fuck are you doing here?* She waited.

The cop said, "Look, lady, I've no patience left. I can't trust myself to be civil. So, why the hell-fire-fuck are you driving around Detroit in a red convertible? Hoping to squeeze in a short tour of the local riots before the nine o'clock curfew? Jesus!"

"No, sir," said Maggie with more force than she intended, "I've been to one police station and two barricades trying to deliver four cases of pop. I heard you were thirsty. Everyone took a few cans and asked me to deliver some to the next police barricade, then the next. I have three cases of Coke left. They're for headquarters. I hope this is my last stop."

"You crazy beautiful woman, you could've been shot. Coke? Really? Coke?" Looking across the street at the rifles pointed their way, he yelled, "She's got three cases of Coke!"

The cop unloaded the cases then looked at Maggie with gratitude if not respect. He said, "I guess good Samaritans come in all shapes, sizes and sports cars. I promise I'll never jump to conclusions about a pretty woman in a red convertible again. Ya done good. Now, get the hell outta here."

Just then, a group of ten Negroes approached them with their hands up, arms stretched high. Behind the prisoners, five cops pointed shotguns at their backs. The rifles in the windows turned in unison to follow them. No one spoke. Maggie watched as the group entered Headquarters through a side door reinforced by prison bars. When the door slammed shut, Maggie felt the cold click of steel slide down her back.

2

Who's on First?

The largest riot in the nation's history is over. The 82nd U.S. Airborne musters out of Detroit. Curfews are eased. Thousands of sightseers are bumper to bumper in the riot areas. Dead: 43, Injured: 1200, Arrested: 7231, Stores looted or burned: 2509, Families rendered homeless: 388, Damage to property: $40–100 million.

—Teletype, Sunday, July 30, 1967

JULY 1967—Sitting at the downstairs kitchen table, Maggie stretched her legs across the adhesive-backed linoleum tiles she and Aunt Jo had pieced together. The tile mocked wood with its highly exaggerated deep and uniform engraved lines—a magnet for breadcrumbs, dust motes and who knew what else. Checking her legs for black stubble, Maggie could feel the yellow wicker chair leaving a crisscross pattern on her *thunder thighs*, a family trait with mixed blessings. And, as much as she loved her thick black hair, she despised the coarse shadow it left on shaved legs. In the winter she could hide the stubble under knee socks. In the summer she was SOL. Maggie sympathized with her heavily bearded male friends. What a drag! Every three days she wore jeans to avoid having to shave. This would be a jean day.

When the rioting started, Aunt Jo bolted to visit her family in Windsor. Maggie enjoyed the time alone, but looked forward to having her back. The house and decor was *very* Aunt Jo — filled with stones, shells and driftwood from The Great Lakes, table cloths from India, faded chenille bed spreads, spindly house plants frantic for sunlight, photo collages and macramé hangings. Aunt Jo brought new meaning to the word eclectic.

Maggie was seldom alone at the house, and for the first time in almost five years she felt like an intruder. This time, Aunt Jo's possessions seemed more intimate while she was away. Maggie wondered if it was time to see a shrink or just finish her graduate program. Once Maggie graduated and got a real job, she'd give up the dormer at thirty dollars per month and find a place of her own. As much as Aunt Jo loved her and seemed to enjoy her activism, Maggie thought she'd welcome a return to solitude.

The riots were over, but Detroit was in ruins and nothing had been resolved. Maggie's sadness was taking up far too much time and space. One recurring bright spot was the cop with platinum blond hair and laser blue eyes who said he'd buy her a Coke this fall. Sam. There was something about him that made her smile. *Crap*, she thought, *I'm feeling keyed up about someone I barely met and may never see again. Am I that desperate?*

Maggie was pulled out of her reverie by the phone. "Hello!"

"Hey, Maggie. You okay?" It was her sister Isabel from Westland.

"If you're asking if I'm being held hostage by a bunch of rioting, militant blacks with big-ass fros, the answer is no. In fact, I'm sitting here checking my legs for stubble and feeling sorry for myself because I'm alone. Boohoo, as if I have any real problems. What's going on in Wasteland these days?"

"Well, thanks for calling to let me know you were okay. I was so freaked out. I tried a dozen times last week, but couldn't get an answer at Aunt Jo's. Finally called Angelo and he said you were 'busy changing the world.' Christ Maggie. Lots of fear mongering and survivor guilt in the burbs. The mayor wants us to keep our kids indoors because, and I quote, 'the niggers from the city are threatening to kidnap our babies.' I could hardly believe my ears. I told Eddie this was our chance to get rid of those pesky little ankle biters!"

Maggie had long thought that anyone who met Issie learned first-hand what the word "irreverence" meant. "Issie! I know you're kidding, but if anyone heard you say that you'd end up in the cooler." Unable to curb her laughter, Maggie realized her attempted rebuke sounded more like applause.

"So seriously, what's it like in Detroit?" asked Issie, "I'm not about to join the gawkers but I want to know how you are. I've been worried."

"Crazy times. My only effort to change the world was to make sure the cops had something to drink. I didn't want them shooting innocent people because their brains were fried. So, on Tuesday I picked up four cases of pop and delivered them to police stations and barricades between here and downtown. I thought I was fine until I entered the war zone. No shit, Issie, there were trucks filled with little boy soldiers and guns. On the way, flimsy wood barricades were set up to stop traffic. No water. No food. Everything was closed down, like some bubonic plague wiped out a million people. Downtown was so dark from smoke it looked like night. Guns were sticking out of windows everywhere. Then, I saw a group of Negro men with their arms stretched to the sky. My heart split open and my arms and legs felt like rubber. I'm not sure how I made it home. I don't remember driving."

"Oh no you don't, get back here! Sorry Mag, got to go. The boys just ran outside naked. I'll call later.

"Well, if it isn't Florence Nightingale!" Clyde called out as he was feeding another pizza into the oven. With his white jacket, dark chocolate skin, hazel eyes and a tight, manicured fro, Clyde looked like he just stepped off a Broadway stage. Tall, thin, muscular, he moved like a dancer.

"Well, if it isn't the disappearing cook! Where the hell have you been? And, what's with the Florence Nightingale thing?"

"I'm talking about the special delivery of Coke to police head-quarters. What was that about?"

"Holy crap! How did you find out?"

"Huh. You didn't recognize me in the dusk, hands up, on my way to hell?"

"In the round up? Why didn't you call out, say something?"

"Say something? Like 'Yoohoo, Maggie dear, could you please tell these nice police officers I'm one of the good guys?' They said if we moved a hair they'd blow our fucking heads off. No way in hell was I going to call out to a white girl in a red sports car. I may be stupid, but this boy's mama didn't raise no fool."

"Oh god Clyde, sorry. I was scared half to death. I can't imagine what it was like for you. What happened?"

"Some of my friends from the hood and I decided to check on the older neighbors, see if they needed help. The National Guard rent-a-cops thought we were looting, loaded us into a wagon and took us to headquarters. We were locked in a holding cell, standing room only. No water. They gave us some broth and crackers the next day. No way I wanted Blanche driving into the mouth of hell to spring me. She called Angelo this morning and he bailed me out. I was lucky. Some of those guys are still in the slammer."

Maggie paused to look him in the eyes and said, "Clyde, you have no idea how glad I am that you're okay. You know how I hate feeding the pizza oven."

"What crap, Soulier, I feel the love." Clyde laughed, "You're my first, my last and only white woman. No one could ever replace you."

"Right. Well, if you ever decide to dump that gorgeous wife and your three adorable sons, let me know. I was worried about you, Clyde Daniel Webster."

"Now don't be gettin' all sentimental with me. I've got work to do."

"Church tonight?" asked Maggie.

"Yep. It's gonna rock!"

Maggie decided to walk to church. It was only a few blocks and she'd spend that much time unlocking and locking the gate to pull her car out of the backyard. Rather than change clothes after work, Maggie kept the jeans and replaced the stained blue tee shirt with a white cotton gauze top trimmed in orange and turquoise rickrack, her gypsy blouse. The air was calm and the smell of smoke hung like dirty laundry against the cloudless sky.

Hope Chapel, a nondenominational Christian church, occupied a small one-story yellow brick building along Fort Street. An abandoned Sunoco gas station to its north provided parking. The Chapel's basement had long served as the neighborhood community center. Alcoholics Anonymous, Head Start and a number of small local nonprofits, without bricks and mortar, used the building and donated what they could afford. Detroit's Freedom Riders were scheduled to meet at 7:00 p.m. on the second Sunday of every month. This meeting, the fifth Sunday, had been added to talk about the riots.

The basement was filled with excited chatter and nervous laughter. The ashtrays were already overflowing and the click of Zippo lighters and the snap of matches sounded like percussion.

Maggie thought *a social scientist would have a field day with this kinetic energy.*

In a large room, fifty gray metal folding chairs faced two portable banquet-sized tables. Four beat-up mahogany banker's chairs, left by the building's previous owner, were reserved for the speakers. A low-ceilinged furnace room provided a reception area, with an old kitchen table for coffee, cookies and name badges. Its recently painted tan concrete block walls supported a new bulletin board that held notices for upcoming meetings, a few job postings and dozens of offers for lawn mowing, cleaning and babysitting. In the center of the bulletin board a color photograph of Dr. Martin Luther King, Jr., from his 1963 March for Freedom in Detroit, was carefully framed with purple grosgrain ribbon and silver tacks. A small, dismal bathroom under the stairway boasted a toilet with no lid and a commercial size sink for heavy mopping. Keeping up with the demand for toilet paper was impossible and regulars knew to bring their own tissue. Upstairs the small Chapel, with its mismatched old pews and benches, was off limits for meetings but open for local performances of all kinds.

"Hey Maggie," yelled Clyde. "Come here! I've got someone you need to meet."

"Sam, I'd like you to meet Marguerite Soulier, better known as Maggie. Maggie, this is Sam Tervo."

Sam was dressed in faded Levi's with a braided brown leather belt, a white button-down shirt, and brown loafers with no socks. *Tan for such a toe-head,* Maggie thought. His phosphorescent eyes looked as though they were on fire. Maggie could not find her voice. Neither of them extended a hand or said hello. Clyde was stunned. He'd never seen Maggie behave rudely and Sam seemed pinned to the floor. "Is everything okay?" asked Clyde.

Maggie finally said, "Clyde we need to talk." She grabbed his elbow and pulled him toward an empty corner in the meeting room.

"Maggie, what the hell?"

"How do you know him? He's a cop!"

"What are you talking about? He's not a cop."

"Oh Christ, I bet that's why you got picked up for looting. He works the other side."

"Maggie, believe me, he's not a cop. I've known Sam for years. We go way back. What's this about?"

"I don't know what you think you know or don't know, but he was at a police barricade the day I delivered Coke to Police Head-quarters. He aimed a gun at me. He's a fucking cop!"

"Oh my god, Maggie. He joined the National Guard to avoid the draft and help pay for his MBA. I don't know why he was at a police barricade, but I can guarantee he's one of us. He's tireless in his work for civil rights—totally, scarily, unafraid to take on any-thing or anyone. That's why I thought you'd like him." With that, Clyde took a deep breath and straightened his shoulders. "Whew. You had me going for a minute there!"

"Sorry, I was certain he was a cop. Talk about whew. I'm relieved!"

When they returned to the reception area, Clyde headed for the coffee and Maggie looked around the room. No Sam. "Shit, damn, hell," she said to herself, "I screwed that up." Someone tapped a teacher's desk bell to begin the meeting and Maggie found a seat in the center of the room next to a chain smoker with a red plaid beanbag ashtray balanced on her knee.

Clyde began the meeting with a short prayer. "Please God, lighten our load and help us see the brother and sister in everyone. We ask that you bless the work of Dr. King and help us remember the path to love is through peace. And, we ask you to bless the hearts of black militants so they might find peace in their hearts and join us in our work for equality. Amen." Prayers at these meetings were punctuated by affirmations like *Yes Lord, Praise God, That's Right.* Clyde once said the power and community of this ritual was manna for the Civil Rights Movement.

Blanche, Clyde's wife, stood up and began singing "We Shall Overcome," the Freedom Rider's anthem. Maggie thought Blanche's voice, always haunting, was more beautiful than ever, as if she were channeling Mahalia Jackson. The hush in the room felt sacred. Visions of burning buildings and riots—the chaos—reduced to a shadow. After the crowd stood and sang the last verse, Maggie thought about Sam's comment to her last Tuesday, "I'm here, in my body." Someone in the row behind Maggie touched her elbow. She turned. It was Sam, in his body.

Maggie missed most of the meeting because she was surfing the idea of Sam. She imagined she could feel his energy, his heat. *Okay*, Maggie thought, she was *very* desperate, but her imagination had not had this much fun in months! She couldn't remember the last time she'd thought about her libido, much less felt it. The noise and cigarette smoke dropped away. All that remained was her, Sam and the energy between them. It seemed like enough.

3

Let the Games Begin

Injustice anywhere is a threat to justice everywhere. We are caught in an inescapable network of mutuality, tied in a single garment of destiny. Whatever affects one directly, affects all indirectly.

—Dr. Martin Luther King, Jr.

JULY 1967 — "Maggie," Sam said as he tapped her on the shoulder. "I think Clyde's trying to get your attention."

Maggie looked up to see Clyde pointing at her. She raised her hand in acknowledgement and Clyde said, "We're looking for volunteers to help victims of the riot who need temporary shelter, income, food or help filing claims for services. Any chance you could act as the go-between the city and this group?"

Damn, thought Maggie. Clyde knew her history of avoiding any and all work with government bureaucracies, but he also knew she was a soft touch. Maggie stood up and said, "Clyde, if you can find someone to share this responsibility, I'd be happy to help. I work nights and my last year of school starts in a few weeks, so it's crunch time."

Before Clyde could ask the question, Sam stood up and said, "Clyde, I'm in the same situation with school and work. Why don't Maggie and I join forces, and between the two of us, we can make it happen."

Maggie saw Clyde squint, as if he was having a hard time understanding what Sam said. After an uneasy, chair-scraping, throat-clearing pause, Clyde said, "Great Sam, thanks."

Clyde looked at Maggie and his expression conveyed, *what the hell's going on here?* But said, "Maggie, does this work for you?"

Maggie looked at Sam, then turned back to Clyde and said, "Sure. Sounds like a plan." Always certain of herself, Maggie felt her knees weaken and her heart race. *Holy crap*, she thought, *get a grip. He's just a guy.*

When the meeting was adjourned, the chain smoker next to Maggie introduced herself as Jean and offered to help. Maggie was anxious to catch Sam before he left, but said, "Sure, give me your name and number and I'll call if we need help." Pulling long drags off her cigarette and balancing the ashtray on her knee, Jean began digging in her purse with her free hand for a piece of paper and a pen. "Look," Maggie said, "why don't you leave your name and number with Clyde and I'll get it from him."

"No, give me a minute, I know I've got a pen in here somewhere." It had only been a few minutes, but Maggie felt like it was taking forever. Finally, Jean handed her a scrap of paper. Maggie smiled, thanked her and walked as fast as she dared toward the reception area. Before she reached it, Clyde stopped her to thank her for taking on the assignment then said, "What's with Sam offering to help? Did you two make nice with each other?"

"Clyde, I need to run, but yes we made nice. He seems like a good guy. Sorry for the melt down."

"No problem. If it hadn't been a week since I'd been home, I'd have you over for a wrap up."

"Thanks Clyde, but I really do have to run." Maggie headed to the reception area, which was now empty. *Damn* she thought.

On the sidewalk only a few people lingered because a curfew was still in effect. It was risky to drive after dark. Maggie began her walk home. Two blocks from Aunt Jo's, a 1962 white Chevy Corvair pulled up and stopped next to Maggie. Sam shouted, "Hey Maggie, need a lift?"

Maggie walked up to the car, leaned in and said, "Thanks, but I'm only two blocks away from my pad."

"Then why don't I buy you that Coke I promised?" His smile was contagious. Maggie could not have contained her smile if she'd tried. Her heart and mind were in a reckless duet.

"Sam, there's a curfew to consider." Smiling, Maggie realized she'd made her statement sound more like a question.

"I've considered that but I'd really like to talk and exchange phone numbers. Hop in. I promise I have no ulterior motives."

Before Maggie opened the door and slipped in, she tucked her lips between her teeth to rein in the impulse to say, *well if that's the case then forget about it!* Signs of life included a small roach clip in the ashtray and a map of Detroit folded under the passenger's sun visor. The inside looked as if it had collected more than its share of ash and dust from the fires. But, it was Sam's aftershave that claimed Maggie's attention. *Old Spice.* She remembered telling Issie that *Old Spice* made her swoon, turned her into Hedy Lamarr on a raw silk chaise.

As Sam pulled up to Aunt Jo's house, Maggie's first thought was, *this house never looked smaller or tackier.* Her second thought, *what the hell am I trying to prove?*

"Nice," said Sam, "great neighborhood, big lawn, lots of shade! Wait'll you see my crib, it's a dump but the price is right. Are we okay sitting out front? Anyone waiting for you?"

"We're good. My Aunt Jo is my landlady. I live in the attic and she throws me a few scraps of food every now and then." Maggie was cheered by Sam's laugh. She thought *wicked looking and he's got a sense of humor.* "Seriously, Aunt Jo went to Windsor when the riots started and I'm not sure when she's heading back. She might be home now."

"Wouldn't she park up front?"

"Nope, doesn't drive. She takes the bus or asks friends or relatives to give her a lift. That would be *me* most of the time. I'd invite you in if there wasn't a curfew."

"Do you offer rain checks?"

"At a premium."

"I wouldn't expect less." Sam thought, *sweet Jesus, I've met my match!*

Both were quiet. Sam cleared his throat and Maggie reached to open the car door. "No, don't," said Sam. "Could we just sit here and talk for a few more minutes?"

Maggie looked at Sam and realized she was far more interested in kissing him than talking. In spite of her feminist views on sexual prowess and power, she usually waited for the guy to make the first move. *Oh crap*, she thought, *so I get rejected. I've been rejected before.* "I know this is crazy, but I'd like to kiss you."

"I like crazy."

"Me too," said Maggie as she took Sam's face in her hands, tumbled down those fire-eyes and gently kissed his lips. When she started to pull away, Sam put his hands on her shoulders and kissed her with such excruciating tenderness she felt tears form in the corners of her eyes.

"Maggie Soulier, I want to get to know you better. I'd camp out in your front yard if I could, but I don't want to scare you off. How about a date?"

"I've never dated a cop, but I might be tempted."

"Ah, the draw of a uniform. I get it. Handcuffs, that whole thing?"

Although not visible, Maggie felt the blush under her olive skin. "Nah, more the appeal of investigation, discovery," she countered, a quick but awkward recovery.

"Better yet! So there's no misunderstanding, and in the interest of full disclosure, I'm not a cop. I have no handcuffs. I'm a reservist in the National Guard, but that doesn't make me a soldier. I'm on the dole to help pay for my education. To quiet any residual guilt, I've made a pact with myself to make enough after I graduate so taxes on my higher income will more than cover any ill-gotten gain."

"Smart move, Tervo. And, in the spirit of full disclosure, I'm a Canadian and I'm not sure I want to live and work in a country that enslaved Negroes and continues to oppress non-whites. There's so much to love about America, but the bigotry, greed and corruption is totally fucked up."

"You're singing from my hymn book, Maggie, but this is my home and I'm committed to civil rights."

"Hmm," said Maggie as she started to open her door. Sam jumped out of his side of the car and met her at the sidewalk. Without further words, they walked to the front of the house.

Maggie moved a weathered St. Francis statue on the porch with her foot, picked up the hidden key and unlocked the door. As she turned to say good night, Sam embraced her. She felt the whole length of his body against hers, about six feet of him to her five feet six inches. The hollow below the open button of his shirt was exposed and Maggie kissed him there, then kissed his muscled neck. The smell and texture of his skin felt familiar, as if she'd done this before.

Sam's arms were wrapped around Maggie's waist. He felt the rise at the small of her back and his thumb moved to stroke the skin under her waistband, just above her tailbone, an area Maggie called her *Bermuda Triangle*. She wanted to swoon, to invite him to her mattress on the floor in the dormer. But, the thought of black stubble on unshaved legs pulled her back to the porch. Maggie reached for Sam's hand and said, "This is way too nice to stop, but I'm not going to jump in the sack with you."

"We can take our time." He looked at her number in ballpoint on his left hand and asked, "Dinner Wednesday?"

"Wednesday's good." Maggie walked into the house, closed the door behind her and gave way to wobbly knees as she slid down the door's back. Sitting on the floor, arms and legs akimbo, she whispered, "holy mother of god."

The phone rang Monday morning before Maggie was out of bed. She raced downstairs but missed the caller. *Damn,* she thought, *it could have been Sam* then quickly reminded herself she was not going to sit around waiting for a guy to call. As Maggie started heating water for coffee, the phone rang again. The wall phone was next to the pantry. "Hello!" said Maggie.

"Hi, sweet one. Did I get you up?" asked Aunt Jo.

"I just woke and couldn't get downstairs fast enough to pick up. Where the heck are you? I've missed you."

"Here in Windsor. We could see the smoke and flames from the park along the river. What a mess! Did it reach our neighborhood?"

"Nope. We're fine. Freedom Riders met on Sunday and as usual they're organizing and mobilizing. I said I'd do liaison work with the city to help streamline services."

"Sounds like Clyde lassoed you again. How's he doing?"

"Lots of excitement there, but it can wait until you get back."

"Good idea. These long distance charges are ridiculous when I can see Detroit across the river. Any chance you can pick me up on Wednesday? Uncle Cyp said he'd give me a ride to the station when he gets off work about five. That would get me to the other side of the tunnel by seven."

Damn, thought Maggie, *there goes date night.* "Sure, Aunt Jo, no problem. If I don't hear from you I'll be there at seven."

"Great! If something happens and we run late, should I call you at home or Angelo's?"

"Umm. Try here first and if I don't answer call Angelo's. You can leave a message with Angelo or Clyde if I'm busy."

"Will do. *Au revoir.*"

"*Au revoir,* Auntie Jo."

The kettle on the stove was whistling, letting off steam. Maggie looked for something to throw.

Okay, Maggie thought, *I need to focus on options.* Maggie fixed herself a Maxwell House Instant Coffee and sat down at the table and began penciling her options:

1. *Call Sam and work out alternative.*
2. *Call Sam and have some options ready, like —*
   a. *Change in plans, how would you like to meet Aunt Jo?*
   b. *Change in plans, what if we picked up Aunt Jo together and grabbed some dinner?*
   c. *Change in plans, I have to pick up Aunt Jo Wednesday night. How does Tuesday night look for our first date? (Too forward, invitational!)*
   d. *It looks like Wednesday won't work. What works for you?*

Good grief, thought Maggie, *no wonder Clyde assigns me liaison work. I'm like a robot!*

The phone rang again. "Hello," said Maggie.

"Hey Maggie, Angelo here. Can you come in early today and help in the dining room? We just took a reservation for twenty at five o'clock. Some kid's sixteenth birthday party."

"Sure, Angelo. Four o'clock okay?"

"That's my gal, see ya then!"

Enough, Maggie thought, *I'm over thinking a simple date. Whatever happens happens. No more romanticizing.*

After Maggie finished her third cup of coffee, she surveyed the tattered house and decided to do some deep cleaning, maybe pick up some fresh flowers for the kitchen table and a new plant for the living room. *Okay,* she thought, *who am I kidding? I'm building stage sets for Sam to feed my imagination and breathe life into my drab existence. Time to face facts. I'm about to throw myself off the proverbial edge for a little mojo.*

4

The Fallout

Just one week after the riots, "For Sale" signs in Detroit's white neighborhoods have become endemic. Developers in the suburbs are filing plans, throwing up houses, schools and shopping malls. Detroit's city fathers are concerned a mass exodus portends devastating financial and sociological risks to the city's future.

—Detroit Weekly

AUGUST 1967—Maggie woke thinking about Sam. *Screw him.* It was nine o'clock Wednesday morning and she'd not heard from Sam since he left on Sunday night. *The good news,* she thought, *no cliff jumping.* When the phone rang, Maggie flew to the kitchen. "Hello!"

"Hey Maggie, sounds like you're out of breath. What's happening?"

"Oh, Issie, I thought you were this guy I met. The one who'd carry me off on his magnificent steed; but of course, I keep forgetting I'm not in a fairy tale. Shit."

"Well, at least you're meeting guys. Twenty-three may seem old, but I know women who got married in their thirties!"

"Issie, I don't feel old, just lonely. My college friends are working on cruise ships, at camps or missions in South America and I haven't seen my friends across the border in months. Maybe I'm just bored. What's going on in Wasteland these days?"

"Nothing, just wanted to hear your voice. Kids are driving me nuts and Eddie is trying to convince me we should buy a Harley because it would save a ton of money on gas. I think he forgets we live in the northern tundra. What's with guys and Harleys? Do they think they'll grow a bigger set of gonads?"

"I dunno. I'm too down to be good company. Shit, Issie, I really wanted this guy to call."

"Who is this dude?"

"Sam. Sam Tervo. Drop-dead good looking. He was at one of the barricades when I was making my Coke run during the riots. MBA candidate at Wayne, civil rights worker, reserve in the National Guard. I think he has some lame job like mine. We didn't talk jobs. He and Clyde have been friends for a long time and Clyde respects him. He's smart and wickedly funny. I'd forgotten I had a libido. Oh, shit. We were going to go on a date tonight but he never called. No word. He could be dead for all I know."

"If he's all that and more, there may be a good reason he couldn't call. Give it time."

"Well, we're supposed to do some work together, one of Clyde's assignments. So I may get to see him again. I built it up in my mind and that's where it hangs; making up stories about where he is, what he's thinking, doing. It makes me feel like a sixteen-year-old."

"Hey, this is all good! It sounds like you're really attracted to this guy. Don't make up stories. Wait and see what happens. *Let it be, let it be, let it be, let it be. . . .*" sang Issie.

"Oh my god, what did you do with the money mother gave you for singing lessons?"

"I know, terrible mistake. Let me know if you hear from Sam. I could use a good love story."

"Don't count on it. This whole thing is such a head-trip. I pick up Aunt Jo tonight so will check with you later this week."

"*Plus tard,* Marguerite."

"*Plus tard, ma chère soeur.*"

After Maggie hung up, she looked around the kitchen. The floor was as clean as it could be. On the table, a lime green vase filled with orange day lilies reflected the morning sun.

When Maggie showed up for work that day, Clyde left to take care of some personal business and Angelo asked her to cover the kitchen. As usual, it was slow until about five then things started to get busy. Maggie reminded Angelo she had to leave at six to pick up Aunt Jo. Angelo said, "Tell her to take a cab and come here. I'll pay for it."

"Angelo, I can't do that. She's going to have a ton of luggage and food and who knows what else. I can't ask her to take a cab. I'm happy to drop her off at the house and come back here around eight, eight-thirty."

"Fergetaboutit," said Angelo, mimicking Hollywood Italian.

"Angelo, I can drop Aunt Jo off and be here by eight-thirty the latest."

"Naw. It won't kill me to work the kitchen for a few hours. You go, enjoy your Auntie. If she has any of those killer éclairs, it would buy a lot of forgiveness."

"I don't know, Angelo. Those Windsor éclairs are a rare delicacy, but since it's you . . ."

"Go on, get to work. I said I'd work a few hours, not the whole goddamn night."

Maggie loved Angelo's curmudgeonly nature. It always felt like a delicious peek into his closely guarded soft underbelly.

On the way to the tunnel, Maggie found her thoughts drifting to Sam. She couldn't believe she so misjudged him and the connection she felt. *Damn*, Maggie thought, *I'm twenty-three and way too old for these kinds of romantic games. I want to find someone to love, marry and raise a family with. Unless Sam's dead or unconscious, there's no reason for not calling. What an asshole.*

Aunt Jo was just getting off the bus when Maggie arrived. Almost fifty, Aunt Jo was hard to miss with her long, straight, premature white hair in a loose pony tail, red lipstick and her signature black shift, black flats and bright colored shawl. Never married, Aunt Jo's uncommon beauty and keen humor defied terms like *old maid*, *spinster* or *crone*. Once Maggie's dates met Aunt Jo, they often chose to hang out at the house and shoot the breeze with her over the kitchen table.

"Hey, Aunt Jo!" Maggie cried out and waved. Other than her one suitcase, Aunt Jo had three small paper bags. One was from the French Bakery. Maggie took her suitcase.

"How was your trip, Auntie Jo? Any rioting, burning or looting along the way?"

"Oh, Maggie, I've missed your humor! My sister Minnie is losing hers. It was good to see her and Cyp, but I think I'm getting too old and impatient to deal with Minnie's constant complaints. I never realized how particular she was about everything, from how I peeled potatoes to how Cyp folded the newspaper."

"You're not too old, just more savvy about Aunt Minnie's attempt to control the world. I sometimes wonder why Uncle Cyp doesn't change religions so he can get a divorce."

"I think Cyp has other ways to express his life force. Minnie's a test of wills, but my guess is he loves the Minnie he married . . . somewhere inside this Minnie. Very deep inside this Minnie!" laughed Aunt Jo.

"I guess. Did I tell you I met someone?"

"A special someone?" asked Aunt Joe.

"I thought so. His name is Sam. He showed up in my life then disappeared. We were going to go out tonight but he never called. I'm bummed. I liked him so much."

"Well, honey girl, if it's meant to be and all that. There's nothing you can do to force love. It either is or isn't. I know that doesn't fit so well with your power to move mountains, but this is different. This needs to steep and settle and evolve. It may not happen on your timetable, or at all. But, if it does, it'll be worth waiting for. This is one of those times to let it go, to trust the universe or god or whatever you believe in to bring you what you need."

"That's what Issie said—actually sang. Oh, Auntie Jo, I'm glad you're home. I feel like I'm falling apart."

"My sense is there's more here. Maybe, instead of falling apart, you're falling into place and you just don't know it yet."

"I hope you're right. You hungry?"

"I have six éclairs—two for you, two for me and two for that rapscallion boss of yours. Did he blackmail you again?"

"Is the Pope Catholic?"

When Maggie pulled up to the house, a white Corvair was parked on the street. "Oh god," exclaimed Maggie, "that's Sam's car. Let's park in the driveway. I can pull the car in the back later. Damn. I smell like a pizza!" Worried she might hyperventilate Maggie eyed Aunt Jo's paper bags.

"Well, there you are. He's on time for his date. Stay calm and invite him into the house. I'll make some coffee and you get cleaned up. We'll share the éclairs when you get down."

"Aunt Jo, I think he's getting off too easy. He didn't call. What the hell?"

"For what it's worth, if you panic he'll panic. Stay calm and see what he has to say. You don't have to make any decisions right this minute. *Capisce?*"

"*Capisce*," said Maggie as she threw open the door and grabbed Aunt Jo's suitcase from the back. By the time she turned around, Sam was standing on the sidewalk with a bouquet of orange day lilies.

"Be still my heart," Maggie whispered to herself as Sam cut across the lawn to the driveway.

"If you take these flowers for your Aunt Jo, I'll carry the luggage," said Sam. Maggie made the exchange without words and headed to the house. Turning to Aunt Jo, Sam said, "You must be Maggie's Aunt Jo. I'm Sam. I don't normally show up without calling, but I wanted to apologize to Maggie in person. If this isn't a good time . . ."

Aunt Jo interrupted him. "Nonsense! Let's go in the house and unload this stuff. We can give Maggie a few minutes to catch her breath. She's been running all day."

As Aunt Jo chatted her way to the kitchen with Sam, Maggie slid into the bathroom. No shower. Maggie didn't want Sam to hear the pipes clanking and think she cared. A quick sponge bath, deodorant and a clean top to get rid of the pizza smell would have to do. Then decided on tangerine lipstick to set off her aqua top. This time, Maggie was pleased to have the self-imposed discipline of hairy legs on a jean day.

"That's an incredible story. I had no idea how you and Maggie met," said Aunt Jo.

"What blew me away was how much fun it was to laugh together, as if the world wasn't falling down around us. In the heat and emotion of violence, there's no place to hide or release fear. That's why guns are so dangerous and war is so freaking impersonal. Everyone is in the open and holding on to fear. When Maggie showed up in a red convertible filled with pop in the middle of the storm, the fear lifted and I reclaimed my self. I don't think I've ever laughed that hard."

The teakettle was whistling and three mismatched cups sat on the counter for instant coffee. Aunt Jo got up to pour the water and set out three chocolate éclairs on different colored Fiesta Ware dessert plates with red linen napkins and mismatched silver forks. Sam's orange day lilies rested in a yellow water pitcher on the counter, an identical bouquet dressed the kitchen table. Looking around, Sam thought an accountant's eye would focus on the lack of uniformity, but an artist's eye would experience the color, warmth and life of this tableau.

Maggie walked in the kitchen just as Aunt Jo set the third place setting. Sam could not take his eyes off Maggie. Aunt Jo could not take her eyes off the two of them. The air in the room purred with anticipation.

"Hey, Maggie, have a seat," said Aunt Jo. "We're going to get into the éclairs while they're fresh. Sam told me how you met. What a wild story! I had no idea you'd ventured into the battle zone."

"I didn't tell you because I didn't want you to worry. It was nuts, but at the time I wanted to help the cops stay hydrated and calm. I didn't want them to start shooting because they were irritable. Tensions were high enough."

"You saved what little sanity I had," said Sam. Aunt Jo laughed and Maggie couldn't suppress a smile.

"Well, I won't argue with you there," said Maggie.

"No, I imagine not," said Sam. He could feel Maggie's coolness while he took in her beauty, intelligence, humor and lovely curves. He knew Aunt Jo was watching him, trying to take his measure.

Once Sam bit into the éclair, he silently blessed all things French. The three scraping forks continued well beyond the last morsels. Aunt Jo said, "We have three éclairs left. We could hold two for Angelo and split the third one three ways."

Sam jumped up and said, "Done!"

In no time they were, once again, lost in the sensation of all things creamy and chocolate.

Maggie thought there were few culinary experiences as sensual as eating éclairs—*vive l'éclat de l'éclair!* Which, in the strict English translation means: long live the brightness of the flash. Maggie tucked that away for a future poem.

Sam thought he'd be happy sitting at this kitchen table for many years.

Aunt Jo thought, *hang on to your Birkenstocks, Maggie, and don't look over the edge.*

Sam opened the gate while Maggie drove her car in the backyard and raised the convertible top. The curfew had been moved back to eleven and that gave them about two hours before Sam had to head home.

Now that she and Sam were alone in his car, Maggie found it harder to be calm. She agreed with Aunt Jo that acting from panic wouldn't help, but she didn't like to be taken for granted. If Sam treated her like this before their first date, then she sure as hell couldn't expect it to get better.

Sam turned into the Sunoco parking lot next to Hope Chapel. "I'm not sure where we can park in this neighborhood, but I wanted to look at you when I apologized. Is this okay or is there a better place to park?"

"This works."

Sam turned off the car and settled sideways in his seat to face her. Maggie turned toward him, crossed her arms and nodded.

"Listen, I was expecting you to tell me to get bent but instead your aunt invited me in. It was nice to spend time with her. She's smart and beautiful . . . like you." Maggie remained silent and tried to ignore the gymnastics in her heart, stomach and head.

"Before I explain my disappearance, I want you to know I'm seriously attracted to you. I don't know if I can't or don't want to let you out of my mind. Either way, we've been spending a lot of time there and I want to get to know you better.

"Last Sunday night I received a telegram ordering me to report to the National Guard Building on Eight Mile Road at o-six-hundred hours Monday morning. The telegram instructed me not to tell anyone, including spouses, families and employers. The National Guard would handle notifications after we received our final orders. I had no idea what was going on. I thought the United States had been invaded or we were being shipped off to Vietnam or Cambodia on some secret mission.

"Long story short, I spent Monday at the National Guard Building with other Guardsmen debriefing the riots—more like *rehearsing* for a debriefing. Late that night, we were loaded on busses and heading to the MEP Station in Lansing. MEP stands for Military Entrance Processing, where we spent the night. All day Tuesday, we had the same debriefing with Governor Romney, Mayor Cavanaugh, state and federal military chiefs and a number of other officials. Afterward, we spent a second night in Lansing and were bussed back to Detroit on Wednesday. During the entire process, we were restricted from contacting anyone for any reason. The government did not want the press to get wind of the debriefing until they heard it first. That is why, dear Maggie, I didn't call. It frustrated the hell out of me that I couldn't reach you. I hope you'll give me another chance."

"Oh, Sam, no one would ever accuse me of being a romantic, but I was so looking forward to seeing you. I even cleaned the house! By this morning, I was totally pissed off at you, and pissed off at myself for trusting you and romanticizing about our connection. I did, do feel a connection, but I'm a little burned right now. Not sure what I want to do. Part of me wants to jump your bones and another part wants to run for the hills. I want to kiss you and slap you. Does that scare you?"

"Yes, it scares me, but I don't want to let government paranoia about the press mess up a good thing. I hope you don't run for the hills. Take whatever time you need. I'd like to start over," said Sam.

Maggie thought the intimacy and thrill of being heard, exposing vulnerabilities and risking rejection was mind-blowing. She'd never met anyone who seemed so unafraid. In the past, with other guys, Maggie might have insisted they jump through hoops. Somehow she knew Sam was not a hoop jumper. She wanted to believe he was a truth teller.

"Where were we on Sunday before you left? Could we start there?"

5

Cliff Jumping

We have to see that riots grow out of intolerable conditions existing in all our cities, and also out of centuries of neglect. The tragedy is that the riots aren't going to solve the problems. . . . They only intensify the fears of the white community while, in many cases, relieving its guilt.

— Dr. Martin Luther King, Jr.

NOVEMBER 1967 — Sitting Indian style on the floor in his white skivvies and a tattered gray Wayne State sweatshirt, Sam sorted through his albums looking for Nina Simone.

When Maggie first saw Sam's place in Highland Park she was horrified. She wasn't blind to the wretched poverty in Detroit, but she'd never *entered* the slums. Sam's apartment house, a tan-brick, soot-covered building, was constructed in the early 1900's without any relief to its four flat, bland sides. Slivered and battered window frames served as archeological evidence of the multiple times they'd been repainted shut and re-pried open during the past fifty-plus years. Most windows were propped up by tin cans, but some held small sliding-window-screen inserts from Woolworth's to provide ventilation. The hallways and lobby were dank with the odor of people living in close quarters. Animal, vegetable and mineral smells blanched together in a perpetual alchemy of life and decay. And sounds. Sounds merged in ways Maggie had never encountered. Cries of pleasure and pain, music and plumbing, cats and babies reverberated in a hauntingly beautiful, warped cacophony of life. Maggie's first reaction was flight. Yet, once she entered Sam's third floor apartment, *place* was no longer part of the equation.

Maggie sang, "Bird's flying high you know how I feel—bump-ah, bump-ah, bump-ah." Dressed in a pink Flower Power sweatshirt and white Lollipop briefs, Maggie swung her hips low and slow with the taunt of a burlesque queen. "Fish in the sea you know how I feel—don-cha know." Putting her nose to Sam's nose, Maggie twirled away, her shoulder-length black hair moving with a drum roll of bumps and grinds, as she sang out "hip swing, hip swing, hip swing—it's a new dawn, it's a new day, it's a new life for me—you know what I mean—and I'm feeling good—bump-ah, bump-ah, bump-ah."

"What am I doing looking for Nina Simone when you're right here with all this sass and jazz?" Catching Maggie's ankle on the last *bump-ah*, Sam said, "Come here you green-eyed witchy woman."

Maggie knelt in front of him and realized getting lost in Sam was becoming an addiction. Nina Simone could wait, food could wait, homework could wait, sleep could wait, but her hunger for Sam couldn't. Maggie pulled herself up on Sam's lap and wrapped her legs around his waist. She smiled as he moved closer. Sam ran his fingers along her shoulders then down her arms to her hands. Taking her wrists, he raised Maggie's arms over her head and gently lifted her sweatshirt, kissing the tender skin from the crook of her elbow to her shoulder.

Hands, hips, torsos, necks and mouths began moving to a silent rhapsody—like kettledrums, violins and trumpets seeking a crescendo. Time stopped. All that existed was the syncopated movement of skin, bone, muscle and breath. Maggie whimpered, "holy mother of god."

Sam cried, "Jesus, Maggie, you're killing me," before they broke into laughter—sounds that fed the jukebox of this hungry tenement.

Maggie nuzzled Sam's neck, breathing in the musk and salt of an ocean, then hurried to the bathroom to wash up and remove her diaphragm. She was always famished after sex. Instead of a cigarette, she wanted three sliders from White Castle.

"Hey Tervo, I'll pick up lunch at White Castle."

"Hey Soulier, I'll take a rain check. I've got to crack my econ books and study for the final."

"Shit. Why does it always feel like we're stealing time to be together? I know we've got to study, but we act like we're breaking a promise, cheating on a betrothed. Hmm. What would this illicit sex be called? An extra-curricular affair?" teased Maggie.

"We could always get married and sign up for married housing on campus. Cheap and convenient! We could park the cars, even sell one, and walk to class."

"Tervo, that has to be the lamest marriage proposal in the history of humankind!"

"Yep. I imagine. But here's the thing, we both know we're heading there and why not do it now? That way we sleep together every night and graduate before the next century. Can you believe 2000? We could have grandkids by then."

Maggie knew she was over the moon, but she wasn't stupid. Sam fired all her pistons—looks, intelligence, humor, kindness. For some reason, she was certain he shared her same sense of mysticism and pragmatism—open to new things, new ideas and new adventures. While conceding her universe of men was limited, Maggie was convinced she'd never find anyone else she'd want to spend her life with. She was ready for Sam's proposal, marriage and cohabitation, especially the cohabitation.

"Sam, I love the idea of sleeping together every night, but give me a break. I'm a woman and wannabe poet. When it comes to things like marriage proposals I need a little more juice."

"Okay, I'll work on that after I study for the econ exam *if* you promise to say yes. In the meantime, we need to get our application for married housing in before the December 1st deadline."

"Oh, *mon dieu*! I'm not sure I'll survive the tsunami rush of romance here. A *conditional* yes, depends on the proposal," said Maggie as she hopped around the small room to collect her jeans, shoes and coat. Flushed from the heat of their lovemaking, Maggie glanced out at the cold, gray day. She wanted to cling to the afterglow as long as she could, carry this sense of bliss a while longer. When she got home she'd try turning her feelings into an *aubade*— her assignment for a poetry workshop that week.

Sam was sitting at a nominally constructed cinderblock and wood plank desk when Maggie tipped his chin up, gave him a chaste kiss, then copped a quick feel between his legs and said, "*adieu*." Sam reached to pull Maggie to his lap but missed as she darted out the door. Sam stared at the wall and shook the smile off his face before he looked down at his econ book and began to read.

On her way home, Maggie was shaking her head and laughing to herself, or at herself, thinking *I'm ready to jump off the freaking cliff and have no idea why I think I can fly!* Maggie wasn't sure where her certainty came from, but she knew her relationship with Sam was far more important and complex than physical or sexual attraction. They had a familiarity and intimacy that spoke of lifetimes, if not ages. Sam said it felt as if they'd known each other in a previous life. Maggie rejected the idea of reincarnation because she thought *who in their right mind would want to come back and do this again?* But she agreed with Sam, this was not the first time they'd known each other. Maggie had been blinded in the past by lust, but not love. She wanted to believe her Chakras were fully open now. Or, the planets were perfectly aligned for her and Sam to meet. Or, she and Sam shared some primordial stardust that fed their conscious and unconscious memories. Maggie thought being a writer worked remarkably well when life got messy. She could create or remake her own reality.

As Maggie daydreamed about how others would respond to their marriage plans, she imagined Issie saying *go for it*. Aunt Jo would say *trust your self*. Sam's brother Kenny would probably say *fucking* A. Clyde would be elated. But most of their friends and relatives would be flummoxed. She could hear them saying *Maggie and Sam always seemed so levelheaded. Is she pregnant? What's the rush?*

Writing an *aubade* turned out to be trickier than Maggie thought. The challenge was crafting something that was sensual, even erotic, but not pornographic. After her fifth, or was it sixth draft, Maggie smiled, ran her hand over the blue-lined page, blue-inked words, before she closed her eyes.

Morning Prayers

Light slides through bamboo blinds as I trace the angles of your uncovered
frame — hinged shoulders, elbows, hips, gnarled hands and knees.

Last night you folded and cradled me, whispered against my skin; our words
tumbled together, turning the dial of a padlock, riding the tension, opening.

I pull the blanket up, stretch myself along your back and
    close my eyes.
The dreamer knows images are lost upon rising.

Clyde organized The Detroit Eight (The Eights) to make strategic decisions for Detroit's Freedom Riders. The name was based on the number of members but more importantly provided a moniker that wouldn't raise alarms on work calendars. Sam and Maggie were ostensibly invited because of their role as liaisons to riot victims. But, there was more to it than that. The NAACP and MLK's lieutenants were modeling and encouraging mixed race committees. Clyde first checked with Maggie and Sam to see if they were willing to be *the token but highly valued whites* before he appointed them to The Eights. Until now, conversations about the need to reach out to the suburbs and form mix-raced coalitions to keep Detroit vital had been exploratory. Now, it was generating serious attention and support from the big guys, including civil rights leaders, trade unions, industrialists and others with known mafia connections. In spite of the money being made by white flight, some of the power brokers had too much invested in Detroit to see it fail.

Sam told Maggie he'd meet her at Clyde's for The Eight's fourth monthly meeting, but planned to leave early to pick up some hours at work. Too many nights with Maggie had taken a financial toll. This would be the first time Maggie and Sam saw each other in the evening without spending the night at Sam's. Right now, his place was their only option. Aunt Jo would have thought nothing of Sam spending the night in Maggie's room, but she had too many Catholic relatives, neighbors and co-workers. The last thing Aunt Jo needed was a reputation for operating a *den of iniquity*. Maggie knew the Catholic Church would go kicking and screaming through the feminist movement. Good Catholic girls didn't jump in the sack without a prayer, promise and wedding vow.

Maggie knew her and Sam's current arrangement couldn't last long; they were ready to play house, with or without a license. Married housing at Wayne State made sense, but it wasn't the only option. At first Maggie thought she'd move into Sam's apartment, with all its smells and sounds. On second thought, she realized it was totally out of the question. Sam's place would be too expensive, as they'd both need cars to get to school and work. And, because of crime in the area, Sam had to rent a locked garage to protect his Corvair from being cannibalized for parts. The locked garage for his Corvair cost more than Maggie paid Aunt Jo for rent each month. She couldn't fathom what it might cost for a TR4.

6

Bootlegged

This is our basic conclusion: Our nation is moving toward two societies, one black one white — separate and unequal.
— The Kerner Report

NOVEMBER 1967 — Although Clyde referred to his neighborhood as *The Perpetual Petri Dish,* it was an oasis in post-riot Detroit. The streets were wide, trees lush and the houses well maintained. With thirty homes in a two-block area, the homeowners knew one another and looked out for each other. Clyde once said, "Here's the math. Whites own ten houses but white families only occupy five of the houses. Of the five, only one white family owns the house they live in. The other four rent their homes from white owners who fled Detroit after the riots." Clyde's own house was a bright yellow asphalt-shingled bungalow with white shutters and a black door. When Clyde referred to his home as a "crib," Sam would say, "you mean cab?" One of those tired, but expected, ritual jokes that caused group groans. Watching them over the past few months,

Maggie realized Clyde and Sam were masters at demonstrating the power of quirky humor to break down racial barriers and quiet egos.

"Hey Maggie," called Clyde as he opened the door. "Sam just called and wanted me to tell you he can't make the meeting and will get with you tomorrow."

"Damn. He's been so buzzed about dissecting the Kerner Report. I'm chomping at the bit to see it."

"Speaking of chomping, Blanche put out pigs-in-the-blanket, crackers, cheese and of course rabbit food—what you French might call a very *petite day joiner*. Work today?"

"*Très petit dejeuner*," laughed Maggie. "As to work, nope. Thought we'd be busy before Thanksgiving but Angelo said chill. He's got me down for two, four-hour shifts during the week and eight hours on Saturday. Good schedule, much less crazy than it was."

"I'm not giving up any hours right now and my guess is the rest of the crew is doing the same. Unemployment is so freaking high that Angelo only has to think replacement and he's got fifty cooks and a hundred waiters at his door," said Clyde.

"Clyde Daniel Webster, are you kidding me? Angelo would close his doors before letting you go."

"Strange things are happening, Maggie Soulier. It ain't what it seems. Go get your *day-jew-nay*, however the hell you pronounce it, from the kitchen and bring it to the dining room. Might be a long meeting."

To Maggie, The Eights were a curious anthology of people. Clyde and Blanche Webster, with their three young sons in a quiet Detroit neighborhood were the median. Blanche ran a daycare center in the basement at Hope Chapel and was active in all things involving children, education and women's rights.

At the far left, Robin and Willie Johnson, mid-thirties and childless, liked to walk on the wild side. Both were into recreational drugs, including LSD for 'spiritual treks.' Robin baked and designed special event cakes for weddings, funerals, confirmations, bar mitzvahs. Her jewel tone colors and cake shapes were off the charts and she'd attracted the rich and famous, including the Motown crowd. But Robin had no interest in empire building and refused to take more than three clients each month. Willie, a local celebrity, was the Zamboni driver at Olympia Stadium. He loved to dress in Red Wing red—red pants, red shoes, red socks. Willie never took time off when the Red Wings had a game and rarely called a backup for their practices. The backup drivers were relegated to cleaning the ice from one a.m. to six a.m. when the arena was rented to amateur teams. A Detroit icon with a smile that lit up the ice arena, Willie, 'Mr. Zamboni', was often invited to emcee small events or serve as the Grand Marshall in local parades. Unlike Robin, Willie loved the smell of greasepaint and the sound of applause. Clyde used to worry about Willie's discretion, but after ten years, he'd finally relaxed his guard. Robin and Willie spent most of their time, money and energy pushing for prisoner's rights, monitoring police conduct, arrest records and criminal court cases. But Willie knew decriminalizing recreational drugs, especially pot, was the ticket to freedom for most brothers. He returned to this arena time and again, bloodied and broken, wrapping his fists for another round. The Johnsons' many connections to the media and defense bar morphed into one of the Freedom Riders most coveted, surprising and effective power caches. Doors and file cabinets opened, information was leaked and tweaked in this underground swap meet.

Remaining at the 'near right' were two single females and Maggie's best friends. Loretta Hood had owned and operated a hair salon just west of downtown called SistaHood for more than twenty years. Before the black-is-beautiful movement gained momentum, Loretta had, one-by-one, begun changing the look of blacks in Detroit. Her customers walked out with Afros, dreadlocks and hair woven with beads, feathers and ribbons. Loretta's own hair was nappy, shorn like a sheep. She said the contrast worked. Her customers were ready for Motown, the cover of Ebony, a late night at the Latin Quarter.

Stella Webster was closer to Maggie's age, tall, thin and gorgeous. She married Clyde's cousin Odell when she was only sixteen. Long-story short, Odell learned his trade in the tenements, dealing and using heroin. After they married, Odell's addiction arced and he began beating the crap out of Stella. Clyde and Blanche took her in when she was seventeen. With their help, Stella attended Eastern Michigan University on college grants and scholarships. After getting her undergraduate degree, Stella went on to earn an MBA from Wayne State. She now worked as a mortgage closer for American Savings and Loan in Detroit. Not into risk-taking, rebellion or even peaceful protesting, Stella's contribution to the cause came through her clarity of communication and attention to detail. Her competency in accounting and knowledge of contract law were invaluable. As for Odell, the last anyone heard he was serving time at *Dehoco*, the Detroit House of Corrections, for armed robbery.

Compared to other members of The Eights, Maggie thought she and Sam moved along the continuum from 'median to left' when it came to taking risks and protesting—but skirted the 'near right' when it came to jobs and life styles. Both she and Sam were more focused on equal employment, equal pay and housing opportunities. Maggie's mind was wandering. She reminded herself to *pay attention and take notes; Sam will want a blow-by-blow of the meeting.*

After ten minutes of catching up with one another, Clyde knocked on the table and cleared his throat. "I've asked Stella to give us some background on the report because, unlike me, she knows how to be succinct. And, because you're all so damn shy, she'll help me lead the discussion. To tamp down any wild-ass expectations, it'll take months to sort out all the details in this report. Our job is to identify and grab the low-hanging fruit and get started before opposing forces set up their defenses. Stella?"

"Thanks, Clyde. In short, because the NAACP has contacts deep within the Johnson administration, the Freedom Riders were able to snag a bootlegged copy of Kerner's Summary Report of the riots. The copy is in draft form. We don't think its been swept by the FBI, or others who might insist on editing it for the 'public good.' The full edited report, expected to be more than 400 pages, will be available for purchase after its release in February. In the meantime, we have one draft copy to begin our discussions. We won't make copies and ask that you not take any notes. I'm sure it goes without saying that any talk about this report outside The Eights could put innocent people at risk and jeopardize our work. Questions?"

"How do we know this isn't a plant?" asked Willie.

"We don't. If it's a plant, the person who gave us the copy might be involved. If not, he might lose his job for turning it over to us. We might get some adverse publicity, but there's nothing illegal about accepting a copy of this draft report," said Stella.

"Bottom line, we don't want anyone losing their job and we have enough adverse publicity without creating more, which is why we can't talk about it outside this group. *Capisce?*" said Clyde.

"Bro, you gotta drop the Italian. You're beginning to sound like Angelo," said Willie. Clyde responded by tapping the table with his middle finger.

Loretta asked, "If we don't cover the core issues tonight, will we schedule an extra meeting or wait until next month?"

Stella looked to Clyde and he replied, "Lets see what we accomplish tonight. I'm open to an extra meeting if that's what it takes. More questions? Okay Stella, let's grab some fruit."

"Three basic questions were addressed: What happened? Why did it happen? What can be done to prevent it from happening again? We'll zero in on the last two questions. Why did it happen? No surprises here. The report found 'race prejudice . . . threatens future . . . white racism . . . explosive mixture . . . pervasive discrimination and segregation . . . black in-migration and white exodus . . . massive concentrations of impoverished Negroes in cities.'"

Maggie was trying to take it all in and make mental notes to cover with Sam. The Eights were transfixed. It was so quiet Maggie could hear Marmalade, Clyde's old collie, snoring in the kitchen. Maggie thought, *Kerner said exactly what we've been saying for years. Finally, it seems, the Feds got this right.*

Continuing, Stella reported, "What can be done to prevent it from happening again? 'The major goal . . . single society . . . open opportunities . . . eliminating barriers. Lastly, increasing communication across racial lines to destroy stereotypes, to halt polarization, end distrust and hostility, and create common ground for efforts toward public order and social justice.'"

Maggie said, "Are you fucking kidding me? Does this mean we aren't alone in this fight?"

Stella looked to Clyde who said, "Maggie, it's filled with hope, but there's one recommendation that gave me the creeps the first time I read it. By the third or fourth read I started to get it. No protest march, this action is more like flying to the moon or writing a symphony. It'll take a lot of time and finesse, but we gotta do it." Taking the copy from Stella, Clyde turned to the middle of the report and read: "'We can pursue integration by combining ghetto enrichment with policies which will encourage Negro movement out of the central city areas.'"

"Now before anyone goes ballistic," said Clyde, "the report supports this recommendation as '. . . the only possible choice for America . . . a policy . . . designed to encourage integration of

substantial numbers of Negroes into the society outside the ghetto.'"
To Maggie, the key words and phrases hung like confetti.

"In my first read I thought, those S.O.B.'s want the cities to themselves," said Clyde. "After I reread it with the supporting comments,
it's clear the effort to achieve equality must include integration. An
all-black Detroit will create a bigger ghetto. We need to integrate
and that means bringing the city to the burbs. Comments?"

Willie said, "It creeps me out *with* the reasoning. It's like hens
chasing the goddamn foxes to the suburbs. What the hell? Why
shouldn't Detroit be the first black city? I say it's about time. Why
not?"

"So, Willie, we draw our lines in the sand and then what? We
design a new flag, set up boundaries? Form our own armies?" said
Blanche. To me the whole point is to find some way to live together.
No more craziness."

"Willie Johnson, Blanche is right. We can't do this shit any
more. If peace is an option it's gotta be our goal. I'm not fighting
for a piece of property. I'm fighting for equal rights. Just so there's
no doubt, I think the only way to equality is to prohibit same-race
marriages, so we all turn honey-colored mulatto. Then we could
smoke weed, dance and make love instead of shooting each other,"
said Robin.

"Robin Johnson, now what poor white boy do you have your
eyes set on?"

"Willie Johnson, you do make my heart sing, but if it was law I'd
be forced to marry Elvis," winked Robin and everyone at the table
dissolved in laughter at the idea of Robin marrying a white boy from
Tupelo, Mississippi.

7

Adulterated

The racial hysteria among whites fleeing Detroit for the suburbs in the post-riot period added to the greater fear and racial hysteria of whites living in the suburbs.

—Detroit Weekly

NOVEMBER 1967—Heading northwest on Grand River Avenue, it was hard to avoid the aftermath of July's looting and burning. Newscasters described this area as 'war-torn' and Sam thought the remains of the S.S. Kresge store near Joy Road looked like a bombed out ship, its hull ready for demolition. How many times had he and his brother Kenny sat at Kresge's soda fountain sipping root beer floats or eating hot fudge sundaes? Speaking of Kenny, Sam thought *what an asshole. Last time I lend him my car!* After all their arguments, Kenny had once again tucked a roach clip in the ashtray. The last thing Sam needed was to get stopped for a traffic violation and arrested for possessing drug paraphernalia. If he got booted from the Guard, he'd lose his tuition benefits. Kenny made good money at a tool and dye shop, but burned through it like who laid the rail. His story this time was his 1965 VW had been impounded for unpaid parking tickets. It'd been months since Sam saw the VW and he had no doubt it'd been repossessed. Sam thought, *shit, mooching is one thing, lying about it pushes it to a whole new level.*

As Sam approached Outer Drive, Grand River looked cleaner, stores were open and holiday decorations signaled a return to normalcy. Sheer Juice, the company Sam worked for, occupied a small two-story white cinderblock office building retrofitted with a loading dock facing the back alley. Unlike neighboring retail stores and offices with plate glass windows, Sheer Juice's daylight slogged through glass-brick windows and frosted-glass doors, giving it a modern architectural mien, but no invitation to enter. When Sam asked the Plant Manager, Louie Zito, "what's with the no-see glass, especially upstairs?" Zito said, "we gotta protect our proprietary interests in the preparation and bottling of Sheer Juice." Sam almost laughed because Zito's response was so *noir* paranoid and illogical. Sheer Juice was just juice.

Four parking spots at the back of the building were reserved for the President, Comptroller, Plant Manager and Administrative Assistant. Parking spaces up front were reserved for customers and subcontractors during the day and for employees who started their shift after six p.m. Because of school, Sam preferred the late shift; parking up front was a nice perk. For that matter, his job was a perk. Thanks to Angelo and his connections, Sam was not flipping burgers or delivering pizza, but working for a company that promised to build his resume during graduate school. Although most of his assignments were mindless, he was exposed to processing, marketing, sales and distribution. And, at times, he was asked to do some basic office and accounting work. On the rare occasion when Sam worked a day shift, he'd take applications and interview hourly workers. It wasn't rocket science, but with the right spin, his experience would look mighty good on a resume, even open a few doors.

Zito saw Sam park his car and was waiting at the front door to let him in. "So, where the fuck you been?" asked Zito. "You get hit by a car or what?"

"Hey Zito! Thanks for holding my place. I don't know what the hell I'd do if I didn't have you kicking my ass every week," laughed Sam.

"You ass-kisser. Won't work. I've got all kinds of shit for you tonight to make up for your piss-poor attendance, so don't even think about leaving before it's done. *Capisce?*"

"*Capisce.* Anything, my night is yours."

"Yeah, well don't fucking stretch the clock. It won't take all night. Follow me."

The loading dock was filled with five-gallon blue containers made of heavy-duty molded plastic. Each container had "DEPC" stamped in white block lettering. Zito said, "We're working with one of the giant beer companies to extend the shelf life of fruit juices. I can't say who but you've heard of 'em. Deal is fucking huge. Cha-ching! It's top secret. You say anything to anyone and you get a pair of cement shoes. Got it?"

"Sure, Zito. This is a good thing, right?

"Yeah, asshole, it's a good thing. Here's what I need you to do. Take all thirty-six of these jugs to the processing area and line them up in front of the first three juice machines. Okay, numb nut? That means twelve jugs in front of each machine. They're heavy as brick shithouses so take them one at a time. It's 6:15 now. I figure five minutes for each trip to cover breaks, so three hours max plus two hours for payroll. I've got stuff to do, so I'll lock the doors and be back by eleven to help you wrap up. Questions?"

"Not that I can think of. You home if I need to call?"

"You call my house and I'll break your fucking kneecaps. My wife thinks I'm working."

"Nice, Zito. You're getting laid and I'm busting my ass."

"Well, you know what they say, 'time and service,' that's why I get paid the big bucks. You can wipe your ass with that MBA," laughed Zito as he headed for the back door.

For the first time it hit Sam that the executive parking spots in the back were strategic. These guys could come and go without being seen. Plus, it was no secret the administrative assistant position was filled by a revolving door of young, pretty, buxom babes.

Damn, thought Maggie. It was after ten and she hadn't heard from Sam. She hoped he'd call so she could do a brain dump of the Kerner Report before she forgot. *Screw that*, she thought. Sam's job was so closely supervised he wouldn't call. Maggie hadn't met his boss and had no interest in meeting him. According to Sam, Louie Zito was a misogynist and banterer. Maggie couldn't decide which was worse, but thought she could take misogyny better than bantering. She'd be glad when they were done with these part-time, labor-intense, mundane jobs. Compared to Sam, Maggie felt lucky. Although her own work was a drag, she stayed with Angelo because she liked him and Clyde. Yet, she dreamed of the day when she wouldn't have to arrange another slice of pepperoni on a pizza, flush out the coke machine or clean up after a bunch of ankle biters. Delivering pizza wasn't bad, but being female was a nuisance. Maggie had some close calls with sofa jocks who'd been drinking and watching sports on TV all day. More than once, some nimrod grabbed her arm and insisted she stay and earn some big tips. In the coldest voice Maggie could muster, she'd say: *My boss Angelo Ciccerelli is connected, if you get my drift. If I'm not back in ten minutes he'll send his hit men out looking for me.* Worked every time. But now, Maggie wanted out. Six more months and she'd have her Master's, and she hoped, a job teaching poetry.

Maggie heard the phone ring and Aunt Jo called upstairs, "are you awake?" Racing down the steps, Maggie began organizing her thoughts about the meeting.

"Hello," said Maggie.

"Hey, Maggie, hope I'm not calling too late. You got a few minutes to talk about tonight's meeting?" said Clyde.

"Sure. I'd love to. I've been trying to keep my thoughts organized to talk to Sam later tonight or tomorrow. He's still at work."

"I know we didn't say much about it at the meeting, but Carl Stringer's white power group, Avenge, is gaining momentum. He and his pocket-protector revolutionaries want to arm whites and keep them in the city. According to their pamphlet the scare tactic is: 'If Detroit becomes black, guerilla warfare will be taken to the suburbs.' Maggie, based on the color of *your* skin, sorry, is there some way you can get more detail about the members, plans and strategy? Stringer and most of his recruits work for the city or county. Whatever you discover will be more information than we have, which are sound bites from radio and newspaper interviews."

"Sure, let me give it some thought. I know a few people at the city and Aunt Jo has some friends with the county. I'll keep a low profile."

"Thanks, Maggie. I don't want to tip our hand and give them more power because they think we're worried, but we need to know what we're up against."

"Sure. I'll talk to Sam about it. We'll keep you in the loop and let you know before we do anything too crazy. How're you doing?"

"Unbelievably good. I think the shock of the riots and my arrest shifted my perspective. Everything seems a little clearer. There's no doubt we have to move our work to the suburbs. The questions now are: how, when and whom."

"Don't be putting my name next to the *whom*."

"Maggie, when have I tried to force anyone to do anything they didn't want to do? Give me a break."

"Why do I hear alarms going off?"

"Maggie Soulier. You hurt me to the quick."

"Like hell."

Just after Maggie bounded up the stairs, the phone rang again. It was Sam.

"Hey, babe, I only have a minute but called to say good night. I've got less than an hour to finish up and I need two. How was the meeting?"

"It was good. I wish you could have been there because I'm not sure I can do it justice. Clyde just called and he wants me to do some espionage."

"He called the right person. Listen, let's wait until we've got more time to talk about the meeting and this new undercover assignment. I just want to hear your voice and tell you I'm thinking of you, loving you . . . methodically undressing you in my mind."

"Where are you? My libido just started pacing back and forth, back and forth like a caged lion."

"Lioness, it's a good thing you're not here right now. I'd lose my job for sexual horseplay or harassment, whatever it's called. Do you think there's a law against raunchiness? Maybe tomorrow. Let's see if we can find time for a nooner in the back seat, under a blanket. Wear a skirt."

8

Light My Fire

The time to hesitate is through. No time to wallow in the mire. Try now we can only lose and our love become a funeral pyre. Come on baby light my fire.

—The Doors, lyrics from *Light My Fire*

DECEMBER 1967—"Hey, Loretta. What's up?" said Maggie

"Hey, bride-girl, what are you doing calling me? You ready to make that long walk down the aisle today?"

"Very funny. My walk will be to the Justice of the Peace if we get there before it closes for the holidays. I'm freaked. Do you have time for lunch today?"

"On your wedding day? Sure, baby, I'll make time. Do you want me to call Stella?"

"Yes, please. Sorry for the last minute cry for help. I don't think I want to back out; I just need friend power to keep me from hyperventilating all day."

"Listen, I only have one appointment after lunch and she's a regular. I'll get rid of her. That way we'll have the whole afternoon if you want."

"Thanks, Loretta, I'm a wreck. Sorry I didn't call earlier but I thought I could handle this like any other day. Aunt Jo's busy making dinner for everyone and she talked Robin into making a cake. A cake! I gotta get outta this place, if it's the last thing I ever do."

"The Animal's got nothing on you, chickadee. Let's meet at Hudson's Piccadilly Circus, the cafeteria on the mezzanine, at noon. They won't kick us out. We'll take as long as we want, shop if we feel like it. We can wear our 'going to the chapel' dresses in case we run out of time."

"Oh god, I feel better already. I'll put you and Stella in charge of reminding me to get to the JP by four o'clock," laughed Maggie.

"No sweat, Maggie, we'll make it happen!

Sam had the day off and too much time to think. *Marriage! What in god's name am I doing?* Last night, Zito and some guys from the dayshift stayed late to celebrate Sam's last day as a 'free man.'

The upstairs conference room was set up with cans of Schlitz Beer on ice, pretzels and a large relish plate.

"Hey, dickhead, what red-blooded man is walking down the aisle these days? Lot's of broads out there hopping on the free-sex bandwagon! 'Make love not war,' that kind of shit. Jesus, Tervo, you nuts?" said Zito.

"Might be, but there've always been broads on the free-sex bandwagon if you're just looking to get laid. I thought it might be fun to live with someone who speaks in complete sentences and makes me laugh."

"What a putz!"

"You got my number, Zito," laughed Sam.

Many of the dayshift guys knew Sam, shook his hand and wished him luck. Sam thought they seemed sincere but awkward. It was unusual for Sheer Juice to host an employee party and Sam was sure these guys would much rather be heading home than drinking free beer.

After forty-five minutes, one can of Schlitz floated in the melted ice and salt crystals bore scant witness to the empty bowl of pretzels. The relish tray was stripped bare. Sam felt a little buzz from his three beers, which was unusual. He'd always handled booze well, especially beer. The dayshift guys headed out and Zito said he'd be back before midnight to 'unlock the cage.'

Before Sam made it out the conference room door, the latest in the string of administrative assistants walked in. Sam recalled meeting her on her first day, *Carla*.

"Hi, Carla," said Sam.

"Hey, Sam, I hear you're getting married tomorrow. Congratulations!"

"I am. You married?"

"Divorced," said Carla.

"That must be tough," said Sam, thinking of ways to make a graceful exit. Carla's eyes were 'raccooned' in black liner. Her mini-skirt and low-cut sweater left little to the imagination. Sam always felt uncomfortable with women who were into exhibitionism—women he found both hard to look at and hard *not* to look at.

"Not really. We had an open marriage and we were both fooling around the whole time. We're better off single."

"I can't imagine Maggie with another guy. I'm sure I'd be too jealous."

"Yeah. That sometimes gets in the way. Roger walks around with a hard-on and for me it was a relief. Not that I don't like sex,

58

I do. I just don't want someone jumping my bones three times a day."

Sam was torn between staying, to see where this conversation went, and walking out of the room. The beer buzz wasn't strong enough to leave this to fate. It was his decision. He decided to let the drama play out a little more.

"Three times a day?" asked Sam. He was curious and decidedly horny.

"Not every day, but most."

Sam couldn't keep his eyes from dropping to her full breasts, small waist and narrow hips. Carla's assets were above the waist. Small hips and skinny legs never turned him on, but this conversation and the possibility of one last fling before he and Maggie married was almost more stimulation than he could bear. Sam didn't kid himself; he knew Carla was both producer and director of this scene.

"One last beer, it's yours," said Sam.

"Sure. I'm off the clock."

When Sam handed Carla the beer, it slipped through his hands and they both grabbed for it and laughed. Sam noticed Carla's small mouth filled with large, slightly bucked teeth. Something about this combination sent his imagination into orbit.

"So, what turns you on the most?" asked Sam.

As if on cue, Carla closed and locked the conference room door and knelt in front of Sam. He closed his eyes as she unhooked his belt, unbuttoned his pants and unzipped his zipper. Sam knew he should stop this. *What if Zito returned?* But he didn't care. He felt Carla pull down his khakis, then his skivvies. He could feel the air on his naked and very hard penis. Then nothing. He looked down and saw Carla pulling off her sweater. Her breasts were spilling out of a black lace bra. Sam watched as she dropped her bra straps one at a time and freed her enormous—*what?* Sam thought *boobs, tits, jugs, hooters, rack, knockers?* Sam lost all sense of time, date and location. He was no longer in a conference room at work. He'd been transported to another place. Carla smiled, grabbed his hand and pulled him to the floor. Minutes, hours passed. Nothing mattered except this erotic, sensual exchange of skin, organs, bones—knockers, nipples everywhere.

When Sam came to, he was lying on the conference room floor, his shirt off and his pants wrapped around his ankles. No Carla. The table had been cleared, and except for his awkward state of dress, nothing looked out of place. *What the hell* thought Sam as he checked his watch. Two hours had passed since Carla first entered the conference room. His head throbbed as he tried to recall the details of . . . *what? Oral sex? Intercourse? Some fantasy? Crap.* Sam ran his hand along his penis to see if there was any sign of orgasm. None that Sam felt. *Did Carla wash me off before she left the room? What the fuck? There was no way three beers would make me drunk enough to pass out, but Carla didn't know how much I drank. She may have freaked and left me on the floor to sober up.* "Son-of-a-bitch," he berated himself, before he noticed a red blinking light in the upper corner of the room.

An easy walk in flats, but grueling in three-inch heels, Stella offered to spring for a five-minute cab ride to the Justice of the Peace. When the cabbie heard Maggie was on her way to get married, he shut off the meter and said, "This might be your last free ride!" Which launched another round of giggles. The afternoon had been a therapeutic girl's day out. If Maggie had written a screenplay about it, she'd call it Women Who Flirt With Marriage.

"I'm the last person to ask about marriage. I never thought, dreamed, hoped it'd work for me. When I got pregnant with Marcus there was no way I was going to marry his sorry-ass daddy. Too many smart women I knew ended up with a man who couldn't keep his pecker in his pants, much less support a family," said Loretta.

"Y'all know my story and I've no intention of making that mistake again. I'd rather be a nun, and I'm not even Catholic," said Stella.

"Okay, is this some new, perverted, zany approach to cheering up a bride on her wedding day? Is there a hidden *Candid Camera*? Geez, you guys!" laughed Maggie.

"Sorry, Maggie, I got carried away. I'm sure Sam's the exception. He sure as hell is a looker!" said Loretta.

"He's that," said Stella.

"Crap. Seriously, who knows? I don't buy into the belief some guy's going to carry me off to his castle to live happily ever after. That's such bullshit. My life's never been a fairy tale and it would be scary to imagine Sam cast as Prince Charming. I'm not a romantic. But deep down I long for a home, family, happiness, security. Okay, maybe I'm a little romantic," said Maggie.

"I want that, too. I can give myself home, family, happiness, security. I think the danger is looking for someone else to MAKE me happy. That's the dark pit," said Loretta.

"I think men are the dark pit. Maybe I'm gay," said Stella.

"All men?" asked Maggie.

"Probably. I mean, well, maybe Sam's a good guy, but he's a guy—testosterone, ego, dick. I don't think guys can help it. I think they're hard-wired to act first, then think," said Stella.

"Ah, Stella, you were only sixteen when you fell in love with Odell. He was an addict. You might change your mind if you find a guy who was brought up in a good home and had a decent education," said Loretta.

"Well, SistaHood, sounds like you be talkin' outta both sides of your mouth," said Stella.

"Maybe. But maybe Sam and Maggie belong together. There's something there. I think Sam's a good man," said Loretta.

"He can be an asshole, but he's a good man," agreed Maggie.

Loretta raised her now empty cardboard cup of coffee and said, "Here's to Sam, an asshole and a good man, and to Maggie, for her fearless love. May they find a remnant of marital bliss."

Maggie thought that Loretta and Stella gave new meaning to irony and insolence. Somehow, this rude cocktail of attitudes gave Maggie a sense of comfort she wouldn't have found through empathy and kindness. *Thank god I have friends like Emily Dickinson's poetry, a bit untamed and slanted.*

Odors from decades of cigar smoke and the accreted scent of Murphy's Oil Soap gave personality to an otherwise drab lobby. The elevators to the Justice of the Peace Office on the third floor were gated with uniformed attendants. Maggie, dressed in a red velvet mini-dress, had splurged on black diamond-patterned silk hosiery; a black lace garter belt; and black *peau de soie* heels. During lunch, Maggie snagged her hose just above the hemline and Loretta stopped the run with a touch of clear nail polish that pulled her skin when she bent her knee. Stella's beige crocheted mini-skirt with matching jacket; long pearl necklace; button pearl earrings; and spike heels gave her that irresistible allure of innocence and naughtiness. Loretta, rarely understated, was dressed in a fitted gold lamé jacket with matching bell-bottom pants and high-heeled boots. Maggie could feel eyes turning as they walked through the lobby—wild, colorful birds against the drab navy blue and brown clothing of the proletariat.

Sam and Clyde were sitting on a bench in the hallway when they exited the elevator on the third floor. Dressed in dark suits and lost in conversation, they both dropped their jaws when they looked up. At first, Sam blushed like a teenager having impure thoughts, ran his hands through his hair and looked away as if he didn't recognize these three wild birds. Clyde was mesmerized, gave a low whistle and said, "goodness, gracious, great balls of fire."

Finally, Sam stood up and looked at Maggie as if she had just come into focus and said, "Babe, you look beautiful. I was worried you'd change your mind."

"I thought about it but decided what the hell, I might as well marry this poor Yooper. No one else will."

"Ah, Maggie, I knew I could trust you not to get caught up in this lavish ceremony."

"Did I tell you I love you?" said Maggie.

"Come on you two. We don't have all day. The JP said he has a Christmas Party to go to and we're his last gig," said Clyde.

"Maggie, you might want to rethink your attendants. Except for Stella, we are a cheeky bunch," said Loretta.

"Don't sweet talk me, Loretta. I'm the only one here who has a reason to be cheeky about marriage," said Stella.

"You got that, girl. You have the rights; the rest of us are just talkin' trash," said Loretta.

"Ready to get married, Marguerite?" said Sam.

"Aren't we going to wait for Kenny?" asked Maggie.

"No, not today."

Clyde, Loretta and Stella got to Aunt Jo's house first, pulling the reception to the front yard to greet Sam and Maggie when the white Corvair drove up. Although Sam wanted Maggie to wait for him to open her door, Maggie was having none of it and met him as he rounded the car. They kissed to cheers from their friends and relatives who were braving the cold to welcome the newlyweds.

Maggie ran up to give Issie a long hug. Issie and Eddie couldn't make it to the JP in time for the wedding because of the kid's school and Eddie's job. When Issie and Eddie got married, in a small church in Westland ten years ago, Maggie was at boarding school in Toronto studying for finals. Issie once pointed out that both she and Maggie had inherited their parents' disdain for elaborate ceremonies *and* the government's ministerial oversight of marriage.

"Oh, Maggie, look at you—absolutely gorgeous in that show-stopping red wedding dress. You look like a Chinese princess. Red! It will bring you generations of luck and love," said Issie.

"Thanks, Issie. God, I'm so glad you're here. How's everyone doing?"

"Walking on eggs, lots of polite behavior, except for Uncle Cyp who's showing the boys how to stand on their heads in the dining room, while Aunt Jo's trying to set the table."

Sam and Maggie took a divide and conquer approach to greet their guests until Aunt Jo called everyone for dinner. On the way in, Maggie gave Angelo a big hug and thanked him for coming. Angelo grumbled, "Yeah, well I didn't have nothing better to do and your Auntie Jo could use some help." Both he and Aunt Jo pretended they were just friends but Maggie always sensed an undercurrent of something more. Angelo never married. He'd complain, "Wives are a pain in the ass, who needs one?" Aunt Jo never married. She'd complain, "I lost the love of my life to World War II. No man can give me what I lost."

"Mrs. Tervo, how does it feel to be married?" asked Willie.

"Oh, for cripes sakes Willie Johnson, give her a break. She hasn't even been married an hour," said Robin.

"It feels good to hear you call me Mrs. Tervo. A little strange, but nice," said Maggie.

"Well, Maggie, you look like an evening of jazz on a New Orleans' pier—full of music and love," said Robin.

"Thank you for the lovely compliment. I've never wanted a white gown and veil. This is the perfect wedding dress for me."

"Hey, Maggie. Welcome to the family. I'm glad my asshole brother had enough sense to marry up," said Kenny. Kenny had Sam's white blond hair and blue eyes. A little stockier, Kenny's broad shoulders held a suit jacket like a mannequin. He was so ridiculously good looking it was hard not to stare.

"Kenny, where the hell were you? We missed you at the JP office," said Maggie.

"Listen, Maggie, I know my reputation precedes me, follows me, hound dogs me. I want to be a stand-up kind of guy, but I'm a loser. Everyone learns sooner or later not to depend on me or trust me. Sorry. I wish it were different. But know I'm glad Sam had the good sense to marry you. You're the best thing that's happened to our family in a long time. I mean that, Maggie."

"Thanks Kenny. I'm not buying the 'loser' thing, but I'll let you know if I think you're acting like an asshole if you'll do the same for me. Truth is, I've always wanted a brother."

"Christ, Maggie, don't make me cry. It will ruin my tough guy reputation."

"Ah, well, tough guy reputations tend to be squandered. I want to meet the real you when we have some time."

"Sounds good. I'd like to meet the real me one day, too," laughed Kenny.

Maggie looked around the house she called home for the past five years. It felt different now that she didn't live here. Blanche, Aunt Jo and Angelo were busy in the kitchen washing dishes, talking, gesturing. In the background, Maggie heard Aunt Minnie complain to Sam's mother Maija that Jo never has *real* coffee and expects people to drink that instant dishwater. Willie and Robin were on the winterized screened porch playing air hockey with the five boys—Issie's two, Eddie Jr. (7) and Raymond (5); and Clyde's three, Clyde Jr. (7), Clive (5) and Carter (3). Uncle Cyp was conked out on the hammock.

In the dining room, Sam, Clyde and Eddie were gripped by Issie's outrageous sense of humor. Maggie heard Issie talking about her labor pains being three minutes apart when she and Eddie went to the hospital to have Eddie, Jr., saying, "When I heard the woman in the next room wailing with labor pains I told the nurse who was checking me in 'sorry, I've changed my mind.' I got up and headed to the elevators thinking *no fucking way am I going to voluntarily commit myself to whatever the hell is going on in the next room. I may be a little obtuse, but I'm not psycho!*" Although Eddie had heard this story a hundred times, he smiled in appreciation for his wild and crazy wife. For Sam and Clyde, it was their first 'Issie Story' and they were doubled over in laughter.

In the living room, Kenny and Stella made an odd couple. Stella tall, thin, and reserved; Kenny shorter, muscular and restless. Yet, there was something in the way Stella leaned in to listen to Kenny that surprised Maggie. Stella was always so contained and protective of her space. This was different.

"Maggie, my beautiful bride, I hate to interrupt your reverie, but your Aunt Jo wants to talk to us before we cut the cake. I think she's ready to get rid of us," said Sam.

"Oh, husband-of-mine, I will follow you to hell and back."

"Have you been drinking?"

"No, but you can scratch that last statement. I was being a smartass and I should behave with more decorum on my wedding day," laughed Maggie.

"I'll be ready to leave after we cut the cake," said Sam.

"And what then, Mr. Tervo?"

"We drop decorum. According to the Play Bill, after the wedding cake is cut, Sam beds his beautiful and sexy wife."

Aunt Jo's bedroom was like a scene from Dr. Zhivago—snow white walls, blinds, drapes, sheets and furniture with an eggplant colored velvet duvet. In the corner, a gold filigree coat tree held Aunt Jo's panoply of shawls. On the bedside table was a small photograph of Aunt Jo and Phillip Xavier, the man she lost to World War II.

When Maggie and Sam knocked, Aunt Jo hurried them in, closed the door and said, "Please, sit on the bed."

For a few minutes they looked at one another. No one spoke. Then Sam said, "Aunt Jo, we can't thank you enough for this reception. We got to spend the evening with family and friends, people we love. It was perfect."

"Oh, Sam, I was thrilled to give you this party. You may not know how much arm-twisting I had to do to get Maggie to agree. I'm warning you, she's one stubborn Canuck."

"That she is!" said Sam.

Aunt Jo was holding an envelope in her hand and began flapping it up and down. "Okay, I thought I was prepared to give you this gift wrapped in my heart and carried by inspired words. But, here I am numb of heart and lost for words."

"Auntie Jo, it's okay. We love you," said Maggie.

After clearing her throat a few times, Aunt Jo began. "My beautiful Maggie, when you first came to live here I was so afraid. We hardly knew each other, but I wanted this to work for both of us. I wanted us to get along—maybe end up liking each other enough to stay in touch after you graduated." Aunt Jo began flapping the envelope again as tears spilled down her cheeks. "From the start, I began to think about you and what you might need or want. I looked forward to seeing you at the end of the day, talking with you. As the days passed, I realized I was becoming someone else. I didn't expect the joy you brought to my life, or the emptiness I'd feel when you moved out." Aunt Jo looked at Maggie and saw her tears, then she began to sob, "Oh, Maggie, I didn't bargain for falling in love with you and I'm doing a piss-poor job of telling you how important you've been to thawing my ceramic heart and teaching me about life."

Maggie stood up to hug Aunt Jo. Sam felt salt forming in his eyes.

"Oh, Auntie Jo, I know. I feel the same. I worked so hard to resist the temptation of turning you into my mother." Wiping her nose with the back of her hand, Maggie laughed then said, "but you've always been that and so much more—my aunt, my friend, my mentor, my landlady!

"Well, screw the landlady. I want to give you and Sam this gift. I've been planning it for a long time. I thought it would be for graduation but decided it was more important to give it to you now." Aunt Jo handed Maggie the flapping envelope and said, "This is for you and Sam."

The wedding card was simple—gold embossed lettering on the front read *Congratulations to The Bride and Groom.* Inside, a handwritten note read, *To Maggie and Sam, May your lives be filled with all the love, joy and adventure the world brings your way. Love Always, Aunt Jo.* A check for two thousand dollars with the notation *rent plus interest* slipped to the floor. Maggie picked it up and tried to hand it back.

"No, my sweet girl, this was always my plan. The bond we have and the love we share is ours to keep. This check is for you and Sam to spend however you'd like. No strings. Gifts should never have strings."

Just then Angelo pounded on the door and stuck his head in the room. "For Christ sake, they're demanding we let them eat cake. What the hell? Are you guys having a goddamn séance in here?"

Robin's masterpiece rose from the center of the dining room table like a prophecy—five stories of alternating round white cakes and square chocolate cakes. Frosted in green, and decorated with silver and red, each two-layered cake was unique in its design, brilliant in its otherness. At the head of the table, Clyde was holding a knife decorated with a silver bow, a sprig of mistletoe and a few small cranberries.

"Before Maggie and Sam cut into this work of art by Robin Johnson, I'd like to offer a toast to the bride and groom, two of my best friends. How this happened, I have no idea. As much as I'd like to take credit for introducing them, I can't. As you all know, these two unlikely suspects met during the heat of the riots, and like all love stories, there was that one pivotal synchronistic moment when Sam decided not to shoot Maggie. After that it was a wild three-legged burlap bag race to the altar. Maggie pulling one way, waiting for Sam to come up with something better than a lease for married housing as a proposal. Sam pulling the other way, thinking the $110 deposit on the cinderblock apartment was better than reciting a poem or proposing on bended knee. It was hard to watch. You ever see two people with one-leg each in a burlap bag heading in different directions, or spinning counter-clockwise to move forward? It was a sorry sight. I couldn't take it anymore. I laid it out for Sam. I said, *dude, if you want Maggie, you need to ante up more than a month's deposit on a cellblock. Women want love, commitment, fidelity and someone to take the trash to the curb. It's more like a life sentence.*"

Clyde's deadpan delivery was flawless. Laughter was ignited and reached pitch perfect hilarity as friends and family doubled over, snickered and bellowed.

Catching his breath, Kenny said, "Clyde, you'd have to be a fool to try to follow that toast and that would be me." Everyone turned to look at Kenny who'd removed his jacket and loosened his tie. Sam grabbed Maggie's hand and squeezed it. Mama Tervo crossed her arms. The dissipation of so much laughter left a canyon of silence. Kenny cleared his throat and heard the echo.

"As some of you know, I'm not comfortable calling attention to myself or giving toasts. Right now, the silence in this room is turning my stomach inside out. But this is too important to keep to myself. Tonight my brother made the best move of his life. I've known this nimrod since I was born and I have no idea why Maggie would want to marry him. But, bro, I'm in total awe. Maggie, you're the best thing that ever happened to Sam and our family. Welcome to the Tervo clan."

After the toasts, Maggie found Kenny and gave him a hug. "Thanks for the sweet words. I'm glad to be part of the Tervo clan and gain a baby brother!" Kenny grinned and nodded as Maggie made her way to the head of the table. A moment later, Mama Tervo tapped Kenny on the shoulder and whispered, "How many brews didja guzzle down today?"

After the ringing of forks against beer bottles and glass tumblers, Clyde handed Sam and Maggie the knife to cut the cake.

"At last. Free at last, free at last, lord almighty, I'm free at last!" said Sam as he gunned the engine of the Corvair. "Do you think Howard Johnson's has sound proof walls?" asked Sam.

"Why Reverend Tervo whatever do you have in mind?" said Maggie in her best imitation of a southern drawl.

"No preaching, but I may want to get on my hands and knees and howl at the moon," said Sam.

9

Ashes

With this faith we will be able to speed up the day when all of God's children all over this nation—black men and white men, Jews and Gentiles, Protestants and Catholics—will be able to join hands and sing in the words of the old Negro spiritual, 'Free at Last, Free at Last, Thank God Almighty, We are Free at Last.'
—Dr. Martin Luther King, Jr.
Grosse Pointe High School, March 14, 1968

APRIL 4, 1968 ANTE MERIDIEM—Maggie took the day off to bring order to her life. That meant cleaning the apartment, washing clothes, updating her calendar, catching up on correspondence and sorting through the junk drawers, magazines and newspapers—four months of clutter. It seemed liked yesterday when she and Sam gave up the second day of their two-day honeymoon at Howard Johnson's to pack and move into married housing. Which, in retrospect, was dumb on both sides, because packing and moving their combined worldly possessions didn't warrant an entire day or the use of Willie's pickup. The Corvair and Triumph would have been more than enough to haul their scant belongings.

Maggie cranked open the windows in the kitchen and decided to have a second cup of coffee to watch the pale sun coax temperatures past the forty degree mark for the first time that year. Thursday's were Sam's heavy day of classes from 9:00 a.m. to 5:00 p.m. and work from 6:00 p.m. until midnight. It was a good day to get things done. She'd skip her Great Classics course at two. Maggie sat down at the kitchen table and propped her legs on the other chair. *Solitude,* she thought, *how long has it been since I've sat quietly — savored my own company?*

Other than her grandmother's crocheted tablecloth, a wedding gift from Aunt Minnie and Uncle Cyp, Maggie had no trousseau to bring to the marriage. Although she balked at tradition and romantic notions about marriage ceremonies and rituals, not having a trousseau heightened the loss of her parents, her ancestral link. In August 1950, when Maggie was not yet five and Issie twelve, their mother and father disappeared in a sailing accident on the St. Lawrence Seaway. No bodies were ever recovered, and according to Uncle Cyp, neither the United States nor Canadian Coast Guard were able to draw any reliable conclusions about whether the mishap involved accidental drowning, kidnapping or murder.

Raymond and Anna Soulier co-published an independent radical newspaper in Toronto, *L'Empereur Est Nu* — translated, "The Emperor is Nude." Considered a liberal rag by the conservatives, *L'Empereur* promoted the secession of Canada from England. Based on old copies of *L'Empereur,* most of the stories garroted the United Kingdom for its callous bigotry and mistreatment of indigenous people in its colonized nations, including Canadians. One news article claimed: "UK's aggressive takeover of weaker nations is necessary to feed its pathetic national ego and royal burlesque theatre." The monarchy was, after all, an easy target and the paper routinely lampooned the obscene cost and peril of pretending a monarchy made sense in the 20th Century. Under the byline: "Surfing the Moat," *L'Empereur* poked fun at world leaders who went along with this ridiculous fairy tale. At the end of the byline, the reporter proclaimed: "Putain, l'empereur est nu!" Words Maggie and Issie adopted as their secret slogan during their years with Aunt Minnie and Uncle Cyp; words that sent them into dizzying giggles.

To say L'Empereur exposés took no prisoners would be a gross understatement. Fact checking was expensive and nearly impossible. The acid test was, "Does this information sound reasonably true and will it sell papers?" No friends to the social and political conservatives, Maggie knew her parents were harassed by the Royal Canadian Mounted Police; the MI5 in the United Kingdom; and, at times, the CIA in the United States. Twice their home and the pole barn printing shop in the back were raided while the family was visiting relatives in Windsor. Issie remembers Raymond telling Anna to behave as if their home phone was tapped.

Their parents' trip along the St. Lawrence Seaway was to celebrate their fifteenth wedding anniversary. Their only vacation without their daughters in five years. Jacques Ruivivar, a family friend and wealthy patron in Toronto, generously sponsored and promoted *L'Empereur* and loaned his ocean-worthy sailboat to the Souliers for this trip—as he had for a number of the Souliers' family vacations to Nova Scotia. Maggie's father, an expert sailor, had navigated the Great Lakes and the North Atlantic since his teens.

Because the kids were minors, the court relied on the Souliers' *Last Will and Testament* to award custody of Issie and Maggie to their Uncle Cyp and Aunt Minnie. Both girls would have preferred Aunt Jo, but she was unmarried, and according to other relatives, not ready to raise two children. Two years after their parents' disappearance, Issie found a copy of an old *Toronto Tribune* hidden away in one of Aunt Minnie's linen chests in the fourth floor attic of her Windsor home. Issie tucked it under her sweater and raced to the third floor bedroom she shared with Maggie. The front page of the *Tribune* was covered with photos of Raymond and Anna at protest marches and fundraisers. The headline read: "Revolutionary Secessionists Subject of Manhunt." The article explained: "Authorities have reason to believe that Raymond and Anna Soulier were involved in acts of international espionage and contraband." These same sources claimed the Souliers' radical newspaper, *L'Empereur Est Nu*, "was a cover for criminal activities." The Tribune went on to say: "MI5 and the Royal Canadian Mounted Police conducted a thorough search of the couples' home and confiscated all materials important to this inquiry." According to a statement made by the Royal Canadian Mounted Police Spokesman: "the Souliers' bank accounts and investments will be attached. In addition, all possessions and all real property, including the house, its contents and the printing shop, will be sold to offset the cost of the investigation and the search for Raymond and Anna Soulier."

Issie now preserved this yellowed newspaper in a plastic container in her small crawl-space attic in Westland. Maggie thought about the many times she and Issie planned to conduct their own investigation, but life kept them busy with school, ballet, piano, lacrosse and all the extracurricular activities Aunt Minnie collected to keep them occupied or, as she said, *out from under foot*. Yet, every time Maggie thought about the circumstances of her parents' disappearance (she never said death), she regretted she and Issie were not old enough or persistent enough to do some digging. Maggie wondered if Jacques Ruivivar was even alive.

Looking at the clock, Maggie said, "Holy crap!" She'd spent almost forty minutes wandering through the tendrils of her mind. Each tendril hung on to some truth, belief, idea—real or imagined—didn't seem to matter. She was struck by the fact that her little apartment with Sam was her first real home since her parents disappeared. Aunt Minnie's house never felt like home because Aunt Minnie treated it like a museum. Maggie frowned to herself thinking, *even Uncle Cyp, after fifty years of marriage, acts like a tenant.*

Married housing came with a kitchen table and two chairs, a sofa with one end table and a full-sized bed frame—metal furniture with easy-to-clean Naugahyde that stuck to bare skin and turned all clothing into Teflon. Maggie and Sam withdrew one hundred dollars from Aunt Jo's wedding gift, which they renamed *The Trust Fund*, to purchase a new mattress, four place settings of yellow Melmac dishes and four place settings of stainless flatware—all from Hudson's bargain basement. And, at the last minute, they picked up a self-whistling teakettle for instant coffee. No more heating water in a small saucepan.

Aunt Jo also gave them two beat up aluminum pans, a well-seasoned iron skillet, a once colorful Indian bedspread, two sets of slightly worn yellow towels and two sets of white sheets Maggie had used on the dormer mattress. Sam's mother, Maija, gave them two knotty pine bedside tables from Sam's old room and a striped Hudson-Bay blanket that had been sitting in Maija's linen closet for ten years because it had to be dry-cleaned. Maggie coveted it because it was exactly like the blanket she recalled from her parents' bed.

The hundreds of books they were unable to part with filled the built-in bookcase in the living room and provided five table legs to support a piece of plywood they'd found behind Angelo's, which served as a coffee table to hold more books. Because they'd only be there a few months, Maggie and Sam decided they had no interest in throw pillows or wall hangings. They'd live with bare bones until they had a place of their own.

Maggie made a third cup of coffee to sip while she cleaned the junk drawer under the phone, the one Sam used to empty his pockets after work, to toss eraser-less, snub-nosed pencils, scraps of paper and ball point pens with life spans of less than three sentences.

The first scrap of paper was hers.

Thank you notes for wedding gifts—

- ✓ Issie & Eddie—*professionally framed photo of parents' wedding*
- ✓ Aunt Jo—*$2,000!!!!*
- ✓ Uncle Cyp & Aunt Minnie—*$100 + Grandma Landry's crocheted tablecloth*
- ✓ Kenny—*wrought-iron peace symbol (wall hanging? trivet?)*
- ✓ Angelo—*two-week paid vacation!!*
- ✓ Clyde & Blanche—*copy of Khalil Gibran's "The Prophet"*
- ✓ Willie & Robin—*CAKE and two tickets to a Red Wing's game*
- ✓ Loretta—*Loretta-made macramé plant hanger with a spider plant*
- ✓ Stella—*a fireproof lock box for documents*
- ✓ Maija Tervo—*dinner for two at The London Chop House! (Who robbed a bank?)*

Clyde got to Big Boys twenty minutes early. He picked a booth that offered some privacy and ordered a coffee. All morning Clyde had been trying to shake images from last night's news clips covering King's speech to the striking garbage workers in Memphis. Clyde thought King's 'mountain top' speech was the best he'd ever heard; yet, there was something sad and ominous about the look on his face and his choice of words. *Like anybody, I'd like to live a long life . . . I've seen the Promised Land . . . I may not get there with you . . . I'm happy tonight . . . I'm not worried about anything . . . I'm not fearing any man.* There were news clips of the marchers earlier in the day, garbage men dressed for church wearing placards that read, "I AM A MAN." Clyde couldn't think about it without tearing up. *Dear God, what will it take to end this insanity?*

Sam arrived with his platinum hair touching his shoulders. Clyde didn't miss the head turning by both men and women.

"Hey, Sam," Clyde called and raised his hand.

"Hey, Clyde, I'm glad you're able to meet on short notice."

"Glad to get out of the hood. Once you've got kids, the wagon trains tend to be drawn a little closer."

The waitress was at the table before Sam sat down. Smiling, she looked directly at Sam and said," Hi, my name's Sharon. May I take your order?"

"Coffee for now."

Clyde watched Sharon walk away from the table without asking him about his order and said, "I'm not sure I love this invisibility when I'm with you."

"Oh, you'll get used to it. Everyone does," laughed Sam.

"Asshole."

"That too."

"Nice locks, Tervo. Did your barber fire you?"

"Newly married, gorgeous wife, graduate school and second-shift sweat shop labor. The barber can pound sand."

When Sharon brought Sam's coffee, they both ordered Big Boy double-decker hamburgers with extra sauce and onion rings. The same thing they ordered every time they met at Big Boys.

"Did you see the news last night—the clips from Memphis?" asked Clyde.

"Nope, missed it. I met with my study group to crank through some multivariate regression analysis problems to find the standard deviation. What a pain in the ass. I hope to hell no one asks me to come up with a standard deviation after I graduate. I plan to do a total brain dump immediately after finals."

"Tervo, I'm sure you didn't want to talk to me about regression analysis. I've no fucking idea what that even means. What's going on, kimosabe?"

"This is one of those father-confessor things. You're not my father and damn sure not a priest, but I need a friend, someone to talk to. I may be in a world of hurt or not. I don't know, but I need your take, your no bullshit street smarts, to help me think through this."

"Lay it on me."

"The night before the wedding Zito put together a party in the company's conference room on the second floor. It took on a boys-night-out kind of vibe—guys from the processing side of the house, beer, pretzels, that kind of scene. Zito was making fun of me because I was getting married and sex was free on the open market. Talkin' trash. I felt a buzz after only three beers, but hadn't eaten much, so blew it off. The guys headed home and Zito said he was going out and would be back to unlock the doors before the end of the shift. I was the last one left in the conference room. As I headed out, the latest in the long line of administrative assistants, Carla, walked in. Like those who came before her, she had a bodacious rack and liked to strut her stuff. I was trying to make my exit when she started talking about her open marriage that ended in divorce because her husband wanted sex three times a day, but that didn't mean she didn't like sex, blah, blah, blah; and the brain between my legs took over. Before I knew it, she locked the door and was unzipping my pants. Two hours later, I woke up bare-assed on the conference room floor with my pants twisted around my ankles. Someone had cleared the tables and cleaned up. I didn't know what the hell happened. I got up and saw a red blinking light. Fuck. My first thought was someone set me up and taped it. I dressed, went downstairs, did my job and didn't say jack shit to Zito when he showed up. The next day, Carla was gone. Someone new had already replaced her. I didn't ask anyone what happened to her because like some two-year-old, I wanted to cover my eyes and pretend she didn't exist. But four months later, I can't shake this sense of doom. You and I both know these guys are connected and I keep looking over my shoulder, waiting for the ax to fall."

"It's a set up. I don't know what they have in mind or when they plan to spring it on you but it's a clear set up. Someone slipped something in your drink. No telling what the story looks like on tape. You have choices, but none of them good. You can tell Zito what happened and ask his advice. You might get a sense of what you're dealing with or cause the ax to drop sooner. Or, you can ride it out; keep your eyes and ears open. My guess is they need your loyalty and this is their insurance in case you want to break the bond, whatever the 'bond' turns out to be."

"What would you do?"

"As freaked out as I'd be, and believe me I'd be freaked out, I'd ride it out. Remember the cowboy philosopher, what's his name, Will Rogers, once said: 'I've suffered so many tragedies in my life that never occurred.' Might not be that big a deal, but if you act spooked you might end up screwing the pooch. I'd stay calm. Let them make the first move. They expect you to look for a new job after you graduate and I'd stick to that plan."

"I'm such a dickhead. My life was finally coming together and I decide to play with fire. Thanks, man, it's good advice. I know you love Maggie and this was so fucked up."

"Hey ass-wipe, I love both you and Maggie. No matter what you think, this was a set up and whatever drug they gave you messed with your head. Just don't screw it up with Maggie. You'll never find another woman like her. And, as much as I hate to say it, no confessions! That means don't tell Maggie to ease your own guilt. You keep it."

"Got it. She'd be pissed at me, but she's a junkyard dog when it comes to protecting people she loves. She'd raise an army to get to the bottom of this. Maggie's the best thing that's ever happened to me. God knows I'm just beginning to grok what love and commitment mean, but she's the only person I've ever wanted to spend time with, to live with. She's unreal."

"Maggie's real. I don't know anyone more authentic. Love her the best you can."

By the time Maggie finished cleaning, organizing and laundering it was after six and she was beginning to take a certain amount of *Donna Reed* pride in her homemaking abilities. During the weekdays, Sam was never home for dinner, but a lovely dessert to share before bed seemed the perfect way to top off the clean smell of their *petite maison*. Perhaps *tarte citrons*, lemon tarts with stiff meringue? Maggie laughed at herself. All she needed was a freshly pressed apron. She imagined meeting Sam at the door, a clean house behind her, *tarte citrons* on a plate in her hands and an apron barely covering her naked body. Before her mind had a chance to play with that tendril, the phone rang. It was 6:20 p.m.

"Hello," said Maggie.

"Have you heard?" said Loretta.

"Heard what?"

"Oh god, baby."

Maggie's knees shook; her whole body trembled.

"Oh my god, is Sam hurt?"

All Maggie heard was sobbing, her own and Loretta's. Then, an ancient wailing she did not recognize. Was it coming from her? Loretta?

"Please, Loretta, please tell me what happened."

"They killed King. Oh god, Dr. King was shot in Memphis. Baby, he's dying right now. He's dying."

Maggie sat down on the kitchen floor and hugged her knees. She couldn't stop shaking. She couldn't stop crying. The sharp edges of betrayal and loss and hopelessness sucked the energy out of the room.

"I'll be there in ten minutes," a voice said.

10

Resurrection

*In the end, we will remember not the words of our enemies, but the
silence of our friends.*

—Dr. Martin Luther King, Jr.

APRIL 4, 1968 POST MERIDIEM—When Maggie answered the door,
she found Loretta standing outside in a red turban and a flowing
robe from the same cloth, an African queen. Mesmerized, unable
to take it all in, Maggie stood motionless.

"Maggie, you okay, baby?"

"Oh, Loretta, you look so beautiful and strong. I don't think I
can bear the pain of another assassination and more violence."

"Get your coat Maggie. We're going to the Student Union;
and you and me, well, we're going to talk. We're going to listen.
We're going to make damn sure if Dr. King dies, he doesn't die for
nothing."

Maggie knew she looked like a street urchin—uncombed hair,
knee-stained jeans and Sam's old camel-colored chamois shirt she'd

adopted as her own. She grabbed her navy pea coat, closed the door without locking it and followed Loretta across campus to the Student Union. Before they reached the Main Building, Loretta slowed down and slipped her hand through Maggie's elbow and pulled her close. It wasn't that cold, but they were both shivering.

The dimly lit, unheated Union was packed with students attempting to watch television reports on a 19" black-and-white Zenith. Shortly after 7:05 p.m., the newscaster reported that a spokesman from St. Joseph Hospital in Memphis, Tennessee, had pronounced Dr. Martin Luther King dead at 7:01 p.m. Eastern Standard Time. A single bullet had torn through his jaw and severed his spinal cord.

Coverage immediately switched to the White House where President Johnson was preparing to address the nation. A commentator intoned, "We understand the President just talked to Coretta Scott King to express his condolences." A weary LBJ appeared at the podium and asked every citizen "to reject the blind violence that has struck Dr. King, who lived by nonviolence. . . . It is only by joining together and only by working together that we can continue to move toward equality and fulfillment for all people."

But something vast and uncontrollable had already been set in motion. The newscaster said teletypes, from all the major news services, reported incendiary riots had erupted in cities throughout the country. The President had already mobilized National Guard troops to help contain the violence.

Sam, thought Maggie, *he'll be called up*. Maggie wanted to cancel the thoughts that raced through her mind. She wanted to hear Dr. King's call for peace. Not LBJ, not a Texan, and not, god forbid, a shit-kicking cowboy who lifts his hunting dogs by their ears.

Maggie turned when she heard Loretta's voice. On top of a table, Loretta stood like a vision summoned from some past or future that had mysteriously been made *now*. Her twenty-foot shadow cast itself against a windowless concrete-block wall. The room rippled as conversations broke off and hushes foraged toward an uneasy stillness.

"My name's Loretta Hood. I'm a Freedom Rider, not a Freedom Coaster. I'm a Freedom Speaker, not a Freedom Policer. I'm a Freedom Seeker, not a Freedom Hoarder. And I've got something to say." Words rolled in a slow, precise, measured cadence and Loretta's left foot bounced up and down as if it had no where to go. Soon, the fabric of her skirt began to swirl and quiver, like the ground trying to contain the first tremors of a quake. Taking a deep breath, she looked out at the sea of white, black and brown faces heaving together like a building storm. The energy in the room was restless, angry, bewildered. Loretta knew she had to go on, but she had no map, no idea what to say.

"Right now my heart is full of splinters. Right now my stomach is full of fire. Right now my mind is a blank space on a balcony in Jim Crow's backyard. Right now I don't know if there's a god, but I do know a blaze has started on a balcony in Memphis. A blaze has started in my gut. A blaze has started in this room and in every room where people love freedom across this country. And it will not be stopped. Part of me wants revenge, an eye for an eye and a tooth for a tooth. But where does that lead? Gandhi said it would *leave all of us blind and toothless*. But we have a fire to see by. A fire to feed us."

Some of the students moved closer, encouraging her to speak up, say more. "Dr. King taught us how. I want to cocoon myself in his passion. I want to wrap myself in his words. I want to hear with his heart. I want to hear with his heart! Dr. King told us to 'stick with love because hate is too much of a burden.'" Loretta bent at her waist and drew deep breaths, as if she'd just run a marathon.

"But, love. Love is hard. These splinters hurt. This fire burns and a part of me wants to bury myself in Dr. King's grave because love hurts. It turns hearts to stone, blood to bile. But hard as it is, Dr. King would tell us to stick with love. Love is not passive. Love is power. Love can be disobedience—marches, protests, lawsuits!

But love is not hate, fear or violence." Loretta paused to shake off her pain. "You see Dr. King and Gandhi somehow knew that love is freedom and freedom is love. Gandhi's followers started by picking up pieces of salt from the beaches, breaking the Brit's Salt Laws in India. This simple, quiet non-violent act ended years of oppression, one piece of salt at a time."

Loretta stopped talking and scanned the crowd as if she'd forgotten where she was or what she was saying. "Who the hell am I to get up on this table and talk? I don't even know who I am, so why should you care?" Loretta pointed to the students gathering closer, her voice cracking she asked, "Who are we now? Where are we going? What are we going to do?"

Wiping tears from her eyes, she shook her head and took another deep breath. "Dr. King wasn't Jesus; oh no, he wasn't perfect, but he was good. Dr. King wasn't Einstein, but he was wise. Dr. King wasn't Mother Theresa, but he was kind. Dr. King wasn't Houdini, but he knew how to change the world with his magic. Dr. King said 'the measure of a person is not what he does when life is comfortable, but what he does during times of challenge.' I'm not sure of his exact words, but the question is, in this god-awful time of murder, racism and rage, what will we do? Will we stand with Dr. King? Will we stay here and talk, find ways to continue his work, our work? Will we pick up the salt? Will we pick up the salt? Will we?"

Maggie looked around the bleak, cold, cavern-like space. Someone had turned off the television. The quiet felt sacred. In Loretta's own exposed grief and insecurity, she'd given everyone permission to be strong and weak, forgiving and unforgiving, to be broken, to be human. Then, people began to move in an uncertain comfort. They looked around as if trying to get a bead on what just happened. Who was this bold, brazen Negro woman in the red turban and robe? The applause started slowly and self-consciously, then gained speed until almost everyone was clapping and crying.

Maggie jumped into action and got someone to donate paper and a pencil to collect the names and phone numbers of students who wanted to join the Freedom Riders. Loretta was helped down from the table and began hugging the mourners. As she looked each person in the face, Loretta seemed to nod *yes our time is now.*

Maggie wasn't sure if it was exhaustion or exhilaration that kept her up. It was almost midnight and she'd not heard from Sam. If he didn't show up by 12:30, she'd assume he was called to guard duty. A non-believer, Maggie surprised herself when she whispered, "please god keep him safe."

Less than sixteen hours ago Maggie was basking in solitude and the quiet routines of a contrived wife—cleaning, baking, seducing. That was before the maelstrom, before another hero was slain and a new hero rose from the ashes. Loretta, of all people. Her boldness trounced any labels she carried—GED, hairdresser, *small* businesswoman. Tonight, in her red turban and robe, on top of a table, Loretta radiated light and power. Dr. Martin Luther King was dead but Loretta Hood was alive, unafraid to ignite new fires and lead in a time of raw-boned desperation.

Maggie woke at 7:00 a.m. because her left black-watch-plaid, pajama-clad leg kept slipping off the *damn Naugahyde sofa,* her first thought, then *no Sam. The Guard must've called him up. Damn, Loretta will be setting up her salon; Stella working; Clyde with kids, wife, work; Aunt Jo getting ready for her job at Hudson's; Issie wrangling the boys for school.* Maggie groaned at her narcissistic self-pitying in the space of Dr. King's assassination and Sam's guard duty. Who the hell did she think she was anyway? She'd head downtown to the library and read the Free Press to see if there was any news about local riots or the National Guard. Maybe she'd check the library's microfiche files to see if they had anything on her parents or Jacques Ruivivar. Something! Anything! Maggie was determined not to spend the day grieving in a clean apartment waiting for Sam to call. She and her grief would find legs.

"*Bon soir*, Marguerite," called Sam.

"*Bon soir*, soldier boy!" cried Maggie as she slid across the clean tiles in her stocking feet and gave him a hug. "I've missed you. No work tonight?"

"No work. Sorry I wasn't here when you got word about King. Did you call Issie?"

"Loretta called crying. I thought she was upset because *you* were hurt and I fell apart on the phone. Ten minutes later she showed up dressed like an African queen—red turban, robe. It was wild. She demanded I put on my coat and walk to the Student Union. Sam, after Dr. King was pronounced dead, Loretta stood on top of a table and drew a huge crowd of angry students to her like disciples. Before long, everyone was crying and hugging, determined to carry on Dr. King's work. It was crazy. I had no idea Loretta had that kind of power."

"Oh, Mag, I'm glad you weren't alone. Loretta's a freaking sorceress. I've seen her smack down gang members with one glance. She *is* an African queen when her back's against the wall."

"Hungry?"

"Starving."

"Yesterday's stew and day-old bread coming up. Any signs of Carl Stringer or Avenge last night?"

"None. There was talk about a group called the Invaders, in Memphis, who were pushing peaceful protesters toward violence and creating some of their own. The buzz is the Invaders were on the FBI payroll to ramp up the chaos and shut down Johnson's support of King *and* the Civil Rights Movement."

"No shit? What does the FBI have to gain from that?"

"My dear Maggie, J. Edgar is a raving, tight-assed conservative and flaming bigot who thinks civil rights activists are dangerous subversives and communist sympathizers. He'd do anything he could to undermine our work."

"I don't get it. Why would a gay guy in a closet object to civil rights?"

"I hope to hell our apartment isn't bugged. Are you kidding me? What makes you say that?" asked Sam, as he glared through squinted eyes and squeezed her hand so hard it hurt.

"Seriously? You're not worried about saying the Invaders are on the FBI payroll but you're worried about me suggesting Hoover is homosexual? What's that about?"

Sam shook his head and said, "Let's talk about your day. Mine is obviously too full of shadows and boogiemen."

Maggie grinned and said, "Now that you mention it, I ran into some cloaks and daggers today. I spent most of my time at the library to see if I could find out if our city was burning down and dredge up something about my parents' vanishing act. No word on the National Guard, so assumed you'd show up before too long. Then, in an old clipping, I found Jacques Ruivivar, Raymond's and Anna's patron. Tracking the microfiche forward, it looks like he's alive and well in Toronto. More recent articles link him to the FLQ, the *Front de Liberation de Quebec*—a militant separatist group supporting Quebec's sovereignty. No peaceful protests there. The FLQ guerillas, the Felquistes, trained with the Palestine Liberation Organization in Jordan and are hell bent on pushing for a French Quebec. And, get this, one of the Felquistes, Pierre Valliéres, just published a book called *White Niggers Of America*, drawing a parallel between French Canadians and blacks in the U.S. Make no mistake, I'm horrified by their use of guerilla tactics and violence, but somehow more proud to be a Soulier. Make any sense?"

"I don't know. Nothing seems to make sense these days."

"Anyhow, it looks like Mr. Ruivivar is a big time activist or terrorist. Sam, can we take a few weeks this summer and see if we can find him? See what he knows about my parents' disappearance?"

"Sure. We can figure something out, ride into the great unknown; take a look at the latest version of the French Revolution. But first, we have to decide where we're going to live. We only have married student housing until mid-May. I think our best move is to find a rental in northwest Detroit before we buy."

"Moving two more times seems nuts. What if we find the perfect fixer-upper? Why wouldn't we just buy it?"

"Because, my love, we don't have real jobs. Where we work and what we make has a significant impact on qualifying for a mortgage and buying a home."

"Ah, the MBA speak I so love to hear," groaned Maggie.

"I have a few other languages at my disposal."

"Like what?"

"Like what do you think about making a baby?"

"Are you kidding? I haven't even had a real job yet. I can't get pregnant now."

"I'm not kidding. We've been talking about this for months. It's time, Mag. I'm ready. I think you are. Maybe because we both lost parents when we were young. We'll have beautiful, smart, sassy kids. I want to be young enough to play with them, take them places, get to know them."

"Holy crap. I need time to think about this. I mean, I always thought I wanted a child, as in *one* child. But, there are times when I'm not sure. Besides, even if I was absolutely sure I wanted a baby, I want our kid to have a place to call home. It doesn't make sense if we both need jobs before we buy a house."

"In some ways it does. You might not get pregnant right away, but if you do we can make it work. Like teaching a few night classes in poetry so I can be home with the baby. Mag, there's no question. You'll be a great mom."

"You'd do that? Stay home with the baby so I could work evenings?"

"Sure. We want to start a family. There's no perfect time. Why not? Besides, it would be a lot of fun trying to get pregnant."

"Speaking of trying, let me show you what I bought today."

Maggie opened a Woolworth's bag and pulled out an orange and white checked bibbed apron. "I thought you might be impressed by my *Donna Reed* clean house and dinner. This seemed to be the icing on the *éclair*. I could try it on for you," said Maggie with a coquettishness that Sam thought sounded both tender and wildly seductive.

Before she was done speaking, Sam started to unbutton Maggie's blouse. No bra. Maggie unwrapped her wraparound skirt and let it fall to the floor. No panties. Sam's hands began to shake as he slipped the apron over Maggie's head. He ran his fingers along the edge of the bib and turned Maggie around until his hands were resting on her *Bermuda Triangle*. Sam felt a certain *déjà vu* — or was it a flashback? He wasn't sure. The shadows and boogiemen reappeared. The ax seemed to be suspended in air, waiting to drop.

11

Cartels and Conspiracies

So however difficult it is during this period, however difficult it is to continue to live with the agony and the continued existence of racism, however difficult it is to live amidst the constant hurt, the constant insult and the constant disrespect ... we shall overcome ...

— Dr. Martin Luther King, Jr.

JULY, 1968 — "Before we begin, I want to thank Robin, *in absentia,* the only word I remember from high school Latin, for making a cake to celebrate our one-year anniversary as The Eights. She said, wait a minute, here's her note:

> *A nutty pineapple right-side-up cake as a sign of our kickass stick-with-it-ness in this wacko upside-down world!*
> *Peace and Love, Rocking Robin & Red-Winged Willie*

In case you didn't know, the Johnson's are on their first ever road-trip vacation to New York City. Literally, their first ever road trip, first ever vacation and first ever trip to New York City. Robin wanted to go to Mackinaw Island but Willie nixed that by saying he didn't want to be handed a dishtowel when they got to The Grand Hotel. Anyone been to Mackinaw?" asked Clyde.

"As a kid. The island was pure white, including stable hands, busboys, and housekeepers. Lots of rich college types waiting tables. Suit and tie required in the dining room. Prissy as hell," said Sam.

"I went two years ago with Aunt Jo for my bachelor's degree celebration. Whites only north of Saginaw. In fact, I think I was the only brunette on the island. Mackinaw's horse-and-buggy-eighteenth-century motif comes replete with racism," said Maggie.

"I say we all go next year and *replete* ourselves. Order chitlins and greens, dance buck naked around a campfire and drink from the public water fountains," said Blanche.

"Damn it to hell Blanche, drink from the public water fountains? Have you lost your friggin' mind?" said Loretta.

"Someone's gotta do it," said Blanche.

"I'm there," said Stella.

The group's laughter felt forced, it's energy flat. It had been three interminable months since Dr. King's assassination and one wretched, agonizing month since Sirhan Sirhan's bullet took down Bobby Kennedy. Both deaths were still swinging from cottonwoods, oaks and willows in small towns and large cities across the country. The shrouds of these two men hung heavy as civil rights workers slogged through the summer of 1968. People talked about the new Jim Crow—assassins hired by powerful, wealthy cartels. Conspiracy theories made more sense than the random loss of the nation's finest civil rights leaders by lone assassins—JFK, MLK and RFK. Hope plummeted.

Exasperated, Loretta leaned over the table and said "Look at us, catfish picking through rubbish at the bottom of the Detroit River for what? To avoid daylight, oxygen? Who are we waiting for in this dark, airless place? You think Ralph Abernathy is going to lift us out of these dining room chairs?"

"It's a time for mourning. Three months isn't long when we look at over three hundred years of slavery, oppression and segregation. A week after Dr. King's assassination the '68 Civil Rights Act was signed. Two months later, RFK was assassinated. We've been brought to our knees but we haven't stopped," said Stella.

"Stella, we've been down this road before. Three *weeks* is too long. You think George Wallace is mourning? You think his bid for president was slowed down by grief? Or you think, just maybe, he's dusting off his speech about *segregation forever*? I know it's hard, I know it hurts like hell, but we're it. No one's going to do it for us."

"Loretta's right. We can't sit around wringing our hands like a bunch of girls," said Clyde.

"Screw you," said Maggie.

"Maggie, why do you always take my old saws so personally? I didn't mean *you're* wringing your hands."

"Words wield power—like legends, fables, fairy tales. What crap. You're too smart to pretend it's okay to bust an entire class of people."

"Sorry. I can't help being an asshole, which is why I surround myself with bad-ass women."

"You got that right, and you can bet your sorry ass we'll remind you when you forget," said Blanche.

Usually quiet and always kind, Blanche's unexpected barb shut down the room. Through the screens, the sound of crickets took over. Clyde looked down, wound his wedding band back and forth, before he looked up and said, "Back to Loretta's point. No more time for mourning. The polls show Wallace gaining support from blue-collar workers in both the north and south. It's dangerous to blow him off as a joke. Until November, he's got press, microphones and audiences. We don't. We need to get our act together and get the word out. Maggie, where are we on Carl Stringer's pocket protector avengers?"

"Not much going on since they crashed King's talk at Grosse Point High last March. Carl's rabid obsession is dangerous, but most of his co-workers think he's a complete jackass. I'm told people agree with him to get him off their backs so they can get back to work. No one's able to pin down the number of active members in Avenge because it draws crowds from the Birchers, the Klan, Nazis and other bed-wetters. Bottom line, Carl's scare tactics are getting old. My sense is he's more nuisance than threat."

"Let's not get blindsided by the number of whites who talk the talk but hope we stay where we are, in the ghetto and out of their lives. If anyone here thinks Detroit isn't heading to become one of the biggest, meanest ghettoes in the north, think again. We've got to move this act to the burbs. Dr. King and RFK may have been shot by single assassins, but James Earl Ray and Sirhan Sirhan had the support of millions of white racists. These racists might have been silent, they might not have held the guns, but they sure as shit helped pull the triggers," said Loretta.

"And," continued Loretta, "we know there are far too many muckety-mucks who rig the game and call the plays. The FBI sure as hell didn't tell Dr. King about the threats against his life. Instead, Clyde Tolson, Hoover's henchman and not-so-secret-lover, called Dr. King 'the most dangerous Negro leader in America.' Dangerous? Give me a break. This peaceful, non-violent civil rights leader was dangerous? Seriously, who was afraid of Dr. King? The FBI? The Klan? King Henry Ford?"

Sam leaned forward, stretched his right arm across the table and pointed at Loretta and said, "Loretta's right. Tolson's decision to call King 'the most dangerous Negro leader in America' was no misspeak by the Bureau. Tolson took his orders from J. Edgar and J. Edgar wants to rile white suburbia. More importantly, Hoover wanted MLK gone. I confess to being cynical as hell, but the conspiracy here is dressed in neon." Pulling his arm back and looking around the table, Sam continued. "Here's my take. King spent most of his life working on civil rights legislation that attempts to reinstate the civil rights of non-whites and women. Hear me when I say 'attempts to reinstate.' The right to vote was given to Negroes, I mean black men, one hundred years ago. Then, fifty some years later, women got the right to vote. The Civil Rights Act Stella talked about reinstates voting and property rights with sharper teeth. But let's not kid ourselves, it'll take frigging years for court cases to test, argue and achieve what this new Act claims to protect. Right now, our job is to push these fragile eggs through the fallopian tubes of white courts. To, finally, enforce these birthrights. We can't wait for daylight or air or a period of mourning. We've got to grab it and fight for it, or live without it."

"Sam Tervo, is that you or are you channeling Dr. King?" said Stella. "You sound like a civil rights leader."

"No way; not me. Loretta's the leader. I just took what she said and dog paddled through the shallow basin of my mind."

"Sam, thanks for saying 'black men.' So, how about it Sista-Hood, you ready to do some preaching? Next 'Revival Meeting' at Hope Chapel?" asked Clyde.

Loretta looked at her friends sitting around the Webster's dining room table—Clyde, Blanche, Stella, Sam, Maggie. They were a reckless crew of normal, broken, hungry people. Loretta thought, *who are we to think we can flip the switch? And me, I don't have enough time to get through the day.* Before she finished that thought, images of Sojourner Truth and Harriet Tubman tap-danced on her wooly head. Loretta smiled then said, "Hell yes! All you white dudes in my old history books need to move your sorry asses over and make room for Sojourner and Harriet and all those who spent their lives fighting for equal rights. I don't know where I'm going to find the time and energy, but I'm surrounded by friends, and ghosts, who are ready to help me hatch some eggs."

Sam had a hard time believing a year had passed since the riots. The smell of smoke and ash haunted Detroit neighborhoods. Burned out buildings, charred skeletons, stood like ancient ruins—monoliths of humankind's rage against poverty, invisibility, injustice. Just west of the blight, Sam and Maggie had rented a small gray-shingled bungalow on a month-to-month lease. Vacant for the past six months, the house was clean but in deep decline. Door, cupboard and faucet handles were loose; windows sealed by layers of paint or nailed shut; linoleum buckling and wallpaper pealing. On the plus side, it was dirt cheap, only six miles to Sheer Juice and an easy bus ride to The University of Detroit where Maggie snagged a part-time teaching job for the Fall. Poetry positions were legacies. Poets did not give up teaching positions. Maggie soon realized it was a waste of time to surf the obits for dead poetry teachers, because positions were filled before the incumbent gasped his last breath. Like so many before her, Maggie would begin her fine arts career teaching Freshman English. Sam had his resumes out to most of the car companies and a few banks. Car companies paid twice as much for new MBAs and offered more interesting work, better benefits and chances for advancement. Sam was keeping his fingers crossed.

"Hey Clyde, I think the ax is starting to fall. Zito called and wants to make sure I'll be at work tonight. Says he needs to talk to me," said Sam.

"Time for Big Boys?"

"Literally and figuratively. I'm not sure I have a big enough dick to deal with this myself."

"Well, I can understand why you're calling a black guy."

"Thank god. I must have misunderstood Blanche."

"Fuck you, Tervo."

"Noon tomorrow?" laughed Sam.

"I'll be there."

Sam got to Big Boys early. Clyde usually arrived first to steal away from work and family, but today Sam needed some alone time. His shallow breathing wasn't about King, Kennedy or civil rights. His shallow breathing was about his own sinkhole of moral turpitude. In street language, it was the cost of being a dickhead.

"Hey, dickhead," said Clyde.

"You took the words right out of my head."

Clyde faked a punch to Sam's head before he sat down and said, "Let's order. I'm starving."

"You notice any changes here?" asked Sam.

"Hmm. Nope."

"Like I'm the only white guy in the restaurant? Seriously, I thought someone might come up to me and ask if they could pet my blond hair. It's freaking weird."

"No shit. You are. Well, isn't this a black renaissance?"

"That too," said Sam.

A young black woman, in a white cotton blouse and modest navy blue a-line skirt approached the table. She was new. New was written all over her careful grooming, perfectly pressed uniform, sharpened pencil and formal greeting. Clyde was particularly kind and patient as he gave his order. Sam thought restaurant employees were in some secret society. They took care of each other. Clyde, like Maggie, always left big tips.

"Before I mess with your mind, what was going on between you and Blanche the other night?"

"Like what?" said Clyde.

"Just picked up an edge."

"Ah, nothing. She was pissed because I signed up for some additional shifts at Angelo's and she wanted me home to help set up for the meeting. Just the usual three-legged-race for time, space and sanity! We're both working too many hours and as the boys get older there's no friggin' time to get away."

"Sorry. Am I stealing alms?"

"No, asshole. My choice. What gives?"

"Long story. Last night I got to work a few minutes early and Zito met me at the door . . .

" 'Hey ass-wipe, need to talk to you,' said Zito.

" 'Sure thing, Zito.' I thought we were heading to his office on the second floor but he took me to the Conference Room. On the table was a small viewing screen and a tape player. My knees buckled and I thought I was going to upchuck three White Castles.

" 'What the hell happened in this room between you and Carla?'

" 'Zito, I don't know.' Then, I spilled my guts and gave him my story—hopeful blow job, last fling, great tits then the blackout.

"Zito kept shaking his head up and down like he knew all this, like he'd seen it on the tapes. Then he said, 'What about the bruises on Carla's face and neck?'

" 'I don't remember anything after she removed her bra.'

" 'You don't remember choking her, slapping her?'

" 'No way, Zito. I've never hit anyone—man or woman. There's no way I'd hit or choke anyone.' I could hardly form words I was so fucking scared.

" 'Look, ass-wipe, I'm not messing with you. You're in some deep shit, and I can't help you unless you help me here.'

" 'Zito, I don't remember a thing. I woke up with my pants wrapped around my ankles. My head was throbbing. Someone had cleaned the room while I was passed out cold. I swear I'd never hit a woman.'

"Zito patted me on the knee and said, 'Maybe someone gave you a mickey. I don't know, but I saw the tapes and I'm here to tell ya, you held her head like a goddamn vice when she was on her knees. When she tried to leave, you grabbed her by the throat and held her over the table. I've seen some rough sex in my life, sicko porno flicks and all that, but this was hard to watch. You're lucky you didn't kill her. Carla's attorney called the next day and we looked at the tapes. After talking with our lawyers we decided we couldn't afford the bad press. What with the beer company joint venture and all. So we settled yesterday. It cost us a shitload of money. Her attorney said he gave us the *only* copies of photos they took of her bruises, which we all know is bullshit. The deal is you don't even think about contacting her. Got that ass-wipe?'

" 'In spades.'

" 'Now pretty boy, we need to find a way to get you the hell away from Sheer Juice, but within reach if things go south. You've got an interview with Jingo Motors next week. Some piss ant title like Employee Who-Haw for hiring or training, I forget. So, get your resume shined up and make sure you get this job. *Capisce*?'

" 'Sure Zito.'

"Late that night, one of the processing guys, Henry, pulled me off to the side and said he needed to talk. I followed him to the loading dock so he could have a smoke. He told me the new chemical they're putting in the juice to extend shelf life is poison. Might even cause cancer. I treated it like a loyalty test and said it was time to give up his freakin' Dick Tracey comic books. I told him the preservatives are safe."

"So Clyde, my best friend and partner in crime, I'm sitting here wondering if I can trust you. That's how mind-fucked I am. If you're part of this cartel, this conspiracy, you know I'm bought. If you're *not* part of this cartel or conspiracy, you know I'm bought."

"Sad day for us, my friend, but I get it. What you said is between us. What you decide I'll honor. But hear me say this, I am and will always be your friend."

Sam looked at Clyde, then looked somewhere beyond Clyde's view and shook his head 'no.' Clyde turned around to look. Nothing. No one.

"Hey Sam, you want to talk this through? Get my take?" said Clyde.

"Yeah, sure. I'm a mess. Didn't sleep."

"First question, did you see the tape?"

"Nope. Last thing I wanted to do was watch that tape."

"How do you know this isn't one big setup? What if they paid Carla to seduce you after they drugged you up?"

"Go on," said Sam.

"If I wanted to buy your loyalty, I'd think of what's important to you. Number one, Maggie; number two, reputation; number three, job. This is a tripleheader, my friend."

"What about the Henry thing?"

"Well, if Henry was a set up, they might think you've been nosing around. They know you're an activist and you wouldn't let something like that go. That might be a close second in importance to you. But, if this dude was *not* set up, he wanted to send you information because he knows you're an activist and smart and ready to move on after your MBA." Clyde paused for a moment then asked, "Did Zito show you the photos?"

"Nope."

"If I wanted to scare the shit out of you I'd show you the tape or photos, especially the photos. Security tapes tend to be fuzzy and hard to read, but the photos would have sealed your loyalty. Why not show you? Maybe they don't have photos. Maybe Carla was part of the plot to secure your loyalty and she's off on a two week cruise to the Bahamas."

"Here's something I don't think I told you. When I came to, I felt myself to see if I'd come. Nothing. No stickiness, scent, nothing. I may not know my head from a hole in the ground, but there's no way I'd force myself on a woman. Carla showed up at the end of the party, locked the door and unbuckled my belt. I might be an asshole, but I'm not a brute."

"So think about it. Here's Carla freaked out of her mind because you're beating the shit out of her, raping her and she cleans you up and cleans the room before she leaves. I don't think so. I think they want you by the short hairs and the best way to keep you in the circle is to keep you scared."

"You're right. There's no way Carla would hang around to clean up if that's what happened. I'm a total nimrod. I missed it."

"Fear makes us nuts. I know. I've been there."

"In this situation?"

"You are a nimrod. No. Not in this *exact* situation. But I know how fear can make us nuts. You need to find some way to tamp down the fear and pay attention. My guess is they didn't spend this much time and energy for a short-term relationship. They think they've bought you. You think you're bought. For that matter, I think you're bought. I don't know how you unwrap this but you need to look at this long-term. Years. You play it out and don't let them know what you know. Be the nimrod."

"Christ, Clyde, sorry I said I didn't trust you. Other than Maggie, you're my only friend and no way in hell can I tell Maggie about this. You're it."

"Tervo, listen up. You've got to treat everyone you meet like kryptonite. That means *everyone*, asshole. You can't afford another Carla. And, remember, I can't have your back unless you ask for help. *Capisce?*"

12

Evolution

You say you want a revolution—well, you know—we all want to change the world. You tell me that it's evolution—well, you know—we all want to change the world.

—The Beatles, lyrics from *Revolution*.

AUGUST 1968—"Hey, Mag, let's boogie shoo before we miss the revolution. By the time we get through customs and drive two-hundred-fifty-some miles, the French might have planted their flag in Quebec and headed to Toronto." Dressed in a pair of cut-off jeans, a white undershirt, his second-string brown loafers and aviator sunglasses, Sam stood by the raised hood of the Corvair's front trunk sipping coffee, waiting for Maggie to wrangle Aunt Jo's blue Samsonite. Maggie insisted on taking the largest piece for their ten-day trip. When Sam reminded Maggie about the tiny old stairways in *pensiones* and suggested she take two smaller suitcases, Maggie said, "No problem, Tervo, I'll handle it myself."

"Coming!" yelled Maggie as she shoved the clunky suitcase across the tattered linoleum floor. Once she made it to the side door, she had to push the suitcase through first, then down two narrow wood steps, before she could step out and close the door. Maggie's hair, wet from the shower, was in a ponytail filled with brush rollers. The rest of her looked like she stepped off the cover of this month's Glamour Magazine—a new pink and orange striped sundress with orange espadrilles, tanned skin, Hot Pink lipstick and matching nail polish.

Sam whistled and said, "Hot damn. It was worth the wait!"

"*Merci ma chère.* I'm so freaked I can hardly stand it. I've wanted this trip for so long it's hard to breathe. What if we can't find Jacques or he won't see us?"

"Oh, Maggie, it's a moon shot. If he doesn't see us, well that tells us something. We can dig through the libraries, look for friends, neighbors who remember your family."

"I know. I know. But I have to see him, to look him in the eyes and see what's there. From the untrimmed edges of my patchwork soul, I know they disappeared to protect Issie and me. During the Cold War every radical and most liberals were labeled communists. *L'Empereur* was exposing corruption, crushing the establishment. My parents knew they were dancing on the edge of a cauldron. Sam, I know this sounds like a childhood fantasy, but every molecule in my body tells me they're not dead."

"Maggie, we have ten days. The last time I had ten days to focus on any *one* thing was when I was, what six, banging my knees, learning to ride a two-wheeler. We'll find some leads or the leads will find us."

"Do you have any idea how much I love you?"

Sam looked at Maggie and thought, *unbelievable. This drop-dead beautiful, smart, funny woman loves me* then said, "Maggie, of course. How could you not?"

Maggie laughed and said, "Tervo, you are one insufferable, ego-tistical Yooper. It's a good thing you've got the looks to pull it off."

Luggage, books, magazines, a wicker picnic basket and blanket filled every spare inch of the Corvair. On beautiful summer days like this, Maggie missed the Triumph's ragtop. But, after a bitter winter, with several recharges to its fading battery, two flat tires and a few fender benders, she and Sam sold the Triumph while it was worth some money. *Cha-ching!* Another eight hundred dollars added to their savings account.

Maggie switched on the radio to The Beatle's newest record, *Revolution.* It had already become a favorite. . . . *But when you talk about destruction, don't you know that you can count me out. . . .*

After singing their way through Windsor's traffic and smog, the road opened up to miles and miles of countryside. The green pastures and farmlands might have been scenery in France or Brazil or America. Yet, here they were in Canada, Maggie's first home. Tears began to spill down her cheeks, chin, neck, then pooled in her collarbones. She let them flow and experienced, maybe for the first time, the *sensation* of Canada as her birthplace. Her first destination on this beautiful, crazy planet.

"Hey, babe, you okay?" said Sam as he pulled to the side of the road, turned off the car and looked at her. Prisms of light pierced Maggie's eyes, hair and tears. The picks in her brush rollers created some sort of dizzying crown of thorns. Maggie smiled then Sam smiled as they wrapped their arms around each other. In the silence of that simple embrace, Maggie and Sam met one another in a way neither would ever talk about or attempt to describe.

"How about here? We're only an hour from Toronto and about to run out of pasture," said Sam.

"I guess. I'm not sure we should be climbing fences."

"Mag, you of all people? Really? I thought you were hell bent on finding rules to break."

"You're right, what was I thinking? Okay, let's bend and break some rules."

"I've got some rule-breaking ideas," teased Sam as he slid the car on the gravel shoulder and brought it to a sharp stop at the ragged edge of a drainage ditch hidden by weeds.

Maggie whispered, "holy crap, Sam. Don't move. The right front tire is teetering on the edge of a pit at least five feet wide and five feet deep."

Without responding, Sam eased the steering wheel to the right, put the car in reverse and slowly lifted his foot off the clutch as he backed a few inches. Straightening the wheels, he shifted to first gear and barely touched the gas pedal as he crept forward then gently turned left toward the highway. Once he felt the traction of pavement, Sam said, mostly to himself, "Must be a tractor path somewhere down the road." Although he had a reputation for tacking through turbulent winds, Maggie knew to look for that ever-so-slight tightness in Sam's temples when he grit his teeth. It was her cue to back off and trust his compass.

A mile down the road they saw two well-worn tire tracks angled across the ditch and pulled in. A simple metal gate closed off vehicle traffic, but offered an easy climb to the pasture. Maggie grabbed the blanket and Sam picked up the picnic basket.

Up close, the pasture was a carnival funhouse of mud puddles and moguls. What they thought was shining wheat turned out to be thistle. Driven by hunger and an irrational determination to find the perfect spot, Sam charged ahead. Now more than fifty yards away, Maggie saw him turn and run back, yelling for Maggie to get to the car. In the distance a bull was gaining ground. By the time they reached the car they were covered in black silt, their bare legs thrashed by thistle. Both were too winded to laugh but they couldn't help themselves. Choking, coughing and chortling, they chased away any and all romantic notions about pastures and picnics.

When they threw the blanket across the tractor path in front of the car, the bull snorted, stomped his feet and shook his horns from the other side of the gate. "El toro!" laughed Maggie as she made a few moves with her corner of the blanket.

Lunch turned out to be a repeat of the un-pastoral-pasture story. Ice stored in plastic bags had melted and leaked into the wax-papered tuna salad sandwiches. Dill pickles had marinated the already too sour apple slices. Paper napkins, left over from the wedding party, were sopping wet. After they hoovered a small bag of potato chips, Maggie and Sam clicked their Coke cans together in a toast.

"Here's to being chased by a bull; it has a certain Hemingway-esque feel to it," laughed Maggie.

Sam took Maggie's Coke from her hand and placed it beside his on a nearby rock. Stretching out on the blanket, Sam pulled Maggie on top of him. Reaching under her skirt, he hooked his thumb through the crotch of her cotton panties and shimmied them down. The air, sun and risk of being seen had a slow motion effect—like listening to a 78 rpm record played at 33 rpm. Time was unreliable. Aware of the sun's heat, Maggie's weight and the tension of his muscles, Sam began to sit up. The smell of the bull mingled with his own sweat as he eased himself out from under Maggie. On her stomach, she seemed listless, sleepy as Sam lifted her up on one knee then the other. He stripped off his shirt and wiped his face and the back of his neck as he watched a light breeze play with the hem of Maggie's sundress. Time passed, time stood still. On his knees, Sam lifted the back of her dress. Head back, the bull snorted, pounded his right hoof in the ground then bellowed as he slammed his horns against the metal fence again and again.

It was after four when Maggie and Sam found the *pensione* they set up through AAA Travel. Only a few blocks from downtown Toronto, the Yorkville neighborhood had been pegged *Hippie Haven*. The two-story, bay-and-gable house was surrounded by private homes that had been converted to *pensiones* or small businesses—attorneys, photographers, accountants, stationary stores, tobacco stores, head shops—a neighborhood in transition. A small sign at the driveway said: *Parking for Maple Leaf Guests Only.* Other than this, there was no other sign identifying the house as a *pensione*.

A small pebble path led from the driveway to a side entrance with a note: *Mr. and Mrs. Tervo please come in and give me a holler. Thank you, Marc DeVille, Proprietor.*

Maggie and Sam entered a vibrant old kitchen. The ceiling was ten feet high. Cupboards and open shelving held at least three sets of dishes, serving platters and bowls, food, birdseed, table linens and dozens of cookbooks. Pots and pans hung from racks over two well-worn cook tops. A huge butcher-block table, holding bowls of fresh fruit, nuts, tea bags and small jelly jars anchored the room. In an adjoining sunroom there were three tables seating four each. The look, feel and color palate was familiar—Aunt Jo's kitchen on steroids.

"*Bonjour*, Monsieur DeVille," called Maggie.

"*Bonjour*, Madame Tervo. Is that you?" replied a voice from another room in the house.

"Yes. We're here in the kitchen," said Maggie.

A tall man with startling blue eyes and long gray hair tied in a ponytail walked in, shrinking the size of the kitchen with his wave of energy. "Good afternoon! You must be exhausted after your long trip. Please, please, sit down. I'll make some coffee and warm up some of the best banana nut bread you've ever eaten," said Mr. DeVille.

"I'm happy to help," said Maggie.

"Maybe another day. Let me make sure I have the names right, Maggie and Sam?"

"Yes, thanks. We *are* exhausted and coffee and food sound great." said Sam.

"I bet, and please, call me Marc."

"I detect an American accent," said Maggie.

"That's where I spent most of my life. My father moved us to Detroit back in the 30's and I lived there until after the war, then moved to California. After I lost my parents in the late 50's, I decided it was time to get to know my French Canadian relatives. When my grandmother died last year, I was her only living heir and inherited The Maple Leaf. I thought, what the hell, I might as well see what it's like to run a small *pensione* in Toronto. Twenty years of writing ads for cars and cleaning products was frying my brain. I pick up some freelance ad copy for pocket change, but mostly sit on my ass and watch TV commercials. How about you guys, what do you do?"

"We both just graduated from Wayne State. I'm starting a new job for Jingo Motors when we get back—interviewing and hiring. In September, Maggie takes on a few Freshman English classes at The University of Detroit."

"Freshman English, as in 'go shoot yourself?'" asked Marc.

"Pretty close," laughed Maggie. "My first love is poetry but there's a long line of ravenous artists ahead of me."

"Poetry's a tough market. No money but lots of competition. Go figure!" said Marc. Then turning to Sam, he said, "Jingo Motors? I don't know them, but if they're anything like the auto companies I worked with, well, watch your back. I've never met a bunch of executives who spent more time climbing over each other to reach the executive bathroom. Makes you wonder who the hell's minding the store."

"Jingo's too new to have a reputation, but I gotta admire their good judgment in hiring me."

"My husband has no shame," laughed Maggie. "Visions of grandeur or some other pathological affliction. He'll fit in."

"I love it! People are so frigging serious these days. I know there's a lot of shit going down in Detroit but, come on now, slavery ended after the Civil War. Right? Time for the niggers to quit whining and complaining, give up that non-war."

"Banana nut bread hit the spot," said Maggie as she downed her coffee and got up from the table. Even with her tan, Sam could see the blood rising.

"Yep, thanks Marc, we appreciate the welcome but need to unpack before we crash. It's been a long day," said Sam.

"Sure thing. We can talk later. You have the first floor room, far end of the hall. The keys are on a hook next to the door. So there's no surprise, we'll be sharing the loo across from your room. I shower at night. Second floor is booked for the next few months, a young family from Windsor looking for a place to live. Two kids, noisy as hell, but konked out by seven."

"Maggie, we're not selling out. Marc's a Neanderthal and bigot. Maybe both. The world's full of both."

"But that doesn't mean we have to stay under his roof."

Sam lowered his voice and said, "Mag, we're here. We'll be out scouring the city every day. We won't even see him."

Lowering her voice even more, Maggie said, "Really? I would not have been more shocked if Marc confessed to being a serial killer. The minute he walked in the kitchen I was impressed by his looks and energy. I thought hip, liberal, artistic guy from California. A potential friend! My intuition is totally off kilter, which means we are so fucked."

"About what?"

Whispering, Maggie said, "It's *about* being here to investigate the disappearance of my parents and the first person I meet is a serial killer who I immediately consider a potential friend."

"Give me a break, Mag. He's not a serial killer. With his ponytail and blue denim shirt I pegged him as a liberal. We were wrong. Just a warning for us to look beyond what we think we see."

"Tervo, I get where you're going, and I love you for it, but I'm not in the mood to be cheered up. I'd like to relax in my funk and point out that my suitcase made the trip just fine, thank you very much."

"By all means, enjoy your funk and *oh so sweet* revenge. You deserve it. I, for one, will forever remember today as the day you drove a bull crazy and took me to the moon and back. Marguerite Tervo, matador and astronaut."

13

Haute Bourgeoisie

*There are decades where nothing happens; and there are weeks
where decades happen.*

—Vladimir Ilich Lenin

AUGUST 1968—A large carafe of dark roast coffee sat on a low flame
next to a basket of blueberry muffins in a red and white striped dish-
cloth on the butcher-block table. A note from Marc read: *Enjoy!*

"We can do this, Maggie. We're paying for it," said Sam.

Maggie inhaled the seductive bouquet of roasted coffee and
blueberry muffins—aromas that defied definition. Like trying to
describe the color orange. Maggie buried her face in her hands
and said, "Okay, enough. I've been scented into submission. I'm
about to prostitute my integrity for real coffee and fresh blueberry
muffins."

Two of the tables in the sunroom were set with flowers in
wine bottles, bowls of fresh strawberries and pitchers of orange

juice. Compared to their usual fare, this small *pensione* was a five-diamond hotel.

Wiping a stray blueberry off the plate with his finger, Sam asked, "Where to first?"

"Jacques' office. I want to let him know we're in town. A ghost from his past who wants to stop by and learn more about her parents? Does that ring true?"

"It is true. Why wouldn't he buy it?"

"You're right, he'll buy it. He's probably some old dodderer who won't remember me."

"Maggie, his friends disappeared or he helped them disappear. He knows about you and Issie. He might be doddering, but I'm sure he remembers you."

"Oh crap, how will he reach us if he's not in? Should I ask Marc if we can use his phone number?"

"If Jacques isn't in, we can ask his secretary to set up an appointment for tomorrow. If she won't, then we let her know we'll stop by tomorrow to see if he can meet with us."

"Let's 'walk the dog.' If she's French we play by her rules. If she's a Brit we can intimidate her."

"Why am I not surprised to learn the French aren't easily intimidated?"

"Because, *mon ami*, you are married to a matador."

With the AAA maps they marked out a route from the *pensione* to Jacques' office. The mixed neighborhoods along the five-mile drive reminded Maggie of her years at boarding school. The Amadeus School for Girls attracted the rich, famous and impoverished. Its goal was to strengthen education through diversity. Maggie once told Clyde it was her Petri dish for studying the isms—racism, sexism, classism, nationalism.

"This city feels like home to me. I can't believe it's been more than six years since I graduated. It's like no time has passed."

"Mag, you're beginning to sound like my mother."

"Please, no, anything but that!" Maggie cried. "Kidding. It's not that I don't love your mother, I do. It's just that I want to be your wife, which means I can't be your mother."

"It's okay, Maggie. Mom has strong opinions about everything and I know it bugs you. But it's more about insecurity than conceit."

Maggie gave Sam's shirt cuff a tug and said, "Mr. Tervo, one of my non-negotiable requirements was a man who loves his mother."

"And, the other requirements?'

"Sense of humor, sense of self and compassion for others. Oh, did I mention being a hunk and good in the sack and pasture?" laughed Maggie.

Sam's trademark blush translated his feelings faster than his words. "Maggie, I think I faked you out on the sense-of-self piece. Humor is a convenient hiding place."

"You think? Sam, you haven't said anything about the city."

"I know this is a dumb-jock thing to say, but because the Maple Leafs are one of the Red Wing's biggest rivals, not to mention my secret crush on Gordie Howe, I was determined *not* to like Toronto. But I do. Very eclectic and un-zoned, it's got a small-town-kind-of feel. Like Detroit, the neighborhoods give it shape and character. I'm in no way comparing the Detroit River to Lake Ontario, but the shoreline and vibes of this city remind me of home."

"You've got to be kidding. Alex Delvecchio maybe, but Gordie Howe?"

Jacques Ruivivar's company, Zeno Development, was housed in an old stamping plant not far from the lake, near King Street, in an area called Liberty. A three-story, red brick building, it boasted industrial-sized metal windows and iron staircases. Downstairs the showroom housed some of the original stamping machines. Old metal shelving and storage bins held *objets d'art,* including items dredged up from the bottom of Lake Ontario—rusted anchors, slivered oars, wagon wheels, fossils and shells. A reception area and waiting room occupied the center of the room in front of the staircase. Along one wall, there were three small conference rooms. The two outside facing walls invited the wan urban sun and a long view of Toronto's cityscape through its giant windows.

Maggie and Sam decided on business dress *to avoid the stigma of tourists or grave robbers.* (Sam's joke to help Maggie stay calm.) Maggie was wearing Aunt Jo's sleeveless black linen shift with a string of pearls and black flats. Sam was dressed in his gray gabardine interview suit with a French-cuffed white tab-collar shirt, his dad's old silver and copper cufflinks and a steel blue tie.

Seated behind a curved six-foot-long white maple desk, the receptionist looked like a manikin with her short, black blunt-cut geometric hair, classic features and flawless make up. A nameplate read *Emma Stell.* Like a scene from Edgar Allan Poe's gothic fiction *The Tell-Tale Heart,* Maggie imagined her own 'dismembered heart pounding below the floorboards' with such force she was sure the receptionist could hear it.

"Good morning, may I help you?" asked Emma.

"Yes, please. My name is Maguerite Soulier Tervo. I'm the daughter of Raymond and Anna Soulier who went missing about twenty years ago. Jacques Ruivivar was a good friend of my parents. It would mean a lot if he could meet with me while I'm here in Toronto."

Maggie watched the receptionist to see if she reacted to the Soulier name, or the pounding of her heart, and was both disappointed and pleased she did not. She kept reminding herself not to run, to breathe, to act sane.

"Please, have a seat, Mrs. Tervo. I'll see if I can reach Mr. Ruivivar's secretary," said Emma.

Maggie sat down next to Sam and said, "Emma's French. We play by her rules. She's calling Jacques' secretary."

In spite of her attempts to remain calm, both Maggie's knees were bouncing up and down. After they'd flipped through a number of architectural magazines, then *Look*, *Life* and *The Atlantic Monthly*, Emma finally called them back to her desk.

"I just spoke to Mr. Ruivivar's secretary and she asked me to send you up. Her name is Catherine Caron. If you take the stairs, her office is on the third floor to your right. If you want to take the elevator I'll give you other directions."

"The stairs are fine. Thank you!" said Maggie.

Maggie's legs were shaking when she reached the second floor landing. The views of Lake Ontario were spectacular and she and Sam took a moment to calm their nerves. Unlike Sam, Maggie's style was less subtle. She shook her arms and jumped up and down like a boxer entering a ring. Stretching to touch her toes, then the floor, Maggie held that pose for well over a minute.

"Come on, Mag. We're almost there."

It was hard to tell how many people worked in the building, as there was no foot traffic. None. When they made the landing on the third floor, a lovely woman in her fifties was waiting for them.

"Good morning. My name's Catherine and I'm Mr. Ruivivar's secretary, calendar keeper and body guard," she laughed. "Of course, it's very easy to make these things up when you have a boss who is rarely in town and almost never at the office. I do, however, recognize your name Marguerite and my guess is that Mr. Ruivivar will be very excited to know you're in town. May I get you a coffee while I track him down?"

Maggie felt her nerves give up the battle. Her heart rate slowed and air entered her lungs without effort. "Yes, thank you. Coffee sounds wonderful," said Maggie.

Sam was grinning from ear to ear. Maggie thought he never looked so handsome and comfortable in his interview suit. "I second that motion, coffee would be great."

Catherine seated them in a small anteroom inside a suite of offices. When she returned, she had a tray of sweetbreads, fruit, nuts, crackers and cheese. "Just in case this takes longer than we think. Mr. Ruivivar may be in transit somewhere, but if that's the case, I'll at least find someone who can give us his itinerary," said Catherine.

Sam winked at Maggie and touched her knee. She smiled. They understood it would be better not to talk.

By the time Maggie and Sam returned to The Maple Leaf it was after nine. Rather than risk running into Marc, they decided to shower in the morning. After a day of sightseeing, it was nice to stretch out in bed.

"This is unbelievable. Here we are, day one in Toronto, and Jacques Ruivivar has already agreed to meet with us tomorrow. Did I tell you I almost peed my pants?" said Maggie.

"Off the charts amazing. The more I think about it, the more convinced I am that Catherine knows you. Are you sure you didn't meet her when you were a child?"

"Maybe. There's something about her that rings a bell. Probably because she's French Canadian, I don't know. During my six years at Amadeus we might have seen each other in town. Something. Do you think Marc knows we're avoiding him?"

"Do you care?"

"I think I do. Isn't that nuts? Why would I care whether he likes me or not?

"Beats me. He's not anyone I want to spend time with."

"Will you scratch my back?"

"Turn over, Mrs. Tervo."

Maggie turned on her side and began to purr as Sam scratched her back. She felt the glacier of accumulated guilt, insecurity, dread, inaction begin to melt. Tears fell.

"The curse?"

"No, some perverted form of happiness. It's as if I've been holding my breath for the past twenty years because I so want to know the truth *and* I so want to keep the fantasy I created. Today, I finally took down the stage sets, fired the cast and crew. No more pretending. The truth scares the crap out of me but the liberation I feel is happiness. Freedom *is* happiness."

"Let's cuddle, Maggiesan. I want to see how you feel without the stage props and characters." Sam pulled Maggie close and placed his hand on her stomach. Before they fell asleep he said, "Hmm, it does seem a little less crowded."

Catherine was waiting for them when they entered the lobby at noon. Emma was not at her desk and Maggie recalled that some Toronto businesses kept to the European tradition of closing three hours for a mid-day break.

"Good afternoon, Maggie, Sam. Nice to see you again!"

"Nice to see you," said Maggie.

"Lunch is in the upstairs dining room. I'll take you up on the elevator. Believe me, it's a much easier trip to that side of the third floor," said Catherine.

Several doors and hallways later, they reached the elevator. According to Catherine, the elevator measured ten feet by fifteen feet, large enough to carry ten-foot shipping containers with a thirty-thousand-pound payload.

"I was beginning to think we should have dropped breadcrumbs to find our way back," laughed Maggie.

"I used a map the first six months I worked here. Very circuitous! Not sure why, but all kinds of tales about pirates, drugs and weapons. *Très mystérieux,*" said Catherine, "It's one of the reasons I love to work in old buildings—with their secret cubbies, attics and cellars."

The elevator required a different code to operate the gates at each floor. On the third floor, Catherine had a hard time getting the code to work. Finally, there was a loud click and warning bell as the gate opened.

After three more hallways and several turns, they walked into a dining room facing the lake. Wall-to-wall, ceiling-to-floor windows framed two walls. Maggie experienced the kind of 'whoosh' she always felt on ski lifts, acrophobia chased by vertigo. She turned to look at the table and inside wall.

Three places had been set at a large square table for four. Catherine introduced them to Charles who took their drink order, two black coffees. After yesterday, they decided fresh roasted coffee was their new addiction and they'd splurge on a French press and coffee beans before they returned home.

Catherine pulled out a chair and said, "Please, have a seat. Mr. Ruivivar will be here soon. If you need anything, or need to reach me, ask Charles. I'll be in my office, but since you didn't drop breadcrumbs, it will be easier for me to find you. *Bon appétite!*"

"Holy crap, I'm so nervous I can hardly stand myself. Can you tell?" asked Maggie.

"You look beautiful and a little nervous. It's okay. My guess is he'll be nervous."

Maggie caught her breath and stared at the man approaching the table. He looked familiar but she couldn't say why. At six two, with broad shoulders and intense green eyes, he was virile looking in spite of gray streaks through his dark hair. An insignia ring on his right hand caught the sun and triggered a meteoric flash of memory. Maggie's vertigo returned.

"Marguerite Soulier, you are your mother incarnate. I would know you anywhere. May I give you a hug?" said Mr. Ruivivar.

Maggie moved her chair back, stood up and held on to the side of the table as she attempted to locate her feet. Mr. Ruivivar held out his arms and drew her to him. Sam watched as both Maggie and Mr. Ruivivar began to sob. Not cry, sob.

Sam turned away looking for something to distract him, then turned back to experience what he'd later describe as an *awkward intimacy*. Both voyeur and participant, unbidden tears soon began to well up in Sam's eyes.

Maggie and Mr. Ruivivar took each other's hands and stood looking at one another for the longest time. Sam watched Maggie's awe and delight.

"You must be Sam."

"Yes, I am. You must be Mr. Ruivivar."

"Call me Jacques. I know I'm an old coot but the formality of last names is not my style. Please take a load off," said Jacques. "Catherine ordered trout *almondine*. I hope that works for you."

Maggie nodded, tears still streaming down her face. Sam said, "Perfect!"

"Maggie, I can't tell you how glad I was to hear you wanted to meet with me. For too many years I convinced myself that my presence would bring up bad memories so I stayed away. My, you look so much like Anna. How well do you remember her?"

"I'm not sure how to sort what I remember from the photos I've seen and stories I've heard. I do remember her laughter and playfulness which later seemed such a contradiction to the work she did."

"Anna was passionate about everything—life, you, Isabel, Raymond, her work and her play. Most of the time she was good-natured, but doubt I've ever met anyone so fierce."

Sam laughed and said, "Well, let me introduce you to Maggie. She is definitely her mother's daughter when it comes to fierceness."

"He's right. I wondered about that because Issie, Isabel, is so easy going that I thought I was adopted."

"Issie must take after Raymond. When your dad's world was crashing down around him, he'd pick the most outrageous consequence he might face and turn it into a joke. Like, saying he was planning to raise money for his defense by booking bets on whether the CIA or MI5 made the bust."

"Oh, yes, that's Issie! I worry her insane comments about her kids will grab the attention of the child welfare system. She is so irreverent that the word *irreverent* is not enough."

"There's so much I want to know about you, Sam and Issie. How long are you here?"

"Eight more days," said Maggie.

"Good. Let's get started and see what we can plan for the rest of your visit. Are you willing to indulge me in more conversation?"

"I'd love to. I want to learn all I can about my parents and what you think happened on the Saint Lawrence Seaway."

"We'll do it. For now Maggie, tell me how you landed in the States, what you're doing and, of course, how the two of you found your way to the altar."

14

The Dance

So the darkness shall be the light, and the stillness the dancing.
—T. S. Eliot

AUGUST 1968—Sam looked both ways and listened for breakfast sounds before stepping into the hallway. Avoiding Marc and the ankle-biters had become a morning ritual. From the kitchen, the scent of lemon poppy-seed muffins provided a thin patina to the ripe odor of bleached diapers, baby powder, sweaty socks and milk souring in cereal bowls. Sam wondered why kid's sweat and urine smelled so strong. *Darwinian? A way to get noticed before we have verbal skills or the capacity to take care of ourselves?*

Maggie was sitting at their favorite table in the sunroom reading the Toronto Daily. "Hey, Sam, listen to this: " 'Following a number of riots in Europe and Quebec, the *Front de Libération du Quebec* claimed victory after setting off fifty-two bombs over the past twelve months and attracting hundreds of new *Felquistes* in their fight against Anglo-Saxon imperialism.' Holy crap, I had no idea they were so militant."

"Do you think Jacques was involved with the bombings? He's given us the grand tour of Toronto, talked a lot about your parents, but hasn't said jack shit about himself."

"I don't know. Besides, part of me doesn't want to know. I've always held onto the *Ignorance Is Bliss* theory. If I don't know, I can't be touched by it. Talk about immaturity."

"Jesus, Mag, it's not like the FLQ is normal. We might be better off if we don't know."

"What I want to know is whether my parents are alive. That's the question I want to ask but freeze every chance I get. What the hell? That's the whole reason we came to Toronto."

"You've got to ask, but Jacques doesn't have to answer. If he thinks it would hurt you or them, he won't say. Are you prepared for the answer no matter what? I think hearing they're alive in some unknown, remote place might be harder than hearing they're dead."

"Are you fucking crazy? Why would you say that? What on earth causes you to think it'd be easier to know they're dead?"

"Mag, I get that you want them to be alive and have a relationship with them, but think about it. If they've stayed away, it's because they think you're safer or they're safer. If it were easy you'd know by now. Jacques seems to be playing his cards close to his vest. He wants to learn more about you, see that you're safe and sane. If he knows your parents are dead, he'll tell you. If he knows they're alive, but you or they would be in danger if you tried to find them, he might do what he's doing now or lie. If he doesn't know he'll tell you. Shit. I'm talking in circles. Bottom line, Jacques either knows or he doesn't. But, if you ask, and I hope you do, you need to be prepared to *not* like the answer."

"Sometimes I get lost when you think out loud, but I needed to hear that. *Je t'aime mon doux homme.*"

"Mag, I didn't mean to make you cry. What's going on?"

"Crooked thinking—holding on to fairytale endings. Mother and Father reunited with children and grandchildren, front-page news."

"That's a possibility, but whatever we find out is better than being stuck in some make-believe drama."

"Maybe, maybe not. Let's pack the car so we can get outta Dodge after lunch. So weird, but before we left Detroit I had this crazy image of us rifling through books and files every time Jacques turned his head. Holy crap. Can you imagine us trying to break into the Zeno building or Jacques' gated townhouse?"

"No way. Pure insanity."

"Hmm, or picnicking in a serene pasture?"

Sam pulled Maggie up from her chair and gave her one of his mock, back bending theatrical kisses. When he lost his footing they both slid to the floor giggling like ten-year-olds. Neither noticed Marc standing in the door.

"Good morning, lovebirds!"

"Hey, Marc, sorry for the commotion. We got carried away planning our last day in your very hip city," said Sam.

Marc watched Sam help Maggie to her feet then held his gaze a little too long as she leaned over to straighten the skirt of her red handkerchief-print sundress. "Glad you're alive. I was beginning to think of you as my phantom guests. When do you hit the road?"

"Packing the car this morning so we can head out after lunch. If you've got time, we can settle up now," said Sam.

Maggie heard and felt the tension between these two guys. The Maple Leaf would have been so out of sight if it weren't for Marc. Beyond his crass ignorance and racism, there was also a creep factor. More than once Maggie felt her skin prickle when she was in the shared bathroom, convinced Marc was watching her. Sam blew it off by saying, "Marc's so narcissistic I bet he jacks off in front of a mirror." Maggie checked for peek holes. When she didn't find any, she pinned it on the 'Alford Hitchcock Factor'—a childhood spent watching Hitchcock while Issie and Uncle Cyp added their own mind-bending sound effects.

At the door, Sam said, "Sure, Marc, we'll check with you before our next trip." Maggie slowed her step as she approached Marc and said, "Thanks again for the coffee and muffins. It was a nice way to start the day." Stunned by the measure of delight she took in not saying Marc's name out loud, she thought, *yep, immature as hell!*

Gritting her teeth, Maggie hauled her suitcase up on the bed and said "Ugh. I'll be so glad to get out of here. How long do you think Marc was listening before we saw him?"

"No idea, Mag. What were we talking about?"

"Nothing much—terrorists, bombings, a possible murder, breaking into houses and businesses."

"Well, it'll give him something to play with. God knows he has little else going on."

"I guess. Do you think this will be the last time we see Jacques?"

"No idea. Where are you going with this?"

"I don't know. I'm sad. For some reason I want to keep him close—know him better, spend time with him. I'm so messed up. Aunt Jo as my surrogate mother, Jacques as my surrogate father? What's that about?"

"I think it's about my sweet Maggie in search of her self and her family. Neither Aunt Jo nor Jacques have their own children, so it might work."

"Maybe. I could do worse than a mama Jo and a papa Jacques. Maybe write a folk song about them," laughed Maggie, singing, "my mama was a rolling Jo and papa was throwing Jacques."

"I think someone else has done that, but it'd be a good song to dance to. Make it or break it?"

Maggie raised her eyebrows and looked at Sam sideways, as if he was the only one being corny. "Let's boogie shoo, Dick Clark."

Maggie and Sam were ten minutes early when they pulled up to the twelve-foot wrought-iron fence surrounding Jacques' townhouse. The guard at the entrance recognized their Corvair and opened the gate.

Pepe was one of those stout, swarthy, muscular types. Dressed in a black short-sleeved tee shirt and black pants, he wore a white sailor cap and smoked a corncob pipe. Each time she saw him, Maggie fought an irresistible urge to call him Popeye.

"Hey, Pepe, how goes it?"

"Ah, Ms. Maggie. I thought you and Sam would be bored with this city by now. Not like Detroit with all its fancy car makers and big-time crime."

"Pepe, Pepe. You're too impatient. Detroit's a lot like Toronto. Just wait. The mafia will put Toronto on the map before you know it!" chided Sam.

"Yeah, well, maybe I'll get paid more money for protecting Jacques from serial eaters. How many times you been here this week for food?" growled Pepe.

Both Sam and Maggie thought Pepe must be related to Angelo. If not, they decided there must be a school of 'curmudgeonry' for Italian men with certain predispositions.

"Hey, Pepe, we can take you away from all this. Come to Detroit," said Maggie.

"Ah, Ms. Maggie, I've had some good offers in my life but none as good as yours. Maybe next time! Stop by on your way out. I have a little something for you."

With its stone walls, brick floors, dark wood casks, cupboards and furniture, Jacques' kitchen looked like a wine cellar from a 17th century castle except for ceiling-to-floor French doors facing a *bon vivant's* herb and vegetable garden. Copper pots and pans hung from the ceiling. Polished black soapstone counters boasted a stainless steel sink and held two unusual pieces of art. Next to the sink was a bright green and yellow-spotted metal tree python curled for attack; and on the counter under the cupboards, a triangular-shaped stainless steel tray held a large, varnished greenish-white egg from a black swan. Jacques explained the snake and the swan's egg both portend beauty and danger—one more subtle, yet both symbols of nature's determination to be free.

"*Bonjour*, Charles! Are you ready to see us head back?" asked Sam.

"On the contrary, Mr. Ruivivar has never been this happy. Could you stay a few more weeks?"

"We would if we could. How long have you worked for Jacques?" asked Maggie.

"Twenty some years. I was, what do you call it . . . a *stowaway* on one of Mr. Ruivivar's boats out of Cuba. Imagine my surprise when we didn't dock in Florida. For Cubans, Florida and North America are one and the same. Mr. Ruivivar caught me looking for food in the middle of the night and made me dinner. We had a pact. If I taught him how to cook Cuban dishes, he'd hire me on as his 'chief cook and bottle washer.' I had no idea what that meant, but I'm here to tell you it changed my life and my name. I was born Carlos."

"Ah, Carlos! Does he cook Cuban food?" asked Maggie.

"No. Not so big on beans and rice. He hired a French chef to teach me how to cook 'real food.' Now, I manage the kitchens here and at Zeno. Today, shrimp salad, tomato bisque soup and the best croissants in town. And, for desert, *mousse noisette*."

"Whoa! I didn't realize how hungry I was. Will we see you before we leave?" asked Sam.

"Probably not. We should say our goodbyes now. I've got to get back to Zeno for a big gala we're hosting for the Amadeus School tonight."

Maggie slapped her hand on the table and said, "Oh my god, that was my school!"

"Oh, yeah. That's right."

"You knew?"

"Not sure why I said that. I might have overheard you and Mr. Ruivivar talking about it."

Maggie shook her head back and forth. "Hmm, I don't remember talking about it, but maybe."

Charles put his hands in his pockets and started to jiggle some change. "Well, got to run. It was nice meeting you both and hope you have a safe trip home."

"Thanks, Charles. It was good meeting you, and enjoying food from both kitchens," said Sam.

Maggie opened her arms and gave Charles a hug and said, "I hope we get to see you again."

As Charles was leaving, Jacques walked in and Charles asked for a minute of his time. Outside the windows, with their backs to the kitchen, they leaned in to one another as if sharing a secret. Maggie saw Jacques look down and shake his head back and forth.

After a small toast with iced-tea glasses, the conversation began with the future—talk about Sam's new job, Maggie's teaching position, house hunting, family planning. During a pause, Maggie cleared her throat and said, "Jacques, I've been wanting to ask you some questions since we arrived. We've talked around it but I haven't come right out and asked. I need to do this."

"Sure, Maggie. Whatever it is, please feel free. I'll answer any question I can."

"Were you involved in Anna and Raymond's work to secede from Britain and Canada?

"I helped finance their work and provided space, equipment and manpower. So, yes, I was involved."

"The Tribune said they were involved in 'acts of international espionage and contraband.' Was this true?"

"I think that depends on who's reporting and how they interpret law. At some level, I suppose they—we—were breaking some laws, but it wasn't for personal gain. It was because we believed Britain and Canada were imposing their will on indigenous people and French Canadians. I'd say it was a mission for them, more civil disobedience than criminal. But I'm not a lawyer."

"And you?"

"It was also my mission."

"When they left did you know they wouldn't return?"

"I knew it was a strong possibility."

"Why was it a strong possibility?"

Jacques looked up, then directly at Maggie. "Because, dear Maggie, there were a number of threats made against your parents that summer. I didn't know if they'd make it. If they did, I was sure they'd go into hiding."

"Who made these threats?"

"Anna and Raymond pissed off a number of powerful people, including the mafia in Britain, Canada, the States—you name it. They had many enemies because they had dug deep and discovered corruption they weren't looking for."

"Like what?"

"That's all I can tell you."

Jacques' look conveyed a steeliness Maggie hadn't seen before. She decided to resist familiar urges to plead, pout or argue. Instead, she chose to make the best use of the time they had left. She smiled as a thought slid by—*Loretta with hands raised, fists pumping telling her to pick up the salt.*

"Where were they heading? How would you know if they made it or not?"

"They planned to sail along the St. Lawrence Seaway. Beyond that, I don't know. We all thought it best if I didn't. For their sake, for everyone's sake, I'm glad we made this pact."

Maggie felt a heavy silence settle across her shoulders. The weight reminded her of the unasked question.

"Are they alive?"

"There's nothing to suggest they died, but I don't know if they escaped in another boat or were captured. Maggie, if they were captured, it's unlikely they're alive."

Tears backed up in Maggie's throat and she began coughing. Jacques brought her a glass of water and told her to sip it slowly.

Sam wiped his eyes and said, "Jacques, did Anna and Raymond make plans for Issie and Maggie?"

"Yes, of course. When they realized they might have to disappear, Anna left me a copy of their will and funds to help raise Issie and Maggie. After the court appointed Minnie and Cyp as guardians, the funds were transferred to their bank."

"Did the funds cover our time at Amadeus?" asked Maggie.

"No. Amadeus was Anna's brainchild. She wanted a school for girls that provided education, experience and diversity. We all invested heavily in making this happen. I was given an irrevocable lifetime privilege of selecting two girls for every new class. Anna pushed the Board to approve this twist in the bylaws to make sure you and Issie were taken care of."

"So this escape, this boat trip down the Seaway, was planned way ahead?"

"No, Maggie. It was not planned, but it was always an anticipated exit if their lives or your lives were at risk. Your parents didn't leave you to protect themselves; they left to protect you. This is important. Your parents loved you and Issie more than they loved anyone."

"You didn't say 'or anything.'"

"No, I didn't."

"What can I do now? What if they're alive and need our help?"

"Dearest Maggie, you aren't listening. What they want, what they care about, is that you and Issie experience your own lives as fully and authentically as you can. Anna unleashed her power. If she was here, she'd tell you to plant a willow tree on the moon."

15

Black Jack

*Those who dance are often thought mad by those who cannot hear
the music.*

—Unknown

AUGUST 1968—"So, Pepe, change your mind? Ready to move to
Detroit?"

"Sam, my man, there's no one in Toronto who's ready to move
to Detroit. It's a goddamn shooting gallery. Forget the wild west,
Detroit makes Texas look like a pansy-ass state."

"Think about it, Pepe. Detroit's filled with Italians who left that
mafia-infested boot you call Italy."

Yeah, well, that's why I'm in Toronto. Peace loving hippies and
French Canadians holding hands and singing "Oh Canada" and
planting flowers. I'll come visit when I have an insane urge to out-
run bullets."

"Pepe, you've got it wrong. Detroit is just going through a rough patch. You'll see. One day you'll be knocking at our door," said Maggie.

"Ah, Ms. Maggie, don't count on it. But here, I found this envelope with your name on it in an old stable trunk. Looks like a bunch of family photos. I wanted to give them to you before they got trashed."

Maggie had a death grip on the large brown envelope on her lap.

"So, Mag, are you going to look inside?"

"When I'm ready."

"Do you want to pull off the road?"

"No."

"Okay. Well, let me know if you do."

"Damn it, Sam. Will you please stop pressuring me to do things when you want them done?"

"Mag, no pressure. They're your photos. Just thought you'd be anxious."

"I'm not anxious and I don't want to talk right now. I want to breathe."

"Got it."

Sam was glad they left on a Sunday afternoon to avoid Monday's gridlock in the cities. The empty roads and pastures reminded him of the bull and their crazy lovemaking. *No chance for a rerun today.*

After four hours Maggie said, "let's eat before we get to Windsor. I'm hungry."

"Me too, Mag."

Three miles later, Sam pulled into a scenic overlook. It was almost six o'clock. Families were setting up picnic tables, grilling hotdogs. Kids were playing tag or throwing sticks for their dogs to fetch. Sam spotted an empty table at the edge of the small roadside park next to a stream and said, "Will this do?"

"Holy crap, Sam, it's like we just entered a Norman Rockwell cover of *The Saturday Evening Post*. Sorry for being so rotten. I'm a little freaked out and need some time."

"Babe, I got it. Let's eat."

An old willow brindled the light of a late summer day as Maggie opened the boxed dinner and unpacked turkey sandwiches, homemade potato chips, almond cookies and a thermos of coffee. In spite of the heat, a trace breeze from the north carried the crisp scent of autumn. Under the food, Maggie found four sturdy paper plates and four dark gray linen napkins with the Zeno insignia embroidered in white. A small envelope was addressed to *Maggie and Sam*. Maggie opened the envelope and read the card out loud:

My Dearest Maggie and Sam,

Getting to know you over the past nine days has been wonderful, but I want more.

I hope you'll give some thought to getting together over the Christmas holidays. I have a chalet in Blue Mountain that sleeps ten. Let's see if the two of you, Issie and her family and Aunt Jo are up for the trip. My treat.

I've enclosed my business card so you can reach me. (Home address and phone number on the back.)

Bon appétit, dear ones. I look forward to seeing you again!

> *Kindest regards,*
> *Jacques*

P.S. Maggie, Catherine told me you liked our Zeno linens, so I'm selfishly including these so you won't forget me.

"Blue Mountain? Sam I haven't skied in five years."

"Maggie, I don't think this is about skiing."

Coming out of the Windsor Tunnel, Detroit's skyline shimmered like Miami against the fiery horizon of a setting sun. Its burned buildings and abandoned houses lost in deep shadows. By the time they unpacked the car and stuffed their dirty clothes in a laundry basket, it was after nine. The sky was dark. The brown envelope sat unopened on the coffee table. Sam started to ask Maggie when she was going to open it, but checked himself and said, "ready for bed?"

"Are you kidding? Really? You think I'd go to bed without looking at these photos?"

"Listen, Maggie, you told me not to mention them and I didn't. I know this is important to you. I'm trying to be sensitive, but give me a break here. I don't know how to deal. So you tell me what the hell you want from me."

Maggie sat down on the sofa and started crying.

Sam slid to his knees. "Shit, Maggie, I'm doing the best I can. I know I can be dumb on both sides, but I have no idea what you want from me."

"I don't know what I want. I'm afraid to look at those photos. I'm pissed that I had parents who disappeared without saying good-bye. I'm pissed at Jacques for staying away all these years. I'm pissed because Aunt Jo, Aunt Minnie and Uncle Cyp must have known more than they told me. Fuck, fuck, fuck. My whole life is a god-damn lie, and I'm sitting here like a pitiful orphan crying about something that happened twenty years ago."

"Listen to me, Maggie. You were only five when your parents left to protect you in the only way they knew how. My guess is they acted out of courage. Everyone who loved you believed it was the only way to keep you safe. Mag, you're always telling me we have no control, only influence based on the choices we make. You get to choose how to deal with this."

"I will. But not now I'm too wired. I need to crash."

At four o'clock in the morning a light in the living room led Sam to Maggie. Sitting cross-legged on the sofa, Maggie was wearing a black tee shirt with *Make Love Not War* in pink block letters. In front of her, three carefully stacked piles of photos.

"Coffee?"

"Please."

Sam left the French press in the box, heated water in the kettle and opened the instant coffee. When he brought two cups into the living room, Maggie was in the same position.

"Hey, Mag, do you feel like talking?"

"Not sure. It's so weird. I don't think Pepe had permission to give me these photos and my sense is that Jacques, or someone, may have wanted to sort through these first."

"Why's that?"

"Pile one, baby pictures of me, or me and Issie, including some with Anna or Raymond. Pile two, pictures of me as a toddler alone or with Issie. No parents, no adults, just the two of us at different times and in different places. Pile three, pictures of me at four or five alone or with Issie and/or Anna. No photos of Raymond."

"Okay. I'm not sure what you think this means."

"What I think it means is both my parents were around when I was a baby. One or the other was taking pictures. When I was a toddler, only one of my parents was around to take pictures. It could have been Anna or Raymond or someone else. From age three to five, Anna was in a number of photos but no Raymond. Did he become camera shy? Why isn't he in these photos? Who took them?"

"Do you want my opinion or do you just need a listener right now?

"I'd love it if you'd look at these pictures, including the backgrounds, and tell me if anything looks out of whack. I'm nagged by something but not sure what it is. Right now, I need to soak in the tub."

Sam looked at the three stacks and sipped his coffee. As he began to pick up the first pile, he flashed to his meeting with Zito and the unseen photos of Carla. Thanks to Sheer Juice's influence and recommendation, he'd start work at Jingo Motors tomorrow. This afternoon was paperwork and orientation in Jingo's Personnel Office. Almost everyone, including Maggie, saw this job as a major coup. Only he and Clyde knew about the Magic Slate price tag attached to this job. Clyde was right. Sheer Juice did not set him up for a one-shot deal. Sam was indentured. For how long, for how much? Who knew?

Breakfast was Cheerios, milk and toasted Wonder Bread with cold, hard butter. Sam grimaced before he could check himself. This was the primary reason he never played cards.

"Don't even think it Poker Face."

"So no chance you'll learn to make muffins?"

"Quick study. That's what I've always loved about you. Sorry I've been such a shithead. I'm going to get my head on straight, or as straight as I can. Which, is probably not promising much," laughed Maggie.

"Hearing you laugh is enough. I wasn't sure who was inhabiting that lush body of yours and I'm glad to know you're still here. I've missed you."

Maggie sat on Sam's lap, nuzzled his neck and bit his ear.

"Ouch, dammit Maggie, that hurt. Are you in great need of attention?"

"Probably. Do we have time to talk through the photos before you get ready for work, Mr. Young Executive?"

"Yes, but I'm not an executive. I'm an Employment Manager, which is management level, not executive. I understand corporate types are very sensitive about levels, office space and number of direct reports, so please don't overstate my status."

"Okay, so I shouldn't call you Emperor Tervo?"

"Not in public," laughed Sam.

"The photos?"

"I think you're right. There's a pattern based on age. I went through them quickly to see if anything jumped out at me, then looked at each one more slowly. The only curious thing I saw was in the third pile. Look here at these two photos. There's something on the counter that looks like Jacques' metal tree python. Then, in this last photo there's a man's hand with an insignia ring like Jacques'. The hand is too shaded to see if it resembles Jacques'. Most mind-boggling is how much your mother looks like Catherine, Jacques' secretary. That might be why I felt the connection between the two of you. Could be a French Canadian genetic thing, but there's something. Here, look at these two photos of your mother and think about Catherine. Am I off base or what?"

"Sam, I see the tree python and the insignia ring looks like Jacques'. But, I don't see the resemblance between Anna and Catherine. Not sure what difference that makes, but will look again."

"After I shower, I'm heading out. I want to check the routes and neighborhoods near Jingo. Should be home by six. What's your day?"

"Sorting laundry and lots of calls—Issie, Aunt Jo, Loretta and Stella. I know they're dying to hear about our trip. Plus, Angelo will be expecting a call and will no doubt ask if I can cover weekends during football season."

"And?"

"And, we'll see. We just spent a wad of money in Toronto, and treat or no treat, it would be nice to have some money put away if we want to go to Blue Mountain in December.

"Hey, Issie. How's it going in Wasteland these days?"

"When did you get home? Shit. I can't wait to talk but we're heading to the zoo right now—Raymond's Cub Scout Pack."

"Damn. I've got some pictures I want to show you. Why don't you and the boys come here tomorrow?"

"Too nuts. I know it's your hood, but there's no way I'll let the boys play outside. You come here. I'll make a pot of coffee and pick up a Sara Lee coffee cake."

"Are you kidding me? You think it's safe there with all those frigging hillbillies in white sheets?"

"Marguerite Soulier Tervo, I know you love Detroit but it's always spooked me. Come on. You haven't been here in months. We'll both be more relaxed if the boys can play outdoors."

"I'll check with Sam. We're down to one set of wheels, and I'm stuck unless I can drive him to work and pick him up. I'll let you know."

"Hey, Auntie Jo. How goes it?"

"Oh, Maggie. You're back! Darn. I'm on my way to a meeting with a new designer. I can call later. Depending on the day, it might be tomorrow. I miss you."

"Miss you, too. Call when you can."

"Hey, Loretta!"

"Hey, Maggie! I can't wait to talk to you, baby, but there's someone in my chair and two under the dryer. I'm kicking ass this morning."

"No problem. Keep kicking. I'll try later."

"Stella Webster here."

"Hey, Stella. You buried in work?"

"Nope. Just closed my last open file and was about ready to clean up the minutes from The Eights meeting. We missed you guys."

"Missed you! Sam started at Jingo today and I'm knee deep in dirty laundry, but I wanted to hear a friendly voice."

"You first, Maggie. I've been dying to know if you found Jacques Ruivivar. That name is so fine he could be a character in a book or movie."

"Both! He's got silver screen good looks and at least three autobiographies waiting to be written. Let me start from the beginning."

The afternoon sun was blistering. With no trees, shade-less windows and one small table fan to help cool the house, the heat was unbearable. The side door in the kitchen and one window in the living room held the only two screens in the house. Sam said he'd see if he could find two slider screens to prop up the bedroom windows to get them through the last few hot weeks of the year. Maggie tried to imagine turning this paper-thin shack into a home. *Issie's right. Burned out houses, rancid garbage, rats, panhandlers and gangs—there's no frigging way she'd send her own kid out to play.*

A clean tee shirt and cutoffs would have to do. When Sam got home they'd head to the laundromat, start the washers, then pick up some White Castle for dinner. She was already salivating.

When the phone rang at six, Maggie was licking a tablespoon of peanut butter.

"Hey, babe, I'm just leaving the office and I won't be home until 6:30 or so. What's for dinner?"

"Laundry and White Castle. We're out of everything, so we need to stop and shop on the way home. This one car family thing is the pits!"

"Another bullet to bite. Do you want me to pick up some White Castle before I get home? Are you starving?"

"Tempted, but would rather get started on these clothes before tomorrow. Go. Now. Please."

"Seriously, Mag, we can afford Big Boys. We've hit the jackpot. I'm making twice as much as I did at Sheer Juice."

Maggie looked at Sam in suit and tie, sitting next to her in cut-offs and a faded orange tee. He was beaming. *When did he grow past me?* Maggie felt immature, diminished, sullen, like the time she and her best friend Greta ran for senior-class student council positions. It was June 1962, the last day of their junior year. Candidates were invited to give speeches one hour before voting began. Because *voting day* was always scheduled for the last day of school, everyone was hyped to begin summer break. No one seemed to take the speeches seriously, least of all Maggie, who'd been through these elections the past three years and easily won her seats on the council. On this day, like all others, she was dressed in her *de rigueur* wrinkled navy-blue school uniform, matching knee socks and a scuffed pair of penny loafers. Greta, who was running for the first time, showed up looking like Jackie Kennedy—a watermelon pink Coco Chanel knock-off suit with navy-blue silk stockings and three-inch navy heels. Maggie lost her seat on the council and gained respect for the power of bravado. Greta would graduate Harvard Law School in May then head to Washington, DC to clerk for one of the Supremes.

"Seriously, Sam, I've been craving White Castle since we left for Toronto. We can talk in the car while we wait for the clothes to dry."

"Mag, this job is unbelievable! I thought I'd find a bunch of stodgy engineers with slide rules attached to their belts, but it's modern—big windows, wide hallways and white cedar everywhere you look. No mahogany row like the big boys at GM and Ford. I get the sense they take pride in being more egalitarian or at least more democratic. No shit. It's so freaking open it could be a design studio or ad agency. Guys are walking around in rolled up shirtsleeves and loosened ties!"

"Tell me about the employees? Blacks? Women?"

"I didn't run into any women or blacks in management positions. The only person I spent any time with was Maxine, my administrative assistant. She's very cool."

"And?"

"She's black, about our age and irreverent as hell. You'd like her—great sense of humor, straight talk and lots of sass. My guess is you've trained me well to handle this powerhouse."

"Married?"

"Yes, married. Maxine's hot but she's not you."

"Did you meet with your boss? What's his name?"

"Skip Malone. He wasn't in, but Maxine's not a fan. She called him a dip-wad."

"In what way?"

"She said he's a boot-licker who always says 'yes' to new assignments then puts together a committee to do the work and he does nothing."

"No shit? How does he get away with that? I want his job!"

"No, you don't. Maxine thinks they hired me to be his replacement. She's pretty savvy so will keep my eyes open. What about you? How was your car-less day in the hood?"

"Don't even go there. I tried calling Issie, Aunt Jo, Loretta and they were all too busy to talk much less come by. Stella was the only one who had time for me. When I told her about our trip she got diabolical as hell. I think she'd make a better investigator than an accountant. Jesus. She's mystified by the photos but thinks I'm on to something. Which reminds me, Issie wants me to go to her house tomorrow because she's afraid to let the boys play outside in Detroit. Pissed me off at first, but then thought about how I'd feel letting our kid roam around Detroit alone. Sam, we've got to get out of this area before we have a baby. Maybe closer to Redford? Somewhere behind the library?"

"Did you call Angelo?"

"Yep."

"And?"

"And he told me he hired two on-call employees. He bragged about it being a buyer's market—two for the price of one. What an asshole!"

Mag, you and I both know that's how Angelo says he misses you. Did you offer to cover weekends?"

"Nope. I didn't think I could handle another rejection."

"Give me a break. Really?"

"Sam, I'm in a weird place. You're right, it was typical Angelo, but I couldn't deal."

"So, did you look at the photos of Catherine again?"

"I thought I'd wait to see how Issie reacts. I don't want to influence her thinking. And, I'll need the car tomorrow. I could drop you off and head to Issie's. On my way back, I can stop at Woolworths to get some sliding screens."

Sam said, "sure," then reached across the stick shift and ran his hand up Maggie's leg and traced the warm, damp skin under her cut-offs. "Speaking of Woolworths, Mrs. Tervo, do you still have that orange-checked apron?"

16

Close Encounters

Well, let me tell you 'bout the way she looked, the way she acts and the color of her hair, her voice was soft and cool, her eyes were clear and bright, but she's not there.
— The Zombies, lyrics from *She's Not There*

AUGUST 1968 — Built on a cornfield in 1950, Serene Hills was sixteen miles west of Detroit on the flattest piece of land in Southern Michigan. Not a hill in sight. Two greenhorn speculators, wannabe developers, came up with the name after guzzling a couple six packs of Pabst Blue Ribbon and paying homage to soldiers who qualified for VA mortgages. Only two blocks from the main road, Issie and Eddie's small faux-ranch was in the center of this cookie-cutter subdivision. Sixty-four houses shared the same simple design, red brick in front with gray asphalt siding on the back and sides. When Maggie saw a copy of the subdivision plat, with its equal size boxes, street after street, it looked like a checkerboard. Now, after eighteen years, maturing elms, blue spruce, fir and crabapple had transformed it into an oasis compared to neighboring subdivisions built on barren landfills and scrubbed wasteland.

Maggie was struck by how casually toys, bikes and wading pools were scattered throughout the neighborhood. Yet, there was monotony to it, like hitting the same key on a piano sixty-four times. Kids were buzzing everywhere, white kids, moving from one square box to another. An unrelenting, tedious tempo that gave sound to this human experiment of tenement housing with driveways and yards, but no music or color. Maggie's mind tumbled into an old Sunday school chorus of *red and yellow, black and white are so precious in his sight* and tried to bite back judgment. This was, after all, Issie's home.

Up close, their house was showing its age and slapdash construction—screens hanging from the storm door, dry rot on window casings, loose and missing asphalt tiles on the roof, no eaves or gutters.

Issie was sitting on the edge of the concrete porch sipping coffee. Her bare feet bounced up and down under a green and orange flowered moo-moo she'd worn when she was pregnant with both little Eddie and Raymond.

"Hey, Issie!"

Issie smiled, lifted her cup in greeting and said, "Thanks for making the drive."

"You're right, it's been far too long. I almost stopped to call and ask what main road you were off. Then, I remembered Ford, 'King Henry Ford!'"

"Yep. The owner of most of these here 'plant-tation' workers," laughed Issie.

Issie's comment hung in the humid air. The sarcastic edge to her voice and weariness in her eyes denied the laughter.

"Iss, you okay?"

Issie lifted her cup again and walked into the house. Maggie followed.

Inside, the living room was dark. Ten years ago the antiqued colonial furniture and hooked rug looked bright and inviting. Now the beige, brown, and red palate looked like road kill—frayed fabric bled crumbled foam, the rag rug pulled apart like entrails. In the corner, Issie's ten-year-old mother-in-law's tongue, with its long, sharp, succulent blades, was shrouded in dust. Evidence to support its notoriety as *a plant you can't kill*. But the saddest sight was the desolation of the twenty-inch pot that once held Issie's always-bountiful prayer plant, now two tiny orphan sprouts.

"My god, what happened to your beautiful prayer plant?"

Issie looked at the near empty pot then back at Maggie and said, "Neglect. God, Maggie, this has been the summer from hell. Eddie took a voluntary layoff for the model changeover and they haven't called him back. We've been getting by on unemployment checks, but that ends in September. That's another reason I couldn't drive out to see you. We're on lockdown until we can afford gas. The union keeps telling Eddie to 'hang tight, the plant will be calling everyone back before September 1st.' But Eddie's convinced he pissed off the local president when he refused to cover for a stoner who almost shut the line down in June. It's a mess. I'm a mess. The house is a mess and the poor plants are dying from neglect. Coffee?"

Maggie took in the bright yellow kitchen, with yellow gingham curtains Issie made to *catch the morning sun*. Dishes from last night's dinner filled the sink and a load of clean clothes overflowed from a wicker laundry basket in front of the stove.

"Holy crap, I'm sorry. Sam might be able to get him in at Jingo Motors."

"Thanks, but that dog won't hunt. Eddie's got over ten year's seniority at Ford, and it'd be hard for him to go back to the dirt jobs. He's at the union hall today. Keep your fingers and toes crossed."

"This really hacks me off. How long has he been paying union dues?"

"I know. When management isn't screwing you, it's the frigging union. Eddie knows all about the written and unwritten rules. The 'wife me' is proud he stood by his morals. The 'grizzly-mama-bear me' wants to knock him on his sorry, do-good ass. Sit, let's see what's left of Sara Lee after Eddie and the kids got to it."

Maggie and Issie picked at the remains of the ransacked coffee cake with their fingers as they gazed out the window at an uneven ten-foot-square, freestanding red brick patio in the middle of the backyard. Sand, between the bricks, gave crabgrass easy entry to invade this territory, tipping and lifting the clay bricks in an abstract decoupage.

"I call this *Eddie's Venture in Landscape Architecture*. When he started his layoff, he and the boys took the wagon and went from house to house asking for old bricks. I tried to tell him he needed a concrete base, but no, he said he wanted something more natural in the grass so he could mow over it and not have to edge around it. As an afterthought, he snagged a wheelbarrow of sand from a new sub to tie the bricks together. Someone told him the sand would turn to cement once it rained. For real! I swear he'd be the one guy to buy a bridge because he trusts everyone. So, I try to think of it as a conversation piece. It may be our generation's answer to Stonehenge. Imagine the archeologists a century from now scratching their heads and thinking 'what the hell?'"

Maggie loved Issie's stories about Eddie's ventures. Some of her other titles were: *Badass Motorcycling to the Corner Store*; *Backyard Fly Fishing*; *Play Houses in Perpetual Progress*; and *Bondo, The Universal Fix*. Maggie used to beg Issie to put her funny, inventive stories on paper. Issie always replied, "You're the ink-slinger, not me!"

Maggie and Issie had been talking an hour before Issie finally trolled through the three piles of photos between them, while Maggie made her observations and asked her questions.

"Oh, Maggie. What the hell? We've been living in a game of Clue all these years. Did Professor Plum do it with a candlestick in the library? What do you really want to know? The unknowable? Give me a break. Let it go."

"Let it go? Seriously? You don't care? You don't want to know? What if they're alive?"

"Your bag, baby girl, not mine. I spent way too long trying to solve this goddamn puzzle. Seriously, I don't give a flying flip if they're alive or not. If they are, they sure as hell aren't interested in seeing us. Hard enough to live our own broken lives, and for god sakes, don't drag Sam down this perverted road to nowhere."

"Iss, I need your help. You're the only one who knows what was going on during the first five years of my life."

"Marguerite, I love like you like a mother, big sister, best friend. You name it. I couldn't love you more. Because I love you, I'm not going to jump into this quicksand with you. I'll be here to pull you out when you're ready, but I'm sure as hell not going to spend time on two parents who abandoned us or are long dead. Either way, they lived their lives, made their choices. There's not a damn thing you or I can do to change history. Leave it alone."

"God, Issie, why are you so pissed? Why are you taking it out on me?"

"Marguerite, listen up, I'm not going to waste any more time on this mystery. I'll answer your three questions, but that's it. No more."

Maggie squinted her eyes, squared her jaw and stared at Issie. Issie shook her head and started to stand up. "Got it. Just these three questions. Promise."

"Okay. One, Raymond was a lunatic. He'd disappear for days, weeks, sometimes months. Anna told me he was dealing with his demons. But Raymond brought them home. He'd go into rages because the house was a mess, dinner wasn't ready or he couldn't find the front page of the newspaper. Once, Anna and I made banana splits for dessert. Jacques had given her a set of eight banana split dishes he'd found in a restaurant supply warehouse. Anna was thrilled. She and I put them together—vanilla, chocolate and straw-berry ice cream scoops over a banana, topped with hot chocolate, peanuts, whipped cream and a cherry. We called them our *chef d'oeuvre*. Raymond and you were sitting on the patio out back. You must have been three. Anyhow, Anna and I were both glow-ing when we reached the patio and held up our masterpieces. As always, Anna served Raymond first. I saw his face darken. Then, he stood up, tipped the table over and yelled *Conne! Vous savez bien que je n'aime pas les cerises!* So, because he doesn't like cherries, he flips the table, calls her a bitch, bolts into the house and locks the doors. Asshole. He was totally wigged out. You started to cry, which started the whole world crying. Then, Anna put down her dish and took my two and set them on the deck. She turned over the table, shook out the placemats and napkins, wiped the spoons and reset the table for three. Anna called us into her arms and we huddled forehead-to-forehead. She said something like 'Raymond wants to fight his demons. That's his choice. But tonight, pretty ones, we'll celebrate this beautiful world we call home.' Raymond split before we finished our splits. He was gone a lot after that. I wondered if he was at the funny farm. I never asked. Anna never said."

"But you called your son Raymond."

"When I was lost in the quicksand, I'd forget about Raymond's meanness. I'd recall the times when he was sweet and funny. That's what I chose to remember. Maintaining the fantasy was something I practiced for years. Now it's your fantasy Maggie. You're living the one about our parents being the objects of a manhunt by the evil Brits and Americans. Really? Think about it. It's like saying the whole world is mad rather than saying our parents were bonkers."

"That's what you think?"

"Let's stick to your three questions." Issie made the sign of a cross with her two index fingers, as if warding off bad spirits, and chanted, "Avoid the quicksand. Question two—Jacques was a regular visitor to our house in Quebec when Raymond was quote, unquote, travelling. During my first year at Amadeus, Anna, you and I would visit 'Uncle Jacques' at his townhouse in Toronto. You must have been four."

"Are you suggesting Anna and Jacques were a thing?"

"I'm not suggesting anything. Moving back to our script and your last question, I never met or heard Jacques mention a secretary named Catherine Caron. A secretary stopped by his townhouse once or twice when I was there. I'd describe her as short, plump and dowdy. For some reason I had this morbid fascination with her fleshy cheeks, as in ass. In any event, she was the extreme opposite of Anna. That's it, Maggie. *Finito*."

"What about Blue Mountain at Christmas?"

"No way. No more games of Clue, conversations or visitations with the past. From this point on, I want to hear about you, Sam, his new job, your new job, our lives and the future."

For the first time that morning, Maggie felt the tension leave the room. They talked about the plight of infants with doe-in-the-headlight mothers, Pampers versus cloth diapers, cleaning products, then their favorite topic of whether Aunt Jo and Angelo had something going on.

Issie said, "Hah. I can hear Angelo saying, 'So Jo, I got nothing to do tonight, so if you want to check out the sheets on your bed, well, you know how to reach me.'"

Maggie laughed and offered Aunt Jo's reply, "Earth to Angelo. If you want to spend time with me you've got to take me on a date. A date. No one checks out my sheets, *capisce?*"

"A date? Who dates after thirty? I'll bring pizza and a nice bottle of Cold Duck," panned Issie.

Issie then sat up on her knees on the kitchen chair and leaned forward. "How about, 'so, Jo, maybe we could take a nap after church on Sunday and see if we have our own religious experience.'"

Maggie snapped, "Like what Romeo? You want to light my candle?"

Issie moaned as if she was in the throes of an orgasm and said, "Oh god, I love it when you talk dirty to me."

Both Maggie and Issie doubled over in laughter. Play-acting gave them uncensored, creative license and Maggie loved to laze in Issie's lightness, laughter and irreverence. She thought Issie might be right. She'd spent most of her life playing a board game, trying to find parents to fix her world. Too little time in the here and now, and too few banana splits!

On her way out, Maggie crossed the front yard and encircled Eddie, Jr. and Raymond in a close huddle, their heads touching. She huddled long enough to take in the ripe smell of sweat, salt and dirt. Boy smells. Just then Issie slammed through the aluminum storm door waving a cracked and yellowed plastic container that held the tattered copy of the 1950 *Toronto Tribune* with photos of Raymond and Anna, subjects of the manhunt. Visible through the dusty plastic, the date was eighteen years ago to the day.

All glass, the over-sized front doors of Jingo Motors were impressive. They pulled you into a lobby showroom of their latest models. Sam promised to be waiting on the sidewalk. No Sam.

Maggie parked just beyond the entrance and pulled a book out of the glove box. Dr. Spock's 1968 revision of *Baby and Child Care*. She and Sam had decided to take a running start because Sam thought it would take at least two to three months for his rambunctious sperm to find her egg. With the temperature topping ninety, Maggie was wilting. She cranked down both front windows in an attempt to create a breeze. None. Maggie then hiked up her red handkerchief sundress and tucked it between her legs. Her legs stuck together. In desperation, she stretched her right leg over the stick shift at a right angle to the dashboard and propped her heel on the base of the open passenger-side window. Lost in a section about prenatal care, Maggie didn't see Sam and another man approach the car until both bent down to look in the passenger window. When Maggie looked up, Sam's face was stuck in a half smile over the crest of her bare knee. The other man was in full grin. Maggie froze.

"Ah, Maggie, this is Skip Malone my new boss. Skip, this is my wife Maggie."

Any move Maggie made would risk more exposure, so she lowered her book, smiled and said "Nice to meet you, Skip."

Sam opened the door to move Skip back and mumbled something about tomorrow. After Sam closed the door, Skip bent down one more time to stick his head in the window and said, "Nice meeting you, Maggie. Hope to see you again!"

As they pulled away, Sam whispered "I bet you do," looked at Maggie and they both burst out laughing.

"Mag, I'm too new to be asking for favors. Plus, Issie's right. It would kill Eddie to give up his seniority and lose his pay grade, vacation time and bidding rights. He's worked too hard to start from scratch. Besides, if he's made some enemies at the UAW, moving to Jingo won't change that. He's got to make his peace, throw himself on the union sword—whatever it takes."

"Fine."

"Fine? What does that mean?"

"It means fine. What do you think it means?"

"That's it. Fine? No argument, begging, pleading, cajoling?"

"Nope."

"Hmm. Maggie, you okay?"

"Yep. Just turning over my day with Issie and thinking about the Soulier quicksand. Do you think I'm in quicksand and just don't know it?"

"Maybe."

"Maybe? What do you mean by maybe?"

"I mean maybe."

"Okay."

"Okay? Jesus, Mag, I'm not used to you giving up so easily. You're definitely not okay."

"I've been reading Dr. Spock."

"And?"

"And, I'd like to jump your bones, Samuel Tervo. I want to make a baby."

"Here, on the couch?"

Maggie lifted the spaghetti straps on her red handkerchief dress and started to pull it over her head. Sam began unbuttoning his shirt. The heat and humidity in their dingy rental house transported Maggie to Hemingway's house in the Florida Keys. She could hear jazzmen playing in the streets while sea gulls cried and flapped their wings. The sun would set soon. In the Keys, a flash of green light along the horizon would thrill the rum drinkers and sun worshipers. Here, in a tiny shell of a house, crashing waves licked the living room floor.

17

Dead Rabbit

Like a clock whose hands are sweeping past the minutes of its face—and the world is like an apple whirling silently in space—like the circles that you find in the windmills of your mind.
—Noel Harrison, lyrics from *Windmills of Your Mind*

NOVEMBER 1968—"Oh my god, Issie, the rabbit died," said Maggie.

"Holy crap! I don't know if I should offer you congratulations or sympathy. Just pray for a girl. When did you find out?"

"Just now. I got a call from the doctor. Sam's in a meeting and I couldn't stand holding on to this information another second. Why does a rabbit have to die?"

"When are you due?"

"Mid-July. I'm freaking out. But this is good, right? I have the summer off and I can go back to work in September."

"Maggie, whatever you do, don't tell the school you're pregnant. They'll fire you. Do you have to work?"

"God, I don't know. I've got to get off the phone in case Sam tries to call. I'll catch you later."

Maggie sat on the brown tweed sofa she and Sam picked up at a yard sale. Then, the fabric and cushions appeared to be in good condition. But now, with a baby coming, Maggie saw the sofa and the rest of the house with new eyes. *What was Proust's quote about discovery not being about new places, but having new eyes?* Maggie searched her mind without luck. She'd go to the library and look it up later. One phone call, one dead rabbit later, her life already felt different and nothing looked the same. Maggie stretched out on the sofa, laid her hands on her belly and stared at the ceiling light fixture—a terrarium of iridescent blue flies, papery gray moths and one silky orange dragonfly. *Holy mother of god, what were Sam and I thinking?*

When the phone rang, Maggie was standing on top of the kitchen table under the living room light. Three of the four screws that held the glass globe were clamped between her lips as she moved to unscrew the fourth with a metal fingernail file. Dropping the file on the table, spitting three screws into her hand, Maggie executed a backward slide off the table and ran to the kitchen to catch the phone.

"Hey, Mag, what's up?"

"The rabbit died."

"Whose rabbit?"

"Sam, THE RABBIT DIED."

"The rabbit died? Oh my god, the rabbit died! We're having a baby. Maggie, we're having a baby! My heart is beating so hard I wonder if you can hear it. Can you hear it?"

"Hold the phone next to your heart, let me hear it."

After several beats, Sam whispered, "Can you hear it?"

"I think so. Or, it's my own heart. God Sam, we're going to be parents! I don't know if I'm ready."

"Who's ready? How does anyone know if they're ready? When babe?"

"Dr. Stanley said the third or fourth week of July."

"Are you scared, excited, peaceful?"

"All of the above. I was on the kitchen table taking down the globe from the ceiling fixture in the living room to clean it. We're eight months away and I'm already nesting. Do you think I'll become a housekeeper?"

"Not a chance. We're both too laid back. I'm so curious and excited about this metamorphosis, this blind march into parenthood. We're going to have a baby, Mrs. Tervo!"

"Oh god. We moved too fast. We don't know the first thing about raising kids! I was parentless, and you didn't. . . ."

"Mag, seriously? Most of us are lucky we survived childhood."

"Is that your slanted, perverse way of trying to cheer me up? Because if it is, I'm missing the point."

"My beautiful pregnant wife. We're smart, we can memorize Spock; plus, our friends and family will be lining up to give us advice we don't want."

"Ah, yes, advice. Something to look forward to. Speaking of advice, let's wait a few weeks before we tell your mom.

"Your call, babe. How about White Castle on our way to The Eights tonight?

"You're on!"

Maggie loved the drive to Clyde's house, past Aunt Jo's street and Angelo's Pizzeria. Her old haunts. The after-work traffic seemed light for a Wednesday and the starless, cloudy night rested like a pall on the bare trees and empty sidewalks. Due to schedule conflicts, this was the first called meeting of The Eights since their return from Toronto. Maggie knew their ragtag civil rights momentum relied on time stolen from hourly workers, beauticians, maids, janitors, truck drivers and factory workers. Most were from toothless neighborhoods in skeleton cities. Without Dr. King pushing the agenda, work was relegated and measured in random, intermittent hours.

Clyde and Marmalade met them at the door.

"Hey, Marmalade you poor, beleaguered collie. You still hanging out with this bum?" said Sam.

"Marmalade knows he's got a good thing going. What about you Maggie? You still hanging out with this bum?"

"Clyde, are you comparing me to a dog?"

"Oh, shit, I stepped in it again. Of course not, Maggie, I meant you're too good for this cracker."

"Better. Give me a hug. I've missed you!"

"You too, Maggie, especially at work. Angelo's been in a deep funk since you left. If you thought he was a pain in the ass before, wait'll you see him now."

"For real? Angelo told me he hired two people for less money than he paid me. Ticked me off."

"Maggie, you of all people know Angelo was telling you he missed you," said Clyde.

"I guess. Without a car I'm a little homebound. But, I'll pop in one day and we'll let Angelo buy us lunch."

"Do it! Blanche is in the kitchen with Loretta and Stella talking trash, waiting for Robin and Willie."

"Sam, walk with me and Marmalade for a few blocks and tell me what's happening. New job, new digs. I've missed you, my man."

It was cold enough to see breath, silent enough to hear it.

"Job is way better than I thought. Relaxed dress code, guys walking around without jackets. I've even seen a few with loose ties. No shit. I told Maggie it reminds me of an ad agency."

"Seriously, that's your bag? I work in jeans. You want casual, flip hamburgers, make pizzas, dump garbage, mow lawns."

"Got it. I sound like a ditz."

"No, you sound like a suit, part of the country-club set. 'Oh, worries me, I've got a pimple on my ass and I have to wear a tie to work.'"

"Fuck you."

Clyde put his arm over Sam's shoulder and said, "Let's cut to the chase, I love you too much to sit back and watch you become a bigger asshole than you are."

Sam dropped his head on Clyde's shoulder and said, "just my luck to choose a prick to be my best friend. And, not to brag, but I've got an administrative assistant who is 'dy-no-mite.' Smart, sassy, good-looking."

"Please don't tell me you've made her your confidante."

"She's my assistant. Who else am I going to trust?"

"Dickhead. Remember our talk about kryptonite?"

"I do."

"And?"

"And I'm a dickhead. Damn. I don't think I've told her any-thing personal, and I sure as hell didn't tell her about my Sheer Juice fumble."

"Sam, that was not a fumble. More like a hundred-yard dash to the opponent's end zone. It brought you to your knees and who knows how many years on a short leash. You've got way too much to lose to make anyone your confidante. Think about it. You haven't even told Maggie. Or have you?"

"No. Maggie can't know. Not now, not ever."

"Okay then. No word from Zito? No special favors?"

"None."

"Good, except the longer the time and the farther you are from Sheer Juice the more likely you'll forget about treating everyone like kryptonite. You can bet your ass they're not going to forget. You might want to have the word 'kryptonite' tattooed on your left arm."

"I was thinking the word 'dickhead' on both arms."

Marmalade barked at something—a shadow from the street-light, a stray cat?

Everyone except Blanche was seated at the dining room table, including Robin and Willie. There was an air of excitement. The room shimmied with animation and sound.

"Well, if it isn't Daddy Sawbucks. Fancy job, new baby on the way," cried Robin.

Sam looked at Maggie who shrugged her shoulders, held her palms up and smiled like Mona Lisa gone rogue.

"Yep, we're learning how to be grown-ups in spite of ourselves," laughed Sam.

Blanche walked in with a tray of eight stemmed glasses and a bottle of *Boone's Farm Apple Wine*. "Well, it's not champagne, but this calls for a toast!"

Clyde stood up, raised his glass and looked first at Sam and then at Maggie. "My two friends, we've worked hard, labored through race riots, protests, sit-ins and pizza parties for nine-year-olds. We've seen some of the best and worst of humanity. But here you are, bringing your kid into this tilt-a-whirl world. Just when you think you couldn't love them more, there will be the first smile, first tooth, first step, first word. Totally out-of-sight! Kids open the forgotten world, the one hidden from adults. I wish you health, happiness and sorrow. You will have sorrow. But, this kid will give you courage you didn't know you had and teach you about love in ways no one can explain." Clyde touched his glass to Maggie and Sam's glasses. Then everyone began toasting health and happiness.

Loretta laughed as she said, "Here's to sleep-filled nights. Marcus was a night owl, slept all day and up all night. It was a special kind of hell."

Sam whispered, "Maggie, I wasn't expecting this. Did you change your mind?"

"No. We were in the kitchen talking and I just blurted it out. It was as if I was channeling someone else. Freaked me out. Are you okay?"

"Me? I'm on some Timothy Leary LSD trip to the moon and back. Seriously, it's as if I'm out of my body looking at myself from the other side of the room. Who am I now? Who are we?"

The meeting sounded like a recast of everything they said every month, except for the wailing, ranting and raving about Nixon's win. After ten minutes, Clyde called for order. "Listen up. We can't change what is. We can only hope Vietnam will turn Nixon's attention to war games and give us time. Time for what you ask? The Civil Rights Act is a piece of paper. The courts are just beginning to give it teeth. In the meantime, tens of thousands of jobs and honkies are fleeing the city. If you haven't noticed, Detroit is getting poorer and blacker. Bad enough, but the suburbs might as well have twelve-foot barbwire fences to keep us out. Anyone taken a Sunday drive to Livonia, Westland, Farmington, Southfield . . . anywhere outside the city limits?" asked Clyde.

Sam and Maggie were the only two who raised their hands.

"Just as I thought. What's the buzz? Why aren't we darkies checking out these new hoods?"

"For me, it's about time, energy and gas. What could be more boring, and a bigger waste of time, than sightseeing along one of the Mile Roads? I don't think anyone's going to be standing on the gravel shoulder of Seven Mile, waving a handkerchief, hoping I'll stop for a cup of tea," said Loretta.

"Robin and I went to Northland Mall a few times. It's got some color, mostly Jews and Arabs, but we sure did get 'the looks.' I felt like I was stepping on a sidewalk in Mississippi in the early sixties. It does make you aware of your skin tone!" said Willie.

"Willie's right. In Detroit I never think about being black. At the mall, I couldn't *stop* thinking about being black. Pisses me off to be wishing myself white at this point in my life. Lord, god, the next thing you know I'll be praying for blue eyes again," said Robin.

Blanche leaned forward and whispered, "Lois, an old neighbor and one of our white-flight friends in Livonia, invited me to her house for lunch. I can't do it. Scares the bejesus outta me. Brings up all my childhood nightmares from the south. Do y'all know about the cops radioing an NIL code? Stands for "Nigger in Livonia."

"Blanche, are you frigging kidding me? How do you know that?" asked Sam.

"Common knowledge. The NAACP whiffed it after the riots," said Clyde.

"Holy crap! How do they get away with it? Who in their right mind would let this go on?" said Maggie.

"Maggie, you've never been stopped, frisked or dragged to the slammer because your skin's white. Believe me, this ole minstrel song ain't nothing new—same thing, second verse. Doubt there's a white town *without* a nigger code. This might not be the south, but these auto plants are filled with Jim Crows. Southern attitudes and white sheets followed them north, packed in old trunks and piled in the back of pickup trucks draped in a Confederate flag. Same baggage moving into the burbs," said Clyde.

"We're the ones who act like the burbs are wrapped in barbwire. If we're afraid to cross the city limits, we're complicit in supporting this white supremacist, segregated, uncivilized world we live in," said Stella.

Snapping her fingers Robin said, "Complicit? Sister, where in hell's half acre did you come up with that word? And, what does it mean?" asked Robin.

"It means we're helping the crackers maintain their fences. Sorry Maggie and Sam, I mean the bigoted whites. Well, maybe not. Maybe I mean *all* whites. Bigoted or not, when we hold back, keep ourselves separate from whites, it's easy for them to drink the Kool-Aid. Ain't nobody holding up a mirror. If we don't whack through this jungle and pass the talking stick, why would they bother? Which, of course, leads to the question, do we even give a rip? Is it our goal to have whites accept us? And, why do they get to be the standard?" asked Stella.

"Do we give a shit? What do you think?" asked Clyde.

"It just struck me. After all this fighting for equality, which *is* our goal, I wonder if *acceptance* by whites is realistic. I'd like it, but do we need it?" said Stella.

Maggie leaned forward, waiting to pounce. "Probably not. Whites are no different than anyone else when it comes to the survival of the fittest—power and wealth. In Canada, French Canadians are the underclass. In fact, I found out there's a book called *White Niggers of America* about French Canadians. There, bigotry isn't based on pigmentation; it's based on the imagined threat to the Brit's livelihood, to their power to control the wealth. Imagine the Brits worried we French would get too uppity? Little did they know!"

"Girl, you sittin' at the right table then," said Robin.

"For real? Maggie, I had no idea you were French Canadian. I thought you were just some clueless white hippie chick looking for a cause," panned Loretta as the entire group cracked up.

"With that, we'll call it a night. I want you guys to be thinking about how we begin to change the opinion of Führer Nixon's silent majority. We need to tear down the unspoken but very real 'barbed wire,' between Detroit and the burbs, before Nixon trashes the Civil Right's Act. Then, of course, we have to come up with a good name for Maggie and Sam's baby. As we know, honkies do a piss-poor job when it comes to names," said Clyde.

"Amen to that," said Loretta as she hugged Maggie and lifted her off the ground.

Before Sam shifted the car into first, Maggie said, "Let's stop at Aunt Jo's and let her know."

The porch lamp was off but light glanced through the shrubs in front of the kitchen window. Maggie rang the doorbell. No answer. Maggie tried again, still no answer. Maggie pulled her moleskin poetry notebook from her purse and ripped out a blank sheet. As she looked for a pen, the door opened and Aunt Jo smiled at them through the guard-chain gap.

"Maggie, Sam, what a surprise! Hold on and I'll unleash this chain so I can give you a hug." Aunt Jo was in her signature white terry-cloth robe with her hair in rollers. "I'm so thrilled for you both! Issie called and gave me the good news. I tried your house a half dozen times."

"We had a meeting at Clyde's. Sorry I didn't call you myself, but I lost my head and decided to clean all of our ceiling lights. I've got enough dead insects to support six junior high science labs. I hope we didn't wake you."

Aunt Jo tapped the brush rollers on her head and said, "Good grief, I hope I don't scare you. Come in. We'll sit in the kitchen." Without asking, Aunt Jo put on a kettle of water and pulled three cups from their hooks.

"No fuss, Auntie Jo," said Maggie, as she looked at all the familiar surfaces, colors and objects. Was it a lifetime ago when she sat by this phone, willing it to ring, willing it to be Sam?

"So you're due in July. What's your intuition tell you, boy or girl?"

Sam and Maggie looked at each other then, in unison, said, "girl."

"Me too," said Aunt Jo, "a little Maggie!"

"Oh god, let me re-imagine," laughed Sam.

"So, Auntie Jo, what's going on with you? Hanging out with Angelo?"

"Maggie, I know you and Issie think you can turn our friendship into a romance, but that's not happening. I fell in love once and that will keep me company the rest of my life. Angelo is a friend. No more, no less. And, believe me, he's not looking for romance."

"Auntie Jo, how would you know? Seriously. Angelo says the opposite of what he thinks and feels."

"That's his unique charm and it works for me."

Maggie laughed and said, "Sure, Auntie Jo, I get it. Was Issie doing psychic cartwheels over the phone because Eddie's back to work and she has the house to herself? What a mess! In August she was so depressed with him underfoot she almost killed off all her houseplants. Have you seen her? She's so skinny that if she turned sideways, she'd look like a gamma ray. Seriously, her double C boobs wouldn't fill an A cup."

"Okay, in case you two forgot, there's a guy in the room."

Aunt Jo got up and hugged Sam over the back of his chair. Cheek-to-cheek she whispered in his ear, "My dear sweet Sam. If this conversation led to a public service announcement, the tag line would be: *retain your mystery*."

"What was Aunt Jo whispering about?"

"Something about retaining our mystery."

"Aunt Jo's the mystery. I don't understand why she refuses to talk about Jacques' or my parents. She says it's too hard for her. Makes me nuts. Life is a mystery."

"Does Jacques know that Aunt Jo and Issie refused his invitation?"

"I wrote him and said they couldn't make it."

"Maggie, do you want to go? I mean, pregnant and all."

"Sam, don't treat me like I've got some disease. Dr. Spock says pregnancy is a state of health. Besides, I want to get to know Jacques better. I want him in our life."

"What about skiing? Can you ski if you're pregnant?"

"This trip is not about skiing *mon ami.*"

Sam reached over, put his hand on Maggie's belly and sighed.

18

Trapped

I think that when women are encouraged to be competitive too many of them become disagreeable.

—Dr. Benjamin Spock

DECEMBER 1968 — Sam looked at his watch before he called Maggie at the number on the yellow telephone message. Maxine had checked the box next to *Urgent*. It was nine a.m., less than an hour since he dropped Maggie at The University of Detroit for a faculty lunch and end-of-semester planning session. Rather than risk weather and city bus schedule delays, Maggie opted to get there four hours early.

A male voice said, "Good morning, this is the University of Detroit Library. May I help you?"

"Good morning. This is Sam Tervo. I have a message from my wife Maggie who asked me to call this number."

"Of course. Please hold and I'll let her know you're on the line."

"Hello."

"Hey, Maggie, you okay?"

Maggie whispered, "Oh god, Sam. I've been puking my guts out. Can you pick me up? I can't do the bus."

"Morning sickness?"

"I guess. I called the Department Head to tell him I couldn't make the meeting. He pressed me for a reason, then asked if I was expecting. I had to tell him. Sam, he said he was sorry but he'd have to replace me next semester, some rule about the 'impropriety of pregnant women in a classroom.' I'd be so ticked off if I didn't feel like a pollywog in a Mason jar."

"Hang tight. I'll look for you in the library. If I don't see you, I'll assume you're in the ladies room and plant myself between the circulation desk and the door."

Sitting at a well-worn, yellowed oak table near the entrance, Maggie's head rested on her folded arms. Dressed in black, with black hair spilling like ink, she looked like one of the nuns covered in a habit. Sam did a double take before he put his hand on Maggie's shoulder and said, "Hey, babe. How're you doing?"

Without moving her head, Maggie looked up at Sam, her face tear-stained and sallow. The makeup she'd so carefully applied for her 'first professional meeting' smudged her face and mascara left skid marks under her eyes. Maggie said, "If you think I look bad, *ya shoulda seen the other guy,*" then burst out crying.

During the ride home Sam had to stop twice for Maggie. Her dry heaving was punctuated by pleas and obscenities. The few saltines Maggie had for breakfast and the few ounces of water from a library fountain were long gone. "Hey, Mag, this may not be the best timing, but do you want to stop and pick up some White Castle for your lunch later today?"

When Maggie punched him in the shoulder and started to wretch out the window again, Sam said, " Got it. Bad idea."

Sam in a white button-down shirt, wearing his loosened black, gold and blue paisley print tie, cleaned up the dinner dishes after making Campbell's Tomato Soup and grilled cheese sandwiches. Listless, Maggie watched from the kitchen table in navy sweat pants, a red cable knit sweater and an old pair of Sam's wool hockey socks. Ice was collecting inside the windows where the caulking had cracked.

"Mag, I know it doesn't seem fair, but most places won't hire pregnant women. I may not like it, but I kind of get it. It's a distraction, if not a disruption. Seriously. Think about it. A pregnant woman might prompt sexual thoughts, catcalls, you name it. Catholic universities sure as hell don't want to deal with that. Besides, most women quit after the baby's born, which makes this debate a . . . what? An argument about six to eight months of lost work?"

"Sam, really? Who's behind your long hair and sideburns? A pig with a brush cut? This is 1968. We're out of the Dark Ages. At least I thought we were."

"Mag, I'm on your side. But the flipside, whether we like it or not, is the hard reality. This is *still* a man's world. It'll take time for the pendulum to swing."

"Screw it. I'm not going to give up my career because some uptight priest thinks pregnancy is obscene. I'm going to fight this."

"Right, Mag, you want to take on the Vatican between morning sickness and Dr. Spock? Don't get me wrong, you of all people could do this, have it all. But, why when you don't give a damn about this job?"

"Sam, Freshman English is my *path* to poetry, my way to earn stripes. We were going to do this together. You said you'd watch the baby while I taught at night. Now nothing?"

"Babe, if it was up to me you'd be running the poetry department. What do you want? If you want to fight I'll climb in the foxhole with you. If you decide to take this time to work on civil rights, women's rights, motherhood, whatever, we can live without your income. Up to you."

Maggie raised her eyebrows and looked at Sam sideways. He waited for the hook, the wry comment. Instead, she stood up and took his face in her hands, smiled and said, "Samuelsan, we're both fighters and dreamers. Let's keep our feet on the edge of the foxhole and plant a willow tree on the moon."

Morning sickness had no mercy or time restriction. The smell of coffee or cigarette smoke tested Maggie's gag reflex in every bagel shop, restaurant, movie theater, bus, doctor's waiting room, anywhere people drank coffee or smoked, which meant everywhere. Home was Maggie's only safe harbor and keeping her own company was like rowing an anchored boat. Everyone was working or getting ready for the holidays while she spent endless days trying to keep bland food down. After several last minute cancellations to meet for dinner to celebrate the baby, Sam's mother Maija offered she and Kenny would make dinner in Maggie's kitchen and smoke outside. In final settlement negotiations to host, what Sam now referred to as the *Bi-lateral Dinner*, he agreed to re-caulk the windows and mop the floors.

Maggie smiled as she looked around the house—clean light fixtures and floors, ice-free windows. On the coffee table sat Jacques' gift of four gray Zeno cloth napkins, tied in a white grosgrain ribbon; Grandma Landry's off-white crocheted tablecloth; one of Aunt Jo's Scotch Pine candles; and a very pricey red linen tablecloth from Hudson's post-Christmas sale last year. Maggie told Sam it was worth the twenty dollars because it 'lifted her spirits' so Sam christened it *The Red Shroud of Turin*.

Maggie planned to organize and set the table. Sam would pick up wine and beer after work. For the first time in weeks, Maggie looked forward to getting out of her sweats and into real clothes.

When the phone rang at four o'clock, Maggie expected to hear Sam's voice, maybe Issie's. "Hello!"

"Hello! Is this Marguerite Soulier Tervo?" said a man with a deep, baritone voice.

Maggie halted a moment before returning a formal reply in her best aristocratic voice. "Yes, it is. To what do I owe the honor, Monsieur Jacques Ruivivar?"

Jacques' laughter hooked her immediately. "Oh, Maggie, it's so good to hear your voice. I got your letter and it looks like this year's out. A baby? Imagine!"

"It's hard to imagine. With morning sickness, it's a stretch to see beyond the moment, much less seven months down the road. How are you?"

"Doing well, Maggie. I wanted to call before the holidays got away from us. My accountant said there's a small reserve at Amadeus for the Soulier girls—you and Issie. I know it's hard getting on your feet and it sounds like Issie and Eddie have had some financial challenges this year. If you'll send me bank account information for the two of you, I'll split the proceeds and wire the money."

"Are you putting me on? Really?"

"Really, Maggie. I'm not sure of the total, but it's sufficient enough to make sure it gets to a bank rather than risk mail."

"How exciting, found money, like an inheritance from a long-lost relative."

"Well, so it is, the remainder from Anna and Raymond's investment in your education."

"You're right. Issie and Eddie will be thrilled and we have a very empty nursery to furnish. Are you planning to go to Blue Mountain?"

"Maybe. Probably. Being there is like living in a Christmas diorama. Let's try again for next year."

"For sure, Jacques. Have a happy holiday!"

"You too, dear Maggie."

Just as Maggie hung up, the phone rang again.

"Hello!"

"Hey, Maggie. I wanted to warn you before I show up at your house tonight."

"Oh, Stella, we've got plans with Sam's mother and brother."

"I know. Guess who's coming to dinner?"

Before Sam got out of his car, Maggie was standing in the open side door with her hands on her hips, goose bumps multiplying in the arctic air. Maggie's orange and white checked apron covered a thin black a-line dress over black nylon tights with black patent leather go-go boots. Maggie had pulled her hair into a French twist and trimmed it with sprigs of holly leaves and red berries that matched the burst of red lipstick.

"Hey, babe, what's up? You look out of sight, like some Goddess Aphrodite."

"Samuel Tervo, why didn't you tell me Kenny and Stella were dating?"

"What? Where did you hear that?"

"Stella called and said 'guess who's coming to dinner?'"

"No shit? I had no idea. I can't remember the last time I talked to that dickhead. Is this the first time Stella said anything?"

"Yes. Stella claims they didn't want to freak us out so they decided to see where the relationship landed before they told us."

"Since when?"

"Since our wedding, almost a year now."

"Unbelievable. I thought Kenny's absence meant he was back into drugs and no way was I going to spin that roulette wheel again."

"You torqued?"

"No. His business, not mine. You ready to take down Stella?"

"Yeah. I think I am. We're friends. Why wouldn't she tell me?"

"Mag, pretty and smart as she is, Stella is *the* ice queen. Seriously, look up ice queen in the Britannica and you'll find her picture. I don't think I've ever seen her smile, much less laugh."

"I know, but an entire year? By now you'd think the two of them would know if they're a couple."

"Think Kenny. Would you depend on him to get to dinner on time? Now, think about the high probability for break ups and make ups."

"Okay. I get it. You're wrong about Stella. She's super reserved, but she's not an ice queen. In spite of everything, I can't wait to see how they are together. I'm trying to imagine prim and proper Stella with your wild, crazy-ass brother. Who do you think changed the most?"

"Mag, guys always change for the girl. He'll be wearing a dark suit, white shirt and tie."

"Nah. I bet she's in bell bottoms with a suede fringed vest."

"You're on. If you win I give you a back rub; if I win I give you a back rub."

"Ah, Mr. Tervo, you drive a hard bargain."

Maggie pulled the kitchen table into the living room to dress it. She added one white linen napkin for Stella, a keepsake of Mama Tervo's generous wedding gift. Maggie copped the napkin from the London Chop House last May. The truth was, Maggie was about to slip the napkin in her purse when Sam asked the manager if they could buy it. The manager looked around then signaled Maggie to slip it in her purse! Sam called it *The Heist*. Maggie could still taste the medium rare prime rib, twice-baked potatoes, French-cut green beans and hard rolls. After *The Heist* the night air was almost balmy at sixty degrees. Before they reached married housing, Sam turned into Wayne State's empty stadium parking lot. A crescent moon with a brightly burning Venus was holding up the dark blue sky. With the top down on the Triumph, they made love under this symbol of the Libyan flag, or was it a Muslim blessing? In the sated heat of their entwined bodies, Maggie sensed they'd been transported to new lands with *keffiyehs* around their heads and warm falafels in their pockets. The next day, she and Sam decided they'd celebrate every wedding anniversary at the London Chop House— same table, same meal, *for as long as they could masticate.* (Sam's double entendre!) Reservations were set for their first anniversary next week.

For seating, Maggie used the two mismatched kitchen chairs and borrowed three slightly charred card table chairs her neighbor rescued from the burned-out Kresge's after the riots. Maggie thought, *hodgepodge, warm and cozy like Aunt Jo's.* This was the first family gathering at their house—the first company of any kind. Maggie was surprised she felt so jazzed. At a gut level, she thought she finally understood the purpose of house-warming parties. Human energy filled empty spaces, like Sam's old tenement building and its jukebox of sounds, smells, motion—in spite of poverty, in spite of the cold.

"Hey, Maggie, wine and beer in the fridge. Do you need me for anything?"

"Yes. Courage, fortitude and a kiss to build a dream on."

"Seriously, do you need me to do anything? If not, I'm going to wrap the outside pipes. Winter is here big time. They're predicting snow with temps below zero."

"Go ahead. I'm just waiting for your mom to show up and start dinner. I hope we have enough pots and pans."

"As you like to say, oh well!"

Maggie laughed and said, "Oh well!"

Sam was outside when his mother pulled up in her turquoise and white 1956 Nash Rambler Coupe. The car was Maija's earnest protest against the Ford Motor Company. Sam's dad, Otto, started his career building railroads in the Upper Peninsula. Over time, he became well known for his ability to sweet talk insurgent landowners and swing through bureaucratic jungles to get the job done. In 1955, a recruiter called Otto and offered him a job managing the construction of railroad spurs to, and sometimes through, Ford's manufacturing and parts plants. Otto always joked about the Lower Peninsula being a metaphor for hell, but Otto was not without ego. Working for Ford would be like winning the Stanley Cup. Added to the prestige was a salary three times his current pay. Otto and Maija decided to cross the Straits and spend five years in hell for fifteen years of income. The trip back north to copper country would be lined with gold.

Sam was ten and Kenny eight when the Tervos settled into a two-bedroom brick bungalow in Farmington, about twenty miles northwest of Detroit. A small but bustling farming town, their house was a three-block walk to the downtown area with all its usual suspects—a post office, bank, general store, hardware, barbershop, hair salon, movie theater, cafe, ice cream parlor and several churches. One year later, Otto got home from work, collapsed on the living room floor and died before the doctor was called out of a school board meeting and reached their house. Only thirty-six, everyone said Otto was strong as an ox. The doctor said it wasn't a matter of strength, it was god's one-armed-bandit—coronary thrombosis, a clot in his heart. But Maija knew better. For months Otto insisted it was his idea to work seven days a week, twelve hours a day. "I'm young, it'll only be a few more months," he said. After a few more months Otto started leaving earlier, getting home later—more agitated, angrier. Maija begged him to quit, to walk away from 'those goddamn bloodsuckers' and move back to Calumet. Otto told her it was too late; he was hooked on the money and the power. The night before he died, Otto said, "Enough! No more talk about leaving. Maija, love of my life, our days of trying to eek out a living on a dying railroad or salvage copper mines are over. Our life is here."

After his funeral, Maija drove to the Nash dealership and traded in their 1956 black Ford Galaxy for a turquoise and white Nash Rambler. Heading home in the new car, Sam remembered his mom saying, "Ford can go fuck itself," under her breath. That was the moment when Sam quit holding his breath. He knew they'd be okay.

Maggie stuck her head in the kitchen. Mama Tervo was preparing some twice-baked potatoes. As Aunt Jo liked to say, 'Maija strikes a fine figure.' A natural platinum blonde with blue eyes and fair skin, Maija was blessed, or as Maija said cursed, with full breasts and hips. In old photos she looked like Marilyn Monroe. Now, in a too-tight red brocade dress with black suede three-inch heels, graying hair in a bun, and lines in her face, Maija looked every bit of her forty-five years.

"Mama Tervo, you sure there's no way I can help?"

"You and Sam can bring a couple chairs in and keep me company. I don't know where in hell's half acre Kenny is. He said he had to work late but thought he'd be here in time to help."

Maggie gave Sam *the look* and Sam said, "Did Kenny say anything about bringing a date tonight?"

"No way. I've only got enough food for four."

"Ma, Kenny's bringing a date."

Maija stopped scooping out the four baked potato shells, put her hands on her hips and took a deep breath before she turned around and said, "Who's he bringing?"

Maggie looked at Sam and nodded.

"Maggie's friend Stella, he's bringing Stella."

"That pretty Negro girl at the reception?"

"Black, Ma, not Negro."

"Negro to me. What in god's name does that smart, pretty Negro girl see in Kenny? Don't she have a master's degree in something?"

"You mean 'doesn't she have.'"

"Samuel, you don't need to give me no English lessons. I mean what the devil is he doing with a Negro girl who could have any Negro boy she wanted? What's her problem anyhow?"

"Why is it a problem? It's not a problem. People are attracted to each other for all kinds of reasons. She's strong, smart and beautiful. Maybe, just maybe, Stella is what Kenny needs to get his act together."

"Yeah, and maybe people in hell want ice water."

"Ma, that makes no sense at all. Come on. Let's have a dinner to celebrate the baby. Let's give Kenny's relationship some room. If she's as smart as I think she is, she'll drop Kenny and move on. If he's got half a flea's brain, he'll find a way to keep her in his life."

"Mama Tervo, did you see *Guess Who's Coming to Dinner* last year? Spencer Tracey, my all-time favorite actor? Anyhow, he called his daughter's love for Sidney Poitier 'a pigmentation problem.' I agree. Who gets to choose their skin color? Besides, it'll be fun to see them together. We can talk tomorrow and compare notes."

Maija looked at Maggie, then Sam, and said, "I give, but no more English lessons. It really pisses me off." Under her breath, Maija said "Pigmentation my ass." Sam squeezed Maggie's hand and grinned. Sam had warned Maggie about his mother's habit of turning thoughts into words under her breath. Maggie folded her lips between her teeth to mute her laughter and left the room.

By the time Kenny and Stella showed up, Maggie, Sam and Maija had emptied the first bottle of *Blue Nun*. Kenny was wearing a black suit, white shirt and a thin royal blue and black striped tie. Stella was dressed in black bellbottoms, a black turtleneck and a tan suede-fringed vest. Before Sam could take their coats to the bedroom, he and Maggie doubled over in uncontrolled laughter. Tears streaming down their cheeks, Maggie tried to talk, to explain, but the wine and irony were too much. She could not catch her breath.

Stella looked like she was ready to bolt. Maija paced the small kitchen. Kenny finally said, "Okay, you guys, what the hell's going on? What's so goddamn funny?"

Sam put his arm over Stella's shoulder and with a soft tug said, "Oh, Stella, we're so glad you're here. I'm sorry for our bad manners, but we'll explain. You'll love it."

Maggie brought the second bottle of wine into the living room. She kissed Stella and Kenny as she handed them each a glass. "Let me explain."

By the time Maggie and Sam finished telling the story about their bet, and the pleasure they felt when they saw that both had changed for the other, everyone was toasting and laughing. Sam thought his mother's enthusiasm was more about her not being the butt of the joke.

Maggie and Sam breathed easier when Maija managed to fill five plates with provisions for four without repeating her earlier comparison to 'the miracle of feeding the multitudes.' Four twice-baked potatoes became five generous potato pancakes. Four small steaks were turned into slices and served as French dip au jus. One small can of green beans provided a colorful garnish. Maggie took delight when she realized Sam's agility to snag life's curveballs was maternal, and let loose an exalted sigh that Sam had somehow sloughed off the genes that provoked Maija's more sarcastic, complaint-bound nature.

Stella said, "Mrs. Tervo, you are a woman of my own heart. This is not only my favorite meal but the most delicious I've ever had!"

No one missed the wink Sam sent his mother or the smile Maija worked hard to suppress.

Maggie thought Sam saw Stella with new eyes, glimpsing a sweetness and kindness he hadn't noticed before. Sam said, "So,

Stella, how on earth did you two manage to keep a secret for so long with this motor mouth?"

Stella held up a finger as she finished chewing her food, shook her head up and down, and said, "Isn't that the truth? When we first met at your wedding party he was so shy I thought I'd wear myself out getting him to open up. Boy was I wrong!"

Kenny looked at Stella with the unchecked adoration of a stray puppy brought in from the cold. Maija narrowed her eyes at Kenny then turned to Stella before saying, "Motor mouth? I'll be damned. You got this boy to talk? Must be some kinda love!"

"Ma, let it go. Not talking for last few months was the only way I could keep myself from doing back flips down the street and shouting her name."

Stella's dark olive skin turned pink then red. Kenny reached over to kiss her cheek then said, "I told you my family would approve!"

Maggie leaned toward Stella, "How about your family, and Clyde and Blanche, do they know?"

"How do I explain? My parents spent most of their lives running from Jim Crow. Still are. Needless to say, they don't much cotton to my work with the Freedom Riders. So, when I tried to tell them about Kenny, all kinds of hell broke loose. My dad said if I was looking to be lynched then I picked the perfect man. My mom, a lifelong hand wringer, wrung her hands, didn't say a word. They're experts at compartmentalizing. It must have kept them sane growing up on cotton fields in Mississippi. They weren't slaves, but they were. I get their need to break with that past. It's how they survived. Life in Detroit hasn't been a picnic. My dad couldn't get into the plants. He's a custodian at Woolworths. My mom does dishes and mops the floor at the Coney Island below their flat. So they pinned their hopes on me. Sorry, I got carried away. But, no, we haven't said a thing to Clyde or Blanche. Kenny and I wanted to tell you first."

"Oh, Stella, I can't imagine how hard this must be for you both. If you were in Europe it'd be easier. But here, in this back-ass-ward country, bi-racial couples are treated like they're breaking some cosmic law. What the hell," said Maggie.

A heavy stillness settled in the room. Through the ponderous pause, Sam moved like Jacques-Yves Cousteau under water, filling wine glasses in soundless depths. Maggie's stomach churned before she realized she'd been holding her breath, hoping love was not too blind.

Breaking the surface, coming up for air, Sam lifted his glass and said, "To Stella and Kenny for their love and courage. Maggie's right, it'll be brutal. Although I'm in total awe of you both for coming out, I can't help but worry. Our good friend Robin thinks mixing the races is the *only* way to abolish racism. She's probably right. I know you didn't sign up to be pioneers, but here you are. I wish you all the love and peace you can gather up and hang on to." Sam made the peace sign as he sipped his wine.

Kenny returned the peace sign then looked at Stella. "I know this will be tough as nails for Stella, and I feel like a selfish S.O.B. to ask her to be with me and deal with the insults, name-calling, all the bullshit. We've talked this into the ground and there's no way to know how well we'll do until we do it."

Maija turned to Stella and said, "If anyone gives you an ounce of grief, you call me and we'll take 'em out to the back forty and shoot 'em."

"Hey, Ma, thanks. We can use all the help we can get," laughed Kenny.

Stella and Maggie stood up and began to clear the table. As Maija got up to help, Sam said, "Sit, Ma. Let's you, Kenny and me shoot the breeze. It's been way too long."

Before Maggie handed Stella the first clean dish, she said, "God, Stella, I'm sorry your parents aren't on board. If they saw you and Kenny together they might change their minds."

"Not a chance. What my dad said was if I was intent on killing myself he's got some rope in the trunk of his car. He said it would be a helluva sight better than a lynch mob. I know he sounds like an asshole, but it's because he's lived in fear his whole life. My dad doesn't know how to protect me, so he's trying to shock me into his fear. They won't reject me, but it'll be one cold day in Detroit if we decide to get married."

"I wish I could reassure you, but I can't. You're going to get it from both sides—black and white. Sometimes love isn't enough. If you decide it's too much or Kenny's not right for you, for any reason, I'm your friend. I love you and I'll help you any way I can. Sam doesn't have to be in the loop. If you decide to stick with Kenny, I'll be here any time you need to talk, inside or outside the loop. Got it?"

Stella wrapped her long, skinny arms around Maggie and held her tight. She whispered, "I got it. Thank you."

After Maggie threw herself on the bed, in her red flannel nightgown and argyle knee socks, she patted her head, sat up and began pulling the berries and leaves from her hair and unpinned her French twist. "It was so freaking weird. I kept looking at your mom tonight, wondering what she thought about when she was pregnant with you."

"Ask her."

"Maybe I will. So, what do you think about Stella and Kenny?"

"I think Kenny is one *lucky* S.O.B. Not sure I'd say the same about Stella. She's surprisingly funny and not at all an ice queen."

"They're in love. No 'bout a doubt it.'"

"Back rub? Since we're both right, I owe you two."

"Not tonight. I'm a dishrag, a content and happy dishrag, but totally wasted."

Sam spooned Maggie and placed his hand on her belly. He imagined the mystical first home of their child—the soft warmth of the uterus, metronome of the heart and manna through an umbilical cord. "Mag, do you think the baby knows when we're laughing or crying? Does she feel what we feel?"

"Sam, we talk to plants to keep them healthy. It makes sense that we hear sounds and pick up on feelings before we're born. I've already introduced her to classical music, jazz and rock. No rockabilly country. And, please, no polkas! Okay, now I'm babbling, totally exhausted. Good night."

"You too," Sam said or thought he said. His mind was already lost in some psychedelic trip to recall the inside of his mother's womb. The idea of it didn't necessarily gross him out, but the image seemed a little kinky. Sam pulled Maggie closer, slid his hand between her legs and whispered, "How tired are you?"

Maggie answered with a sharp left-elbow-jab to his solar plexus.

19

Tipping Points

Give me a head with hair, long beautiful hair, shining, gleaming, streaming, flaxen, waxen—give me down to there hair, shoulder length or longer, here baby, there mama, everywhere daddy, daddy, hair flow it, show it, long as god can grow it, my hair.
> —Galt McDermott, Lyrics from *Hair*

JANUARY 3, 1969—Maggie woke up thinking about Clyde's New Year's Eve party. She and Sam used to be the last to leave a party. Now they were the first to sidle their way to the front door. Home before the ball dropped in Times Square, sound asleep by midnight. Between morning sickness and fatigue, Maggie felt like she was sleepwalking through life, spending entire days in her red flannel nightgown or sweats. In retrospect, she thought being laid off was a gift, a mystical intervention. Maggie had no doubt that curling up in a fetal position and napping on the floor between her Freshman English classes would have resulted in a very public, scandalous firing. She could see the headlines now—'Morning Sickness Sets

Back Employment Rights for Pregnant Women Another Hundred Years.'

Tucked away in a box, the French coffee press had become what, Maggie thought, *an icon of regrets—a reminder of unrealized, unrealistic dreams?* Like so many of their plans, visions and schemes, this hovel of a house was no Toronto B&B. Breakfast was cereal and coffee was instant. The extra work to buy and press coffee seemed absurd, especially now. Maggie changed her mind about getting organized and let the warped cupboard door dangle two inches from being closed.

During the holidays, Issie surprised Maggie by showing up late one afternoon to drop off some maternity clothes she gathered from her friends. Maggie was in a flannel nightgown, her hair in tangles. Issie shook her head and said, "For kicks, let's turn this scene into a soap opera. Sam spends his days with hip, young, chicks who put on miniskirts, dust their faces with powder, color their lips Jungle Peach and lengthen their lashes with Midnight Black. They bend over to serve him coffee and ask if there's anything else he needs, with an emphasis on *anything else*. One day Sam looks up from his desk, and in the blink of a batted lash and the fresh scent of a woman, he's reminded of his manhood. Later that evening, Sam gets home to find his wife, with matted hair and no makeup, napping on the couch in her thread-bare red flannel nightgown.' Earth-to-Maggie. Pregnancy isn't a nine-month furlough. In case you forgot, Sam is movie-star good-looking, smart and funny. Marriage didn't change that. He's out in the world every day. I get that you feel like crap, but you might want to get out of those flannels and bathe once in a while before someone who does turns his head." Although Maggie replied in kind and mocked her 'swift and slippery decline into ennui,' she had a hard time shaking off Issie's forecast. How could she describe how flat-out, excruciatingly bored she was with herself? *Bottom line*, thought Maggie, *if I think I'm a drag, and act like a drag, I'm a drag.*

Three short rings for their party line jarred her out of her head. "Hello!"

"Jeez, Maggie, were you sitting on top of the phone?"

"Hey, Issie. Just thinking of you. What's up?"

"You sitting down?"

"No. Do I need to?"

"Sit down. You're not going to believe this."

"Okay, Iss, I'm sitting."

"I got our bank statement in the mail today and there's a deposit for twenty thousand dollars on December 22nd. TWENTY THOUSAND DOLLARS! I'm so freaked I don't know what to do. Of course it's not ours, but my heart is racing so fast I had to call. Sweet Jesus, Maggie! I know I have to report it but part of me wants to just pretend I didn't see it and keep it. What would you do?"

"Oh my god, Iss. It's your money."

"Right, Maggie, you want me to spend the rest of my life in prison?"

"No, seriously. Listen. I forgot to tell you. Holy crap, twenty thousand!"

"Stop. What did you forget to tell me? Did you rob a frigging bank?"

"Issie, Jacques Ruivivar called me before Christmas and told me his accountant found some funds in our name. Funds set aside for us at Amadeus. He said he wasn't sure of the amounts, but thought they were large enough to wire to our accounts rather than mail checks. When you and Eddy went to the Indy 500, way back when, and left the kids with his mom, you gave me a signed blank check from your account in case of an emergency. Also known as *The Anna & Raymond Factor* in case you died or disappeared. Anyhow, I had your account number so I sent it to Jacques. I was going to let you know, but between my morning sickness and the holidays I got waylaid. Sorry."

"This twenty thousand is ours? Are you shitting me? Really?"

"Really. I don't have my bank statement yet but there should be an equal amount for me. Imagine, Anna found a way to keep forty-thousand dollars of their estate for us."

"Maggie, are your legs shaking? Mine are chattering. You have no idea how important this money is to us right now."

"I don't think it's hit me yet. It's way more than I ever thought I'd have. Sam is going to freak out. I'm beginning to freak out. I'll call you later."

Good morning, Jingo Personnel, may I help you?

"Hey, Maxine, Sam there?"

"Hey, Maggie! Sam's meeting with the big guys. You need me to pull him out or you want to leave a message?"

"Message works. No emergency. I'm spreading good news."

"My guess is he's on the hunt for good news. With the auto show coming up in a few weeks, everyone looks like they're walking around with wedgies in their patooties."

"Hah! I thought that was their normal gait. How's it going with you?"

"In Skip's words, *fair to middlin'*. Post-holiday blahs. This deep, dark African-skinned body of mine landed in the northern tundra because my grandparents wanted to escape slavery. It might seem like a small price to pay, but I live in duck bumps ten months of the year."

"Duck bumps? You mean goose bumps?"

"Nope, duck bumps. My Texas cousins claim duck bumps are bigger."

"Figures Texas would come up with something bigger. Oh, Max, let's head south for a few weeks. Miami?"

"I'm on it, after the auto show. Just tell me when you're past that gag-reflex thing. Seriously, if I hear someone gag it's all over but the shouting. The last thing we want is a duet."

"Got it. After the auto show, no gagging and no duets."

When Maggie was dialing Sam's office, she'd noticed two gift-wrapped boxes on top of the fridge. Barely visible, the colorful packages were tucked against a bunched up macramé hanger collecting dust and bugs—behind Loretta's neglected, yet lovely, spider plant. Maggie and Sam had decided to wait until they moved to their own house before screwing a big hook in a ceiling. How the plant survived the ice cold drafts and random watering never ceased to amaze her.

Maggie pulled the packages off the fridge and placed them on the kitchen table. Wrapped in red and white striped paper, the largest gift had a hand-cut candy-cane-shaped tag taped to the front that read: *To our baby girl or boy, all my love, Grandma Tervo*. Inside the box, a precious hand-crocheted white receiving blanket and matching cap with white satin ribbon ties, *reeked* of cigarette smoke. Before her gag reflex made a move, Maggie tossed the blanket and cap in the dish tub and filled it with warm water and a splash of Ivory Liquid. Opening the door against needle cold wind, Maggie dropped the box and wrapping paper on the snow-covered side porch. The second gift was smaller, wrapped in silver paper with a blue bow. A matching silver card was signed, *All our love to you and the luckiest baby in the world! Uncle Kenny and Stella*. Inside the small narrow box was a blue felt bag holding a miniature silver spoon engraved 'Baby Tervo.' Maggie ran her finger along the lettering on the handle and thought about the symbolism of this gift. Would Stella and Kenny bring another Baby Tervo into this world? Would a silver spoon hold these same promises?

Maggie thought back to the night of the dinner. There was so little counter space for Mama Tervo to prepare the food in the kitchen, with all the other surfaces in the house covered by books, food or drink. Maggie pictured Mama Tervo putting her gift on the refrigerator and pointing to that spot when Stella and Kenny walked in. When the conversation went in a different direction, everyone forgot the dinner was about the baby. No one asked about the unopened gifts.

The risk of subzero weather did not subdue the menacing sensation that the walls in the house were closing in on her. *Cabin fever reaching some delusional pitch, or new money burning a hole in my pocket?* Maggie wondered. She pulled her navy pea coat out of the hall closet and slipped into a pair of old mukluks to walk to the drug store. *Maybe pick out a new lipstick and grab some lunch at the counter.* Her conversation with Issie made her feel flush. Although she rarely felt poor, Maggie never recalled feeling flush, and searched her memory for what that word meant in Poker. *All the same suit? No, All the same suit in order, like 7,8,9—or was it only face cards? I'll ask Sam.*

Sidewalks covered in ice, Maggie walked on the crusted snow at the edge of lawns. A disturbing kind of pleasure, she loved the sound and shape of each imprint, but thought it was somehow wrong to deface the clean sweep of white snow. Like being the first person to leave footprints in tide-swept sand, or walk across a freshly raked shag carpet. She felt wickedly impudent in this silent space.

Maggie's sense of being adrift on a lonely planet felt familiar. Detroit's brutal winters had the effect of isolating people from one another. With the city's unrelenting din muffled by snow, there were no sounds other than the crunch of each step, thrum of her heart and the vibrato of warm breath against the icy sting of air. No traffic noise. No dogs barking. No other walkers. Maggie remembered a safety film about hyperthermia in high school—for hikers, cavers, skiers or anyone who might get lost or disoriented in the cold. Maggie was bewitched when she heard hyperthermia seduced you to lie down in the snow and fall asleep, like some horrible fairy tale. But, the narrator kept saying, "Killer Cold," like Jack Webb on *Dragnet*, with a bass drum tapping *dum-da-dum-dum*, and her classmates had booed and hooted. But, today, she got it. Maggie felt the undertow of the cold and the beguiling call to lie down for a few minutes and rest. She knew the brain and body would begin spinning cold into warmth, like straw into gold, enough to fall asleep—to fall away from this world. *Whoa,* Maggie thought, *without work, without my own wheels, I'm spending way too much time in the hollows of my mind.*

Just then someone in an old, blue and white banged up VW bus, covered in peace signs and bumper stickers, honked at her. An older woman with a kind face and matching smile rolled down the window and said, "Can I give you a lift?"

Maggie broke into a full grin and said, "You just did! Thanks, but I'm only going to the corner, and I could use some fresh air."

"Girl, you kiddin' me? You must have some Eskimo blood in you. In case you haven't noticed, its ten-effing-degrees-below-zero." Her breath crystallized with each syllable. Maggie gave her a peace sign and the woman returned it, her fingers popping through a threadbare green-knit glove.

Between the extreme cold and overheated store, the windows at Cunningham Drugs were completely fogged over. After pushing through the door, Maggie was relieved to find an open but empty lunch counter. "Hey, Buddy," she called out to the soda jerk dressed in a freshly pressed white shirt with his signature black bow tie.

"Well, up pops the devil! We ain't seen you since the leaves fell from the trees. You lookin' good! What's up?"

"Well, for one, I'm expecting a baby."

"No kidding? You're *way* too young to be havin' a baby."

"You're right. I was hoping you'd notice," Maggie grinned as she hopped on one of the red plastic covered stools and spun around to face him.

"Look at you! You look like a teenager. You think it's too cold for a Vernor's float?"

"Is it ever too cold for a Vernor's float?" Maggie chuckled. "Yes, please. Plus, a cheeseburger with extra pickles and onions, french fries with extra catsup and a side salad with Thousand Island dressing."

Buddy raised his thick, gray eyebrows and looked at Maggie through the yellowed lenses of cataracts, old age and untold pain and pleasure. Buddy had been tending this counter for more than thirty years with love, pride and a dignity born of gratitude for having a job, any job. Maggie couldn't hold back her tears.

"Yep, you expecting!"

"Damn it, Maggie, I've been calling you for the past two hours. Where've you been?"

"Gosh, Sam, I'm fine, thanks for asking."

"Really, Mag? I'm under a lot of pressure with the auto show and I don't have time for games. What's up? Maxine said you had good news."

"It can wait. Go back to work. We'll talk later."

"Got it. You're right. I'm being an asshole. Let's talk when my head's on straight. Tonight there's that dinner with the models for the new models so I'll be late."

"What models and how late?"

"The New York models for Jingo's new car models at the show. I told you."

"I don't think you told me."

"Please, Mag, not now. I'm over the top. As you like to say, I have miles to go before I sleep. I'll be home late. Don't wait up."

"SistaHood Salon, may I help you?"

"Hey, Loretta, I definitely need some help. You busy tonight?"

"No, honey, I'm not busy. You want to get together?"

"Sam's got a business dinner with a bunch of models from New York and I'm royally pissed, lonely and car-less."

"Cold as a witch's tit out there. I'll grab some pizza at Angelo's and head your way."

"Would you? I'm starting to salivate."

"Hang tight. I won't be there till five-thirty, quarter-to-six. Cheese and pepperoni?"

"Add mushrooms if you want. We've got some beer in the fridge."

"Great timing because I need to tap your brain. Some crazy black chicks with hair envy bout ready to tip civil rights on its skinny ass."

"Believe me, my brain is in serious need of tapping. I'm just not sure what you'll find."

"Maxine, Skip wants me to put together separate files for each of the models in spite of the fact that they're all covered under one contract. He said the agency doesn't want to risk the models seeing each other's pay rates. I don't understand. Did we just find out about this?" asked Sam.

"I doubt it. Skip had the file on his desk for two weeks. I have no idea if he read it, but my guess is no."

"Doable?"

"Any choice?"

"Nope."

"Okay, then doable. Let me have it and I'll run copies and put together the eight files. I don't know why we need two models for each car. What the hell?"

"Maxine, you're a wonder! I think the two models cover bathroom and meal breaks for each other."

"Yeah? Well I think there are two each so the models have time to mingle with the dealers and media types."

"Sounds plausible."

"No *plause* about it. It's how it works."

"Max, let go of the morality police routine. It is what it is. Let's get through this year's show, and let me know if you need help."

"You're covered, Tervo. Oh, before I forget, a guy by the name of Louie Zito at Sheer Juice called. Seriously, sounded like some kind of mafioso. Anyhow, he said he wanted to leave a message but then hung up. You want me to get him back on the line?"

Sam shook his head no.

The pizza box looked like it had been licked clean.

"Oh, Loretta, that was so good! I can't believe I inhaled three pieces. I'm going to be as big as a silo."

"You mean barn?"

"That's what you expected me to say so I said something else. Poet games. We all use hackneyed sayings without realizing it. But, when I'm thinking, I try to change it up and find a new metaphor or simile or image. Most of the time they're dorky."

"No shit? I always thought *hackneyed* meant bowlegged or knock-kneed. Like your knees are screwed up. Glad I do hair. All that thinking would wear me out."

"Who're you kidding? I see that mind of yours turning, spinning, rotating . . ."

"More like whirly-gigging out of control. Oh, Maggie, life can be so messed up. Did you hear about the gang of black girls at Cooley High attacking white girls with long, silky, flaxen, waxen—however that song goes—hair?"

"No. Where?"

"In the schoolyard, or on the way to or from school. One girl got her face cut because she started to fight back—badass, gang action. The cops were called."

"What do you want to do?"

"Here's where the brain tapping comes in. We all know black women don't have straight, silky hair. But we're human. These

Diana Ross wannabes *want* what they don't have. So rather than wear kinky, stiff, wooly hair as a matter of black pride, they spend hours, days, months, years trying to look like Sandra Dee. And now attacking girls who do! Maggie, it's pure insanity for black girls to spend half their lives longing for silky hair, white skin and blue eyes. I know. I did it for most of my life. I want *black* to be beautiful. I want these tough looking chicks to know they already got it *going on*. To know they got it *so going on* that the last thing they want is limp-white-girl hair and pink skin. Help me do this. I think it's more important than integrating the burbs. It's a generation of girls we'll lose if we don't start now."

Maggie was tapped and blown away. Like so many times before, she was in awe when she listened to Loretta and saw the world through her kaleidoscope. "Oh Loretta, you're on to something! Here we are trying to bend the calcified minds of adults—people stuck in their ways, scared shitless. Just the idea of bringing young, sassy, strong girls to the table is exciting. They have more to gain and more to lose than anyone."

"It's a mindbender. Let's play with it."

"What if we could get someone, say from the play *Hair* or Motown, to help us open some doors? Your ticket is the salon. But SistaHood means more than a salon. Right? What about *The Black & White SistaHood* or *The SistaHood of Hair*? You could talk about hair, power and diversity as strength."

"And find a white beautician who knows what's going down. Those white girls got to feel like they've been hair raped. Think Sampson and Delilah—hair is power. You don't mess with some-one's hair. If this shit keeps up, we might as well hang up our go-go boots. We gotta get them together in the same room, get them to talk to each other. Talk about being black and white, about being beautiful the way we are. Screw Madison Avenue and Glamour and Vogue; or, better yet, we put pressure on magazines and modeling agencies to hire black models, more Naomi Sims and real women, fat, skinny, curvy."

"Loretta, do you ever feel under water, like you're drowning? You ever think racism is way too big or too much, like there's no way in hell we're going to make a difference?"

"Every day, baby doll. Every day I have to talk to my self. Every day I ask myself the same two questions. *If not me, who? If not now, when?*"

"What if we start with those two questions and talk about the power of peace and understanding in the day-to-day stuff? Then, we could hold hands and sing Kumbaya. Kidding. Too creepy," laughed Maggie.

"You got that right. No Kumbaya. But I like where you're going. We need some honkies to talk to the white girls. I always feel like I scare the Holy Ghost out of 'em. If we could kick this off with a gig, that'd be so fine! I know Willie and Robin have Motown contacts, but I'm tripping on the idea of the musical *Hair*. I wonder how long it'll take to get to the Fisher Theater."

"For real? You think the Fisher has the *cojones* to ask a cast of buck-naked hippies mocking Jesus to play on their stage?" Maggie stood up, pointed to Loretta and began shaking her hips singing, *so you are the Christ, you're the great Jesus Christ—prove to me that you're no fool, walk across my swimming pool.*

"I swear you've got the blackest ass I've ever seen on a white girl. And lord, you do shake that booty like a sistah!"

"No shit? Loretta, I think that's the best compliment I've ever had."

"Here's what I think. I think we signed up for a marathon, but our hair-brained selves are racing to the corner store because we're afraid we'll run out of supplies before we get to the starting line. Before we do anything, and I mean ANYTHING, we've got to get the principal on our side. We get his support or a door slammed in our face. Either way, we'll know if we need to spend money on a new pair of Keds."

"You know how I am about bureaucracies. I'll help on the school stuff, but I promise, I'm no good at jumping through hoops."

"I'll call Blanche. She'll know someone who knows someone, but we need a white person at the table. You can smile, shake your head, bat your non-stop green eyes, whatever it is you white girls do to get what you want. Okay, your turn. Why pissed and lonely?"

By the time Maggie finished telling Loretta about her day, they were both poking fun at the melodrama of it all. Loretta said, "Let's see . . . you walked three blocks in the snow to have a nice lunch at the drug store, bought some Red Hot lipstick, then your husband was too busy to talk to you? That's it? Girl, what do you expect sitting in this rental shack all day talking to yourself? Where's my kick-ass activist friend? I want her back. Get your sorry ass off the couch and do something, even if it's wrong. Write some poems—find a job, volunteer, anything! Don't let that wicked mind of yours turn to silly putty. As for Sam, let him live his life and you live yours. I ain't smoking dope on this one Maggie. Sam's not stupid. Doesn't matter anyhow. Smart people screw up. He's going to mess up and you're going to mess up. That's life. But you, baby doll, got it all. Right now. You might lose it, but you sure as hell don't want to throw it away because your hormones are running helter-skelter."

Sam had eight files in his briefcase as he walked into the Sheridan-Cadillac Hotel. He'd always thought of this place as the *mafioso don* of downtown hotels—lots of glitz, crystal and bravado. The message was: *do not enter unless you plan to spend serious money, keep your mouth shut and tip well.* When the hotel opened in 1924, the Book Cadillac, better known as The Book, was Detroit's tallest building and the tallest hotel in the world. With more than one thousand guest rooms, three dining rooms, three ballrooms, it housed the godfather of all lobbies. Detroit's downtown dwellers knew The Book was the favorite hangout for Abe Bernstein and his Purple Gang, Detroit's answer to Al Capone and his Chicago Outfit. In fact, Abe and Al were friends, as far as friends go in crime syndicates. Majordomo Bernstein, who spent his life dodging bullets, imprisonments and rival gangs, lived on The Book's top floor until he died in 1968 at the age of seventy-six, far surpassing the most generous actuarial tables for gangsters. Many believed Abe haunted The Book, training his eyes on good-looking broads in the lobby, ordaining poker hands in the small salons and taking a sip of each neat Ballantine's 30-Year Whiskey served at the bar.

Dressed in his gray gabardine suit, white shirt, steel blue tie and silver and copper cufflinks, Sam thought his new black wingtips were overkill. *What perverted, psychopathic urge had possessed him to buy a pair of shoes like his dad's?* With each click of his heel across the marble-tiled lobby, Sam was sure everyone knew he was an imposter, a boy pretending to be a businessman. He had no idea he was turning heads because his platinum blond hair was catching the setting sun, or his high Finnish cheekbones were transforming worry into determination, or his fiery blue eyes were silencing detractors and claiming his power.

"Hey, ass wipe, you clean up pretty good. New shoes?"

"Hey, Zito. Yeah, they are."

"I'm sorry."

"Nice. Didn't see that coming."

"Tried to call you today but decided to catch you before the party. I'm here with Carla, and I didn't want you to wet your white jockeys when you saw us. She knows you're here and we're *all* going to keep our distance. *Capisce?*"

"I don't get it. What's the connection? Why are you here?"

"Whose asking, Bozo? Just thank me for giving you a heads up."

"Sure, Zito. Thanks."

"That's better."

This was the first time Sam saw Zito dressed in a suit, and there was no missing the custom-made tailoring. His shoes, soft Italian leather, were the new style low-cut boots. Zito walked liked he owned the night.

20

Sidelined

Capitalism is the legitimate racket of the ruling class.

—Al Capone

MARCH 1969 — "Hey, Clyde. What's up?"

"Hey, dickhead. I haven't heard from you since New Year's Eve. You too important to hang with us regular folk?"

"I've given it some careful thought, but no, not *too* important."

"Nice. I'm weirdly comforted to know you're still a dickhead."

"Then it won't come as a surprise to hear my life's starting to take on water, a lot of water. I thought I could navigate through this squall on my own, but it's beginning to look like my ship's caught in some mother lode tsunami with a bunch of scary-ass rocks along the shore. Or, on the flipside, I'm losing my frigging mind. You got time for a Big Boy summit? I can use whatever sanity, humor or advice you might be peddling."

"Not sure what sanity is these days, but we'll try not to fall down that rabbit hole."

"Right now, falling down a rabbit hole sounds like a good option."

"Hold your skirt, *Alice*. Late lunch today, two o'clock?"

"Thanks, my friend. You're on."

"Hey, Issie, kids at school?"

"*Bonjour*, Marguerite! The kids are at school, what's up?"

"You mean besides being as big as the broad-side of a hay loft? Oh, Issie, I think Sam's having an affair."

"Maggie, when are you going to get yourself a car and get a life? Sam's not having an affair."

"We're saving money for a house. And, as much as I want you to be right, you're wrong. Sam is having an affair."

"Maggie, I was joshing when I said Sam might find someone who bathes. Sam isn't the type. Did he tell you?"

"No, Issie—Sam did *not* tell me. But I know. He's so secretive these days and works late almost every night. When I can't reach him at work, he says he was in a meeting or in someone else's office. I'm not a fool."

"Did you ask him if he was having an affair?"

"I wanted to talk to you first. I can't imagine life without Sam. I'm five months pregnant, no job. I'm not sure I want to bring it up. Maybe I'm wrong."

"I think you're wrong. Besides, the Maggie I know would have already asked him. Your hormones are a complete mess and this is Sam's first year on the job. You don't even know what normal looks like. Find something to do to keep busy. You've got way too much time on your hands. What about your civil right's work? My guess is we still have a lot to do on that front!"

"Everyone's advice, but without a car my options are little and none, or slim and none, whatever that saying is."

"Then get a car. You've got twenty grand sitting in the bank. Take a grand, buy a used car."

"Isabel, you might think you know what's best for me, but you don't. How much of the twenty grand do you and Eddie have?"

"Maggie, that's so fucking unkind. You know we had a ton of bills after Eddie's layoff. And, when I told you he buried us in gambling debt at the track, it was because I trusted you. Why are you trying to hurt me? Never mind, I'm going to hang up before you say another word."

Maggie heard the slam of Issie's receiver and began to cry, then listened as she wallowed. It reminded her of the *cries of ages* coming from the monolith in *2001: A Space Odyssey*—ancient, enslaved souls. Maggie thought she felt her heart fold over and cramp up before the familiar loneliness wrapped her like an old curse. This time heavier, darker, more ominous. *Ominous like cumulous, cumulonimbus clouds turning gray*, thought Maggie. *I'll check the etymology.*

When Sam pulled into Big Boy's, the parking lot was empty. He peered through the winter grime collected on the restaurant's windows to make sure it was open. A narrow slice of florescent found its way through the sludge. March in Michigan was the pinnacle of stir-craziness. Everyone was stretching their necks, arms, bodies to reach freedom from forced-air-heated enclosures and inactivity. Sam looked at his waist folding over his belt and recalled hearing that men with pregnant wives gained weight. Sam was convinced he and Maggie were both suffering from some deep, dark malicious form of boredom. Their conversations were banal, bland, blah. His work was intense and tedious, the last thing he wanted to talk about. And, Maggie with no car, no work, no friends nearby, must be bored out of her frigging mind. Here they were, starting a life together, expecting a baby and the humdrum was deafening.

A knock on the driver's side window jolted Sam back to the present.

"Hey, Tervo! You waiting for a carhop or what?"

Sam climbed out of the car and gave Clyde a bear hug. "Give me a break. I was having the sweetest thoughts about rabbit holes before you interrupted my reverie."

"Let's reverie inside and chow down. Which is what I do now—chow down. Not sure what's going on, but my guess is cabin fever. Every March I pig out like there's no tomorrow or yesterday. I bet I put on ten pounds last week."

Sam pinched his waist and said, "March or Maggie's pregnancy? Not sure which."

"Aren't we a pair to draw to? We're beginning to sound like two old broads," laughed Clyde.

Sam caught a subliminal flash of their future. Twenty years from now, two beer-bellied guys with gray hair, elongated noses and liver spots pinching their waists and talking trash.

Inside, Clyde took off his eight-pound burgundy-colored car coat and threw it on the seat in the next booth. Sam took off his black and gray wool-tweed suit jacket, folded it and put it next to him.

Today their waitress was a skinny white woman—pale skin lit by freckles and frizzy red hair held down by an arsenal of black bobby pins. No greeting, pencil poised over the order book, thin lips pursed, eyes averted, she waited for them to speak. Sam resisted an urge to engage her in conversation about the new wave of bi-racial friends. Clyde ordered for both of them.

Clyde rolled his eyes as the waitress left the table and said, "freeze-dried," their code for unreachable whites or blacks. "What's up man?"

"Wish I knew. Back on January 3rd, Maxine got a call from Zito when I was out. He told Max he wanted to leave a message but hung up. I might've been wigged out if I had time to think, but it was the day of Jingo's Auto Show Pre-Party at The Book. Big promo that night—tall, thin, hot looking models from New York mixing with Jingo executives, ad agency guys, media types and investors. By investors, I mean the whole shebang—mafioso, union chiefs as well as the cobras from Wall Street.

"The night was clear, the moon was yellow and the leaves came tumbling down, or so the song goes. First person I see in the hotel lobby is Zito. He said he wanted to give me a heads-up about Carla being there so I didn't wet my pants. We volleyed back and forth. When I asked him why he was there, he said, 'Who wants to know, Bozo?' I decided to keep clear of him and Carla.

"My job was to set up one of the salons, more commonly known as 'Poker Rooms,' to meet with each of the eight models, get their signatures on a contract, and give them an orientation schedule. The models spend four days getting to know the cars, the media, Jingo bigwigs, go through final wardrobe and fittings, then run through two dress rehearsals. The schedule is non-stop. My job, with Maxine's help, is to make sure this all happens.

"Everything was clicking along until I reached the last model, Ella. I waited fifteen minutes after her scheduled time before I decided to tape a note on the door for her to sit tight if she arrived. In the meantime, I looked for her. Based on her profile and photos, I knew she was a fair-skinned red-haired Cuban. At five-five, she was short compared to the other models. By then it was close to eight and the party in the ballroom was rocking. The other seven models and a few other women, including Carla, were dancing freestyle. Some dudes who knew how to dance, or were so drunk they forgot they didn't know how to dance, were drawn into the mix. The bar on the other side of the room was three deep, with a bunch of guys standing in some sort of a huddle. The huddlers were getting louder and rowdier. As I moved closer, I saw Ella in the center. She was stretched across three fancy bar stools, her black velvet mini skirt over her waist and her red boat-neck sweater pulled down below a pair of gorgeous, mondo knockers. The guys were frenzied—touching, stroking, pinching, pouring wine on her body then finger-painting through it. It felt like some erotic version of the novel *Clockwork Orange*. Ella was laughing and asked if anyone had a stick shift. She was stoned out of her mind. And, I, good buddy, was immobilized and mesmerized. I hated that I couldn't take my eyes away, that I didn't want to or know how to stop myself, or the unhinged rabble-rousers. Then, one of the suits showed her a twenty-dollar bill, rolled it up, pulled down the crotch of her black lace panties and tucked it out of sight. He moved up to her face and unzipped his pants. By now, the guys in the huddle were rubbing themselves or rubbing against Ella's arms, legs, stomach, as if no one was watching. Think about the groans and cheers you heard when Cassius Clay was taking down Sonny Liston. It was that kind of loose, uncontrolled energy, like the room was lifting off the ground. The band got louder and the dance floor looked packed. The suit with the twenty-dollar bill looked like he was going to have a heart attack. The music stopped. In the silence, Ella let go and the suit cried, *holy mother of god, save me*. I turned around and Carla was staring at me. Looking at me in a way that was sober and hard, like she was trying to warn me about something. I must have looked down, because when I looked back she was gone.

"And, the huddle was gone. I don't remember walking away. I saw Ella at the bar chatting up some guy. She was fully dressed in a knee-length velvet skirt, a red turtleneck sweater, nylons and a pair of go-go boots. Her makeup was perfect, her hair neatly combed. The band was playing some Tommy Dorsey thing, no rock. There was no one on the dance floor. I thought *holy shit did I just make up this scene? Am I so slammed by knowing Carla was here that I imagined this whole fucking thing?* I looked at Ella's file in my hand. When I opened it, there was a signed copy of her contract. I raced down to the Poker Room. There was no note taped to the door. Inside the Poker Room the lights I'd left on were turned off. My brief case was on top of the table and locked. My folded jacket was draped over the brief case as if I'd prepared to leave.

"On my way out Ben, the president of Jingo, was in the hallway talking to Zito and Carla. I looked straight ahead and race-walked. My heart was beating so hard I was sure they could hear it. Zito caught up with me in the lobby and handed me a rolled up twenty-dollar bill and said, 'I think this is yours.' I shook my head *no* but the word got stuck in my throat. Zito said, 'Look, ass wipe, we've got the whole fucking scene on tape. We still own you. Don't forget it.'

"I didn't see the kryptonite coming. I don't know how I could have. I'm not sure what they gave me, LSD or some other hallucinogenic, but this was no small-budget film. I didn't call right away because this story makes me sound psycho. I don't even believe it myself. Did I hallucinate the entire night? Since then, there's no doubt I've been sleepwalking through my days. I can't think straight because I keep flipping between here and there, now and then, real and unreal. I'm either totally fucked or crazy as a loon. Maybe both."

"Tervo, I don't think you're crazy. But, you're right. This is no low-ball bid. They want you big time. They had to spend a shitload of money, time and energy setting this up. Why do they want to own you? What do you have that they want? Why would Jingo be involved? What's the connection?"

"That's what I keep asking myself. I've opened every memory of conversations, encounters. Nothing. I don't know what they want or who's involved. At the risk of sounding like a dimwit, I'm a simple Yooper. I have no power, no connections, no mafia contacts, no money, no rich relatives, no inside information on anyone. What the hell?"

"There's something, kimosabe, and it's a big something."

When Sam got home from work, Maggie met him at the door. She was wearing a non-maternity tent dress, jewel-toned paisley on red brocade, masking her expanded girth. Maggie's hair was washed and curled. Her face colored with mascara, eyeliner, blush and red lipstick. Somehow she'd managed to get her swollen feet into the three-inch *peau de soie* heels she wore when they were married. Sam felt like falling to his knees and crying but he didn't want to scare her.

Maggie batted her lashes and said, "*Monsieur*, I know you were expecting your wife, but tonight belongs to me. My name's Colette, and you and me, well, we're going to have a night to remember!"

Sam moved into the kitchen and heard the pressure cooker rattling. He shook his head and said, "Sorry, Colette. That's not going to happen. You see Maggie's the only woman I want." He took off his suit coat and draped it over the kitchen chair. "Come sit down. Once I tell you about Maggie, you'll know why there's no room for anyone else."

Maggie looked at Sam, as if he'd walked on stage before his cue, then blindly followed him into the living room. Sam patted the cushion next to him. When Maggie sat down, the sofa felt like a caress.

Staying in character Sam looked at her and said, "My wife Maggie isn't easy, but I don't want easy. She's a Canuck, a French Canadian, with all the fire and intellect this combo brings. She's drop-dead gorgeous, pragmatic, sassy, wickedly funny and sexy as hell. Did I mention newly rich?" Maggie gave him *the look* and pinched his cheek. Sam pulled her on his lap and said, "It's hard to describe how exciting it is to be in love with Maggie. Every day, when I wake up and see her next to me, I pinch myself. How did I get so lucky? In a world filled with naysayers, chronic complainers and sleepwalkers, I end up with this beautiful, complex person who has the heart, mind and energy to change the world. But look at me. I've been sleepwalking for months because I got lost in someone else's fantasy. For some demented reason, I became more interested in climbing the corporate ladder than climbing into bed with my wife. I made myself miserable. I'm sure I made her miserable. I lost my sense of humor and sense of fun, and maybe I've lost the interest of my incredible wife." Maggie started to interrupt, but Sam placed his finger to her mouth and whispered, "Wait, let me say this.

"My closest friends, including Maggie, know I can be a dickhead. I am a dickhead. But I want you to know I love Maggie far beyond my limited vocabulary, and I'm desperately sorry I got lost in my work. I saw my dad give up everything he had, even his life, for work. That's not the legacy I want to leave. I hope she'll forgive me."

"Oh, Sam. I've been such a slouch the last few months that it made sense you'd rather be at work. I'm starting to recognize myself again, but being pregnant took me down for the count. I let my hormones get the best of me and take me places I didn't want to be. Issie told me I was a mess and I am . . . I was. I thought you were having an affair and it was making me so crazy and wild."

"Babe, not your fault. It wasn't about you. No affair. I'm spending every calorie of energy on work and I've neglected everything and everyone else, including you. No more. Let's find our core. I want to build my life with you, not with Jingo Motors, not with anyone else."

"Build, like layettes? Nurseries? A home?"

"All of the above and more. We're a team. Don't worry and please don't go quiet on me again."

"Yeah, that's pretty funny when I hear it out loud," laughed Maggie. "What, me worry? What, me go quiet?" Putting her head on Sam's shoulder she sighed as she picked up his scent in a way that told her she'd lost it for a while. The baby kicked and turned as if delighted by the remembered voice and balm. Maggie placed Sam's hand on her growing mezzanine. The baby kicked again and again.

21

Mind Over Matter

I freed a thousand slaves—I could have freed a thousand more if only they knew they were slaves.

—Harriet Tubman

JULY 1969—Naked under Issie's threadbare green and orange flowered moo-moo, Maggie propped her chin on her fists inches from the electric fan on the kitchen table. Oscillating back and forth, the steel blades blew a clumsy, waterlogged breeze. Sweat was collecting in every crevice of her body as she looked around the wrinkled kitchen and wondered what happened to the burst of energy she'd had over the past two weeks. The house was spotless, the nursery freshly painted and ready. Sam had cleaned all the light fixtures and boxed as many books as they were willing to give up for a few months. Maggie had scoured every square inch of the pink and black tiled bathroom, cleaned closets, mopped floors, organized cupboards and drawers. On one of their drives to check out neighborhoods in Livonia, they found a sturdy white crib with a matching changing table at a yard sale. Maggie washed both with scalding hot water and ammonia.

Clyde hadn't asked them to consider a move to Livonia. He didn't have to. The Freedom Riders needed a white couple to begin changing attitudes within the suburbs, or as Willie liked to say, *behind enemy lines.* Since Maggie and Sam were the only white couple in The Eights, who also happened to be poised to move west, it was a no-brainer. Based on suburban facts and legends, it seemed clear if they could integrate Livonia, they could integrate anywhere on the west side. Maggie thought life in the burbs signaled death by boredom, but Sam's enthusiasm about having more space, seeing the stars at night and planting a garden gave her a boost. With July temperatures climbing to ninety, the idea of big shade trees almost pulled her over the top.

Maggie reached her hands under her misshapen, domed rotunda to find it sitting low, almost between her legs, then used the width of her hands to see how much space she had between her boobs and the mezzanine. *Dropped,* she thought. Of the many books Maggie read on childbirth and labor, she knew labor might begin immediately, but almost certainly within two weeks. Maggie ran her hands over her damp, prickly legs and decided to take a bath and shave before she called the doctor.

"Good morning, Jingo Personnel, may I help you?

"Maxine, Clyde here. What's the buzz?"

"Work and more work. I'm determined to get a life but not sure how. What's up with you?"

"Work, family and some rare moments of freedom. This whole thing about growing up sure looked good from the other side, but I'm here to tell ya, it ain't all it's cracked up to be."

"Amen. I keep thinking it's going to slow down next month, next season, next year. There's no next. You looking for a toe-headed white guy in a suit?"

"You got it."

Clyde tapped the eraser of his pencil to the beats of the transferring call.

"Hey, Clyde, what's up?"

"Time for another summit. I might be on to something. Blanche said Maggie's got a shower at Jo's on Sunday. I can leave the wrecking crew with the in-laws. Lunch at Angelo's?"

"Sure. With Angelo?"

"No, just us. Got to run. See you Sunday about one."

"Hey Auntie Jo, how's it going? You need help setting up for Sunday?"

"Not for a minute, Maggie. You're the guest of honor. Don't ask again and don't lift a finger on Sunday."

"Cool. I'll flop my walrus-shaped body on the recliner, rest my clubfeet and sip an ice cold Bloody Mary without vodka. A Virgin Bloody Mary?"

"What does that even mean? It sounds sacrilegious. You mean tomato juice?"

"Tomato juice with a Bloody Mary mix, no vodka. Not that I want one. It just struck me as funny, like a *New Yorker* cartoon."

"So how are things between you and Issie? Back to normal?"

"I hope. I'm lucky she's a good cheek turner, because I'm so cheeky. Have I always been this obtuse when it comes to insulting people?"

"Oh, Maggie, anyone who knows you feels your kindness. But, in truth, you're headstrong when you think someone's trying to tell you what to do. Like Anna, maybe all the Landry girls, we're strong willed, we want what we want. The down side is loneliness. Most men don't like strong, independent women."

"Aunt Jo, I can't believe you said that. You of all people! You're strong and independent. Men are always after you."

"Short term, Maggie. Men *see* me as a challenge. When the challenge gets to be too much, they make their exit. Trust me, strong women have to find a way to balance the male ego thing if they want a man in their life. It's too much work for me, but Issie's a good example. She uses humor as armor and lots of care in picking her fights. To Eddie's credit, he understands the importance of comic relief; and so far, hasn't hit the limits of Issie's tolerance for crazy schemes and get-rich-quick plans."

"Seriously? I don't get it. Why would Sam, Eddie or any man want a woman to be weak? Darwin must be pitching a fit in the next dimension. Wouldn't our survival instinct push us to choose a strong mate?"

"Maggie you can take that cockamamie theory and stuff it. I know you understand the threat of strength. I've seen you wield it like a shield and a sword."

Maggie thought dark clouds never seemed so welcome. A foundling wind entered the side door with a trace scent of hibiscus and ruffled the dog-eared pages of Dr. Spock. Defused sunlight not only cooled their tiny home, its camouflage of shadows seemed to mend the buckled linoleum, warped wood floors and peeling wallpaper. Maggie stood in the hall and looked at the nursery. All white semi-gloss walls, furniture and ceiling, with a freshly waxed hardwood floor. A yellow rocking chair from Clyde and Blanche's basement and an African animal print quilt from Loretta gave the room a colorful panache. Ready for the baby's homecoming, Maija's white crocheted blanket and cap waited on top of the changing table.

Maggie sat on the rocker and put her hands on her sinking mezzanine. The baby was quiet, saving energy for a trip through the birth canal. From some very wise, ancient, remembered place, Maggie felt a sense of wellbeing, a knowledge of motherhood that transcended her experience on earth. Maggie *knew* she was a mother and played with the idea that motherhood began *before* birth. Did this connection reside at some cellular level? Had Anna passed her love for her mother to her? Would her love for Anna become part of some complex genetic code she transfers to her baby? Maggie placed her hands together, as if in prayer, and one of Anna's rhymes came to her. Moving her hands to this old cadence, Maggie quietly chimed, "Here's the church, here's the steeple, open the door and see all the people."

Maggie didn't hear Sam come home, or notice him in the hallway when he stopped to listen. Twilight, wending its way through the bamboo blinds, glanced off Maggie's fingertips as she repeated the rhyme. A lapsed Lutheran, Sam never understood the concept of holiness until now, here in this broken little house with no stained glass.

Maggie turned in time to catch Sam in awe and greeted him with a wink. "Hey, Papa, the baby dropped. I shaved my legs and the doctor said 'stay tuned.' Any day now we'll have another mouth to feed."

Aunt Jo's house was filled with summer colors, a chorus of women's voices and a picnic bouquet—scents of watermelon, fried chicken, potato salad, baked beans, an out-of-this-world coconut cake by Robin, and Maggie's favorite, Aunt Jo's rhubarb pie.

Maggie was wearing her one and only maternity dress—a sleeveless, lightweight gray and white dotted Swiss with a white sailor tie. Her packed suitcase was in the Corvair's trunk. If Maggie went into labor with pains five minutes apart, she'd call Sam at Angelo's to

pick her up. From Aunt Jo's, St. Mary's Hospital in Livonia was a
trek, but Maggie had chosen Issie's OB/GYN because he delivered
her two healthy sons without complications. Dr. Stanley assured
Maggie she'd have plenty of time to get to Livonia from Detroit
because first-born children usually meant a long labor.

Maggie thought back to her first day of required prenatal
classes at St. Mary's when one of the nuns greeted the small group
of women and asked them to introduce themselves and where they
lived. When Maggie said she lived in Detroit, there were a few
gasps. Among the group, she was the sole non-Livonian and the
only woman expecting her first child. After introductions, the nun
began with the dress code, emphasizing the importance of pregnant women maintaining dignity and respect for their condition
and its affect on others. Without looking at Maggie, the nun said,
"We find it *obscene* for pregnant women to wear slacks or sandals.
Not only is this offensive to polite society, it creates a safety hazard
if the obstetrician has to cut off someone's clothes to save the baby.
To avoid any misunderstanding, you must dress properly when you
attend these classes and when you arrive at the hospital in labor. If
not, you'll be turned away." Maggie was the only woman in slacks
and sandals, specifically purchased for these classes. Most of her
maternity clothes were borrowed, drab and billowing. Maggie's new
tapered red slacks, matching red and white sailboat print top, and
strappy white sandals better reflected her sense of style and color.
She'd felt fresh, hip, grown up when she dropped Sam off at work,
which made the public humiliation sting more. Before pregnancy,
Maggie would have smirked at the nun and thought, *screw you.*
When this happened she almost cried. What happened to her pre-
pregnancy-kick-ass self? Freedom lurked three-days after delivery
when she and the baby would be discharged, released from the hospital's puritanical rules. During her stay, mothers and babies could
only bond on some rigid schedule set by the nuns—feedings every
four hours at ten, two and six, ten, two and six with no regard for

the baby's hunger or need to be held. One of Maggie's friends from Windsor told her that nurses in the States snapped their sharp fingernails against the soft bottom of an infant's foot to wake them up or encourage nursing. Maggie was horrified. Issie said she was over reacting and it was no big deal, babies survived. Ultimately, Maggie decided she was too tired and intimidated by the nuns to protest these barbaric practices. She hoped words and cooing sounds would be enough to coax her baby to stay awake and nurse while under this black-cloaked regime.

Loretta walked up and hugged Maggie back to the present, before putting her hands on the mezzanine. "Well, it's a good thing you didn't wait any longer to have a shower. Look at you! This baby is halfway down the Erie Canal. We might have to bleach and boil some new diapers and help your Aunt Jo deliver her first baby."

"Hah. My guess is Blanche would take over and have everything cleaned up in time to eat. Your yummy fried chicken?"

"Grease and all."

"Have you seen Issie? She here yet?"

"Haven't seen her. Sit yourself down, I'll get you an ice-cold Vernors."

"How about a Bloody Mary without booze?"

Covered in soot and ash from the riots two years ago, Angelo's Pizzeria looked more like an abandoned tool and dye shop. The gravel parking lot was pock marked and sprouting crab grass. Angelo's 'Shiniest Windows in Tiger Town' looked like collages of fingerprints, pollen, acid rain and mud splatter. So *not* like Angelo who wiped the dust off his shoes six times a day. His employees called him Mr. Clean behind his back. Sam thought Angelo must be sick or depressed.

"Hey, Tervo! What the hell you doin' this side of town? You lost or what?"

"Hey, Angelo. You still in charge of this dump?"

Angelo looked around, shook his head and said, "Hard to believe isn't it? Worked my ass off all these years to keep this place looking like a top and since Maggie left I stopped caring. Not blaming Maggie, but she had a good way of upping the ante and keeping me on my toes. She'd raise one of her eyebrows and without another word I knew it was time to clean the windows. She here with you?"

Sam laughed and said, "Oh, I know that raised eyebrow! Aunt Jo is giving her a shower. Thought you'd know."

"Another bad move. I told Jo it's either all or nothing and she said nothing. Which, of course, meant I had to walk away. I'm such an asshole. Back myself in a corner then watch the fucking house burn down. What can I get you?"

"Coke's good. I'm meeting Clyde at one. You got time to shoot the breeze till then?"

"No can do. I'm the only grunt in the kitchen today. Trying out these new cost-cutting gimmicks. No fucking reason I have to work so hard, but I'm better by myself."

"First, you're full of shit. You don't do better by yourself. Look around. Plus, you're dumb on both sides if you walk away from Jo. Where you going to find another Jo? Crow isn't that bad. Eat it and move on."

"Yeah, well maybe. We'll see."

"Yeah, well maybe my ass. Call her. Go to a movie and sit without fidgeting for ninety minutes. Coming from you, she'll know it's a *mega* mea culpa."

Maggie was surrounded by laughter, wrapping paper, ribbon and the most remarkable collection of baby clothes and furnishings. Issie was last to arrive, pushing a brand new stroller up the sidewalk—packed with undershirts, bibs, infant gowns, receiving blankets, a yellow rubber duck with three ducklings and Robert McCloskey's Caldecott Award winning book, *Make Way for Ducklings*. Maggie's favorite book as a child.

When Aunt Jo suggested a few shower games, there was a deep, visceral group grunt as if everyone had been hit by a medicine ball at the same time. One by one, Aunt Jo looked around the room at her uneasy guests. Then, she threw her arms up as if a tent revivalist had palmed her forehead to cast out evil. "Glory be to god! I forced myself to come up with some games but it was the devil's work. Praise the lord and pass the mimosa!" At first there was an awkward silence. Did the spirit move Aunt Jo or was she just kidding around? Issie's unbridled hoots answered the question, inviting more raucous laughter, until everyone understood Aunt Jo shared her nieces' wicked, bizarre sense of humor.

Blanche lifted her mimosa and proposed a toast. "To our friend, sister, niece," then catching Maija's wave, "and daughter-in-law. May you find your way through motherhood as gracefully as you've earned the love and respect of all who know you! Some of us want to be you. Honestly, a few of us have pushed narcissism to new heights by attaching ourselves to your pregnancy. So here's the rub, we've offered many fine names for you and Sam to consider and we have no idea what you plan to call *our* little boy or girl. Give it up."

Maggie was cheered by the love, and as always, the freedom to say it straight or slanted. "*Merci, mon cher ami!* Naming our baby turned out to be *way* bigger than we thought. As most of you know, we took it on like a community project and risked driving you nuts with our constant need for attention. Although we must have known we weren't the first couple to get pregnant or name a baby, we acted like this was the second coming. So, after unimaginable hours spent interviewing friends and family, debating, pencil tapping, head scratching, playing pin-the-tail on the name games . . ."

Issie interrupted with a "Drum roll please!"

Maggie laughed. "Okay, got it. Anyhow, most of you know Sam and I both thought we'd have a girl, but now we're not so sure." Maggie smiled as she rubbed the front of her rotunda. "Boy or girl—we've fallen hopelessly in love with this child. If she's a she, her name will be Tekla, Tekla Tervo. Tekla's the name of Sam's maternal grandmother, Maija's mother, and I can't imagine a more beautiful name or alliteration. We haven't decided on a middle name. If we have a boy, his name will be Otto, Sam's father's name. Samuel was Sam's grandfather so this continues a tribal practice. I wanted to call our son Samuel, so we came up with Otto Samuel Tervo."

Among the hallelujah chatter, Maija hugged herself, nodded and mouthed, "thank you" across the room to Maggie, who smiled and nodded back.

After Aunt Jo and Issie helped Maggie out of the recliner, the women formed a circle around the dining room table. Robin's round, two-layered, silver-frosted, coconut cake was lit like Cape Canaveral—twelve white candles, in concentric circles, and a taller orange candle in the center, rocket style. Around the circumference of the cake, seven yellow and orange moons were arranged from the waning crescent to a full orange harvest moon to the waxing crescent. Only the unseen new moon was missing.

With the exception of unplugged third-world nations, and conspiracy theorists who thought the moon shot was an international stunt to one-up the Russians, the entire planet was *over-the-moon* moon crazy, collectively holding its breath in anticipation of NASA's moon shot. Maggie loved to say it was *outlandish* to imagine a man on the moon, the stuff of fairytales, Buck Rogers, Flash Gordon. Yet, in three days, on July 16th, Apollo 11, a three-hundred-sixty-three-foot rocket, would be launched into orbit from the Kennedy Space Center with three astronauts dressed like deep-sea divers. If things went according to plan, Apollo 11 would land on the moon July 20th, just one week away.

"Hey, Tervo, sorry I'm late."

"No problem. It's a rare thing when I get to sit and let my mind wander without guilt. Kind of pisses me off when I think about it. What am I doing that is so god-awful important I don't have time to kick back and chill?"

"Amen, brother. You're talking to a swami who's preaching the same sermon, or whatever swami's call a sermon."

"What would a swami call a sermon? A satsang?"

"Could be."

"Maybe Angelo knows."

"You're kidding? What would possess you to think Angelo knows anything about swamis or sermons? Okay, no more mind wandering. You're getting soft in the head. Blanche said she'd pick up the wrecking crew so I have an hour and some change. I'll throw a pizza together and tell Angelo we're planning a demonstration so he'll keep his distance."

"Maggie you look tired. Take a nap till Sam gets here. I've got a rowdy flock of nesters demanding to wash dishes and clean up. My bedroom will be cooler because I've got a window fan. Your choice."

"Seriously, Auntie Jo, you don't have to say another word. My feet are barking and my back is ready to shoot the damn dog."

Aunt Jo's Dr. Zhivago bedroom looked a little tired or Maggie thought, maybe she was tired and her view was tainted. Maggie slipped off her dress and pried off her white flats. Venetian blinds turned down, the window fan pulled air from under a shade tree into the darkened room. Maggie looked at her body with a tenderness she hadn't felt about herself in a long time. The baby stretched his legs and pushed at the underside of the mezzanine. Maggie felt and could almost see the entire outline of a tiny foot, as if the baby was kicking off from the side of a swimming pool or the edge of a diving board! Soon they'd meet. Maggie folded back the dark eggplant quilt and in her maternity bra, underwear and patina of sweat, she and her baby slid under a fresh white cotton sheet. Maggie wanted to hold on to these last few hours or days of in utero symbiosis. For months Maggie had been talking, singing or playing music to teach, delight or relax her child. She thought she was making a connection. Yet, Maggie realized, she had never paused to listen. Placing her hand on the baby's head, Maggie whispered, "If you can, give me a few days to pay quiet attention, to hear your thoughts, to know your soul." Maggie felt certain spiritual awareness was lost upon entry.

Sam didn't know how hungry he was until he inhaled a second piece of pizza before looking up.

"Sam, what do you know about gas lighting? Meaning mind-control, not stove tops or post lights."

"Absolutely nothing. Have no idea what you're talking about."

"Yeah, you do. From a 1940-something movie called Gas Light with Ingrid Bergman. Her husband kept her off balance by changing things around the house, turning the gas lights on and off, then giving her the third degree so she'd think she was losing her mind. People started to call it gas lighting when you mess with someone's mind. And, it's a big deal because the CIA, FBI and mafia are using it to fuck with reality. Like yours, the two times you thought you were set up."

"Whoa. Jump back—the CIA, FBI and mafia? What the hell are you talking about?"

"Sorry. Got ahead of myself. Back to the beginning. A few years ago the NAACP got some of the brothers together to see if we could build a coalition that worked, instead of playing alone in our cribs. We try to get together every month. I'm not saying who all's involved, but we've got dudes from the FBI, CIA, and at least two guys who have major connections to the mob. No doubt we use them and they use us. A crooked, dangerous chess game but we've greased the wheels so long that sometimes we start bullshitting and forget where we are. Bottom line, you gotta take what I say with a grain of salt and a pound of pork belly. That said, this boy's club is the only up close, inside view we get of law makers and breakers."

"So our grass roots movement to improve the world is potted in CIA, FBI and mafia dirt?"

"Tervo, you weren't born yesterday. Staying close to our enemies is a smart move. Believe me, no one is recruiting or evangelizing. These dicks and dons love to strut their stuff, drop names, top each other's brags and trade their James Bond stories."

"But why gas lighting? This mind-control game could take months, even years, before someone gets flipped. If they're trying to mind fuck me, two hits more than twelve months apart won't do it. Although it made me crazy for a few weeks, after a year it loses its hold."

"Here's the deal. LSD and other drugs, hallucinogens, are being used to fast forward gas lighting. So, instead of it taking months or years, it can go down faster."

"And the purpose? Why would the CIA and FBI play with LSD?"

"We'll get there. There's a third piece, exploitation or snuff films. Films so raw, so violent, they knock morality on its ass. Once we had good guys and bad guys playing with mind control. Now it's hard to tell the good guys from the bad guys. What's happening is so hardcore underground that only a handful of people know about it. If either of us opens our mouths we're toast. Look at me, Tervo. I want to make sure you know how fucking serious this is."

Sam stared at Clyde and said, "You've got my attention. I'm scared shitless, but I don't know why yet. How did my name end up on this dance card?"

"I don't know why or how, but know you're a lab rat in some mind-altering game and no one is giving you a choice to opt in or out. The CIA calls it Project MK-ULTRA. At first they wanted to see how LSD and other drugs work during interrogations, a kind of no-touch torture. From there they moved to different kinds of drugs with exploitation films and gas lighting. In your case, they might have drugged you and shown you a film with a bunch a guys hitting on the Cuban broad, sliced with sounds from the Liston fight and porno flicks of guys jacking off. Who knows? They're big into mind-control to build invisible armies. Zombies, guys who could assassinate someone and not remember. They have no memory. No way to interrogate someone who has no memory. The feds are home free."

"Where's the mob in all this?"

"According to the CIA dick, they've been testing LSD and other drugs on mob bosses, like Whitey Bulger, in exchange for shorter sentences. Get this, the mob and the CIA had a plan to assassinate Castro. This mobster was going to have his Cuban hooker bring Castro LSD-laced cigars to set up the kill. The plan got waxed. There must be a connection between LSD, gas lighting, Cuba and you. The problem here is there's no line between the good guys and bad guys, so no one to ask."

"I don't get it. What's the mafia's take?"

"Tervo, the mafia is in the same league as the CIA and FBI. They're all into protecting their territories, building their take-no-prisoners scary-ass reputations and collecting intelligence; or in this case, they're inventing intelligence to mind-fuck the next guy. What do they have to peddle besides influence and power? Total, fucking reapers when it comes to money, fear and death. Based on what I've heard, their poker games are like swap meets to trade techniques for torture, extortion . . . you name it! The mob probably came up with water boarding."

"Why me? Think about it. What the hell does some schmuck like me have that anyone would want?"

"We know there's something. How about Sheer Juice and the new preservative deal? Sounds like big money if no one asks too many questions or blows the whistle. Might be enough money to keep you on a short leash. Or, could be Maggie's parents. Why is their case open nineteen years later? I don't know what's involved, but it must be big. Maggie said they pissed off the CIA, MI5 and the mob. Maybe they think they can get to Maggie's parents through you. Or, maybe they've got some future shock plan involving cars, unions or civil rights. Who knows? I've heard Hoover goes ape shit when he sees whites fighting for civil rights. Might be Hoover has a hard-on for you because your pretty face was photographed in Memphis or Detroit."

"Might be all or none. But if I take this to the extreme, you could be one of the bad guys. What if all you're telling me is more gas lighting? You've shrunk my world, made me think I have no allies, no resources except you."

"Go on."

"We keep coming back to this. How do I know you're on my side, that you're my friend?"

"You keep asking the right question. How do you know? Then again, how do I know you won't bust me on this, take me down, hurt my family?"

Sam looked at Clyde and wondered how the two of them landed here, right now, at Angelo's pizzeria on July 13, 1969. Then Sam wondered who was most scared, a white guy in a white world or a black guy with his ass in a sling? Sam leaned across the table and grabbed the front of Clyde's shirt and whispered, "I know, dick-head. I know because you've always been there for me. I love you, Blanche, the boys. I'd never do anything to hurt you or your family. That's how I know you're my friend."

22

Daylight

You can't ride in my little red wagon, the front seat's broken and the axle's draggin'. Second verse same as the first.
—Camp Song and U.S. Army Cadence

JULY 20, 1969 ANTE MERIDIEM—Up on his elbows, Sam watched Maggie swing her legs over her side of the bed like a human pendulum to reach a sitting position. Gripping her rotunda with both hands, Maggie lifted the weight from her legs before attempting to stand.

"Oh, babe, you look miserable, like a Radio Flyer red wagon with an eighteen-wheeler load. If I could, I'd carry the weight for you."

"My axle's broke and my tongue is dragging, same thing second verse. I can't confirm this, but it feels like I'm caught up in some mad, perverted fluke of nature, that I'm not pregnant and will never, ever again, wear a belt or see the tops of my feet."

"I thought it goes 'the front seat's broken.' Never mind. You want to walk to Cunningham's for lunch and spin around on the stools?"

"I'm desperate to get outta the hood, outta the heat. How about spending the day in air conditioning—the movies, an early dinner at Big Boys? Tonight we can kick back, and from the comfort of our living room, watch twentieth-century pioneers land on the moon. Can you freaking believe it? Millions of people around the world, sitting on their couches, drinking beer and watching men land on the moon."

"Both outlandish and otherworldly! Have you thought about how our lives will change? Once the baby's born we won't have the freedom to see a movie or have dinner on a whim."

"Samuelsan, we can always revert to drive-in movies and car-hop dinners. But no more putt-putt on a whim."

"Putt-putt? Have we ever played putt-putt?"

Maggie started laughing so hard she had to sit back down. "Oh god, the burbs, putt-putt, drive-in movies, carhops! We already sound like two cutouts from suburbia. Do you think it's too late? Have we slipped off the edge? Lost ourselves in some mainstream, colorless monotony?"

Sam couldn't help himself. He fell back on the bed and laughed until he began to cry. Maggie tipped her body sideways then trundled over to look at Sam. She wiped his tears with the tip of her thumb and kissed his forehead. Maggie said, "Was it Einstein who said 'there's no time or space, just now?' Now, when you and I are about to meet our baby on this lonely planet, circling the sun, a rocket ship is heading for the moon. Think of it! All that we thought we knew is changing, we're changing, our lives are changing, our world is changing." Maggie started crying as she kissed Sam's face then nuzzled his neck. She could hear his heart beating and feel the stretch of muscles in his arms as he wrapped them around her shoulders. Sam whispered, "Maggie, I need to tell you something." Maggie began to push away, "Oh god, sorry. I have to pee."

"Hey, Loretta. What's up?"

"Waiting for your call. No baby yet?"

"No baby. Thought I wanted to go to the movies to pass the day, but the pressure of six pounds of baby and thirty pounds of water makes me feel like I have to pee every five minutes. Not sure I'll make it to the hospital without diapers!"

"Yep, getting close. That baby bundle is tap dancing on your bladder. You weepy?"

"Crying over everything—sunlight on withered geraniums, Vietnam, an empty box of Cheerios, putt-putt golf. I'm a walking, talking rodeo of hormones. Even strangers go out of their way to avoid me. Speaking of strangers, have you talked to Stella lately? She and Kenny have both been MIA."

"Talked to Stella last week and it sounds like being an Oreo couple in Detroit is a walk through pur-ga-tory. They're not banned from restaurants, just ignored until they leave. At the movies, they wait in line to be told the show is sold out, at least until they walk away. Fuckers. Kenny has a hard time keeping his cool, so it's a double whammy for Stella. They're talking Canada, Mexico, even Europe."

"We knew it'd be hard, but living it is something else. Imagine being stared at, judged and publically humiliated for doing ordinary things. Does anyone speak up? Try to protect them?"

"Oh god, I don't have to imagine. Been there, live there. Most folk don't have the balls, or ovaries, to speak up. They'd rather live out some fantasy of brotherhood and peace, both blacks and whites. I swear we've got an Uncle Tom for every Jim Crow. When I was fifteen, Ma took us kids to the pool at Rouge Park. Like today, it was hotter than hell. We four kids, my baby brother and two boy cousins, were so hyped about getting out of the tenements and swimming in a real pool. We'd never even seen a pool close up. Ma bought us bathing suits from Woolworths and borrowed her brother's car. She told us to wear the suits under our clothes so we didn't have to change in the locker rooms. My guess is we had a buck's worth of gas and a couple bucks for drinks. We packed peanut butter and jelly sandwiches for lunch. Have you ever been to Rouge Park?"

"Once. It was very white."

"This was in the late 40's, after the war, lily white. The only black person besides us was the janitor. When we walked into the pool area, every head turned and people stopped talking. Total, absolute silence. Ma whispered, 'It's okay. Just behave yourselves and don't make a lotta noise. We got rights. Don't matter.' I sensed the danger but wanted Ma to be proud of me. I took my little brother's hand and walked to the shallow end. As soon as we stepped in the pool there was panic. The other mothers were screaming for their kids to get out of the pool. I heard the words 'niggers in the pool, get out, get out now!' Kids were climbing out, throwing themselves on the edge of the pool rather than using a ladder. One red-faced mother was shaking her fist at the lifeguard. I heard the sharp sound of a whistle, then the lifeguard lifted a bullhorn and yelled, 'Niggers out of the pool NOW! RIGHT NOW! No niggers in the pool!' My mother tried to talk to the lifeguard in his high chair. He tipped his bullhorn down, close to her ears, and shouted at the top of his lungs, 'Get you and your nigger kids away from the pool before I call the cops!'"

"Oh god, Loretta, sorry. What a sick, ugly world this can be. Here we are, going to the moon, and we treat each other like aliens. What'd your mom do?"

"Ma gathered us together and told us to stand tall, put our shoulders back, hold our heads up and walk slow. When we first got to the pool, the quiet scared the crap out of me. On our way out, the quiet felt cowardly. The black janitor, in his freshly pressed one-piece khaki uniform with shiny silver snaps and a name badge, tucked his head down and whispered, 'sorry' as he held the gate open. But Ma, in her faded green and white checked ruffled sundress and straw hat, stood tall, nodded her head and smiled as if she was showing off Christian Dior's couture on a New York runway. On the way home, we stopped for ice cream and Ma told us that we own our dignity, no one can take it away. That's why I keep Harriet Tubman, Sojourner Truth and Ma nearby. They remind me of my dignity."

"Which reminds me why I love you so much. You're lucky you had such a beautiful and wise mom. Speaking of dignity, and my lazy-ass self, did you hear back from Cooley about the scissor talks?"

"Yada, yada, yada. The principal was going to run our proposal by the school board before summer break. I didn't hear back and I was afraid to call. Me, afraid to call! Remember when you asked if I ever felt like I was under water and I said 'everyday?' Lately, it's more like an undertow. I got the impression this sorry ass principal thought cutting off someone's hair was a modern-day Tom Sawyer or Huckleberry Finn stunt. Rather than deal with the issue of racism, he's pretending the recent quiet means everything's okay. It's more of that same cowardly quiet, like my own cowardly quiet when I didn't call. Sorry, Maggie. Here you are, ready to have a baby, and I'm dragging you through my poor-pitiful-me swamp."

"Loretta, we've always had the most perverted and peculiar ways of dealing with our poor-pitiful-me swamps. For these few minutes I stopped thinking about pregnancy, labor pains, or the nearest toilet. I've been such a slouch since we moved here. I've let everything I care about go to seed. But not you; you've been doing the work. You've never been quiet when you needed to speak up. My guess is there's a reason, a sixth sense, for not calling. When I think of this tiny being taking her, or his, first breath on this wild, lush, and very broken planet we call home, I'm more determined to drag these swamps and keep the faith with you until we're done dragging and keeping. Don't let me drop out."

"Baby doll, what on earth are you talking about? You lost your marbles? No way in hell you're dropping out. We're in this together."

Maggie heard the three short rings and tried to ignore it, but their next-door neighbors shared the party line and the same ring echoed through the screens.

"Hello!"

"Bonjour, mon cheri Marguerite!"

"Ah, bonjour, Monsieur Jacques Ruivivar! How are you?"

"The question is how are you? Still with child?"

"Won't be long. This baby is head-down-ready for her trip to planet Earth. Will you be watching the moon landing?"

"Of course! This is very exciting. I hope they find moon people—moon food, moon music, moon language. Audacious to think we're the only life form in this infinite universe."

"Are you suggesting we earthlings are smug and self-centered to think everything in the solar system was designed for our viewing pleasure?"

"Quick study. So, my dear Maggie, you're about ready to have your first child and I'm jumping out of my skin with joy for you and Sam. Once you're home from the hospital and catch your breath, will you please call collect so I can hear the news from you?"

"Absolutely! I'll call as soon as I can."

"Thank you. And, before the year gets away from us, I'd like to queue up for a visit. I've put off some business in Detroit until you're ready for company. Don't panic. I'll stay at a hotel, but would love to meet the baby and catch up with you and Sam. More than that . . . well, we'll talk again when you call. Oops, almost forgot. Catherine wanted me to say hello. She's angling for a reason to join me in Detroit so she can meet the baby. Fair warning, she's an Olympic angler."

Before Maggie reached the phone to call Issie, there was a torrential cloudburst of wind and rain, the kind that turns umbrellas inside out and sends squirrels skittering to lower ground. Holding her rotunda up with both hands, Maggie did a mock race through the house, checking the kitchen, living room and bedroom windows to see if rain was coming through the screens. The two front bedroom windows, with sliding screens, were being pummeled. Using all her strength, Maggie pushed each window up a half inch and pulled in the screens. Then, hanging like a monkey from the top of each frame, Maggie forced them closed, banging her rotunda on the window ledges and leaving her moo-moo soaking wet.

After holding up her moo-moo and wringing it in the kitchen sink, Maggie picked up the phone. "Hey Iss, Jacques just called. Get this, he wants me to call him collect after the baby's born so he and Catherine can plan a trip to Detroit. Seriously, Catherine!"

"Why are you so out of breath? Are you in labor?"

"Closing windows. I can't walk to the bathroom without getting winded. Come on, Iss, tell me what you think."

"Oh, Maggie, I know what you're thinking and I'm not sure what to say. I'm kind of pissed he called when you're about to deliver."

"Well, what do think this means?"

"I have no idea what it means. But there's something I've held back that you deserve to know. Last year, during one of our kitchen talks, I limited you to three questions. What I didn't tell you was how jealous I used to be when 'Uncle Jacques' seemed to prefer you. I can't point to anything he ever said or did. It was more about his face and tone of voice. No doubt Jacques liked me, but Maggie, he adored you. At first I thought it was because you were younger. But my instinct, or major stretch of my imagination, made me wonder, then believe he was your father."

"You actually thought Jacques was my father? Was it just the way he talked to me or was it more? Anything to do with Catherine? Sam's positive she looks enough like the photos of Anna, if you make allowances for some plastic surgery and dental work. Oh god, I'm hyperventilating aren't I?"

"This is all so wacky, like some B-grade pocketbook mystery. I don't know. Keep in mind I was an eleven-year-old who believed in Camelot. I was jealous because Jacques acted like he loved you more. Smoke and mirrors. We were both raised on fairy tales, literally and figuratively, so I don't want you to jump to conclusions. But, you have a right to know, even if it comes from the memory of a screwed up, needy pre-adolescent girl. This might mean something, or it might mean nothing."

By her soft intake of breath, Issie knew Maggie was trying not to cry.

"Thanks, Iss. It's probably nothing."

"Or, my grown up baby girl, it's everything."

After Sam and Maggie devoured six White Castle hamburgers, two orders of fries, and two vanilla shakes, Sam unbuckled his belt and tipped back in his chair.

For the first time in more than a year, Sam felt a sense of power and calm. Maggie's updates on Loretta, Kenny and Stella weren't surprising, but it reminded him of his sidelined commitment to the civil rights movement and all the work in front of them. Sam had the sensation he was outside of his body, watching himself and Maggie at the table. The man he *saw* was no longer a boy. He was a husband, a provider, a civil rights worker and soon-to-be-father. When Maggie told him about the secrets Issie had kept, Sam felt Maggie's sorrow. He was struck by a new awareness that Maggie had lived far too many years with people who claimed to love her, but didn't trust her to know the truth. Sam didn't want to live a lie.

Not with Maggie. Clyde had given him the best advice he knew to give when he said 'tell no one.' Sam didn't want to put any one at risk, but Maggie had to know some things now—not everything, but some things.

"You're quiet. What do you think about Issie musing that Jacques was my father? Crazy or what?"

"I'm drawn to the 'or what.' Sorry she didn't tell you sooner, but get that she didn't want to up the ante on a family history that's already packed with intrigue. Are you pissed?"

"No, for some reason not at all. Might be my age, condition. Maybe motherhood!"

"Do you have any idea how much I love you right now?"

"All of me? The entire eighteen-wheeler load in a wet moo-moo?"

"Yep, all of you and this child who was wise enough to choose you as his mother. Mag, this morning I said I had something to tell you just before you got up to pee."

"That's right, you did. What's up?"

"Unfortunately, I'm going to ask you to take on more mystery. What little I know may frustrate you, but it's important because we have some decisions to make about what we do and who we talk to."

"Tervo, this sounds serious. I hope to hell my schizo hormones didn't scare you off."

"Your hormones might have been a factor, but what I'm about to say is so unreal, unformed, it borders on paranoia and psychosis. Sometimes I'm not sure. I'll tell you what I can and from here on, no more secrets. I need you by my side and I want to be by yours. I'm going to start with the *Reader's Digest* version, then you can ask questions.

First, I learned there's a definite connection between the mafioso at Sheer Juice and executives at Jingo Motors. During the auto show, I found Zito talking to Ben Kabul, Jingo's president, in a back hallway. Zito was with Carla, one of the revolving-door administrative assistants from Sheer Juice. I'm not sure I told you, but the admins were hired to take care of the execs at work and outside of work. Most were young, stacked, slutty-looking girls who wore too much makeup and skin-tight clothes. They didn't get their job based on secretarial skills. Carla was a blackjack dealer in Vegas. One of the recruiters said the admins had to pass the 'elbow test,' which meant if they stood in front of a wall, bent their elbows up and touched them to the wall, their tits would have to touch the wall. I know it's crude and sexist as hell, but I want you to understand the kind of assholes I'm dealing with."

"Assholes and imbeciles. Seriously, with guys like this running the world, no wonder things are so screwed up. Give me a break! Sorry, you were saying?"

"It's okay, Mag. In any event, because Sheer Juice made the introduction to Jingo, I knew they had some kind of relationship, but it's more incestuous than I thought. Without going into a lot of detail, Zito used to play head games with me. He started with chicken-shit things, like gibing me for being a *schoolboy*, saying 'that MBA don't mean shit from shinola.' No big deal, trash talk. Then, he starting messing with me about work schedules and work relationships—who to trust, who not to trust. About the same time, he began to lock me in the shop at night with the dirtiest jobs from the first shift. It was a little creepy, but I was close to graduating and too cowed to complain."

"Whoa! Wait a minute. He locked you in at night?"

"Mag, this is hard enough. Let me finish. One night I asked Zito if I could call him if I had a question. He said he'd break my kneecaps if I called his house when he was out with another broad. No doubt a macho brag about getting a little on the side, but the main message was to let me know he was part of the mob. What happened next requires a lot more time and Clyde's take because it's complicated and more elusive. What's important is both Clyde and I have information that Zito and the mob have started to play with LSD, gas lighting and mind altering to feed the underworld. According to Clyde's sources, this sometimes involves the CIA and FBI."

"Sam, I know you said to let you finish but this is unbelievably farfetched. Are you fucking kidding me? We're talking about the mob, CIA and FBI in the same breath we're talking about our lives? What on earth would bring us to the same place, much less the same table?"

"The best we can figure out is our work in civil rights could be the catalyst or Jingo Motors or Sheer Juice, or my love, it could be related to your missing parents or Jacques. I can only imagine how disjointed this sounds, but the fact is Clyde and I have been trying to put together a scattered one-thousand-piece, monochromatic puzzle. We don't know who's involved and whose not involved. The bottom line is that Jingo or the mob or both are trying to mess with me to keep me off balance and loyal to whatever it is they want me to be loyal to. That's about it. We pretty much have no idea what's going on. Your turn."

"Sam, I don't know where to begin. It sounds insane, freaky and dangerous. What I hear is *they*, whoever *they* are, want to make sure you're on their team. And, right now, you and Clyde have no idea what team they're talking about, who's on the team, what game they're playing or where the end zone is."

"That's the gist of it. I know it makes no sense. What's worse, I don't know when I'm going to be blindsided again. The last thing I want is for you to think I'm pulling away from you or the life we're making. I'm telling you because I don't want to keep secrets from you. You've lived with enough secrets. I need you on my side. Up to now, I've kept things between Clyde and me because I didn't want to freak you out. So, your mood swings may have kept me from telling you. Sorry, babe, to lay this heavy load on you right before labor. But, after Jacques' call, I want to make sure we're safe. I don't know how Jacques fits in, but he may be a link. Clyde thinks the mob or

CIA might be tracking your parents or information they had. I don't want any of us to say or do anything that tips the scale in the wrong direction. Not that I know the *right* direction. There may not even be a direction."

"Samuel Tervo, I love you more than life itself. I'd take a bullet for you. Do you trust Clyde?"

"I do. Is there any reason I shouldn't?"

"None. I would trust him with my life. You couldn't pick a better man for your foxhole. If I'm going to help you fight this battle, I need more guidance. Do I keep my conversation with Jacques casual, banal? Is there a way to measure what I say to keep us in a neutral zone?"

"My beautiful, wise wife. You've got it. We need to find our neutral zone. I have no idea what it looks like, or where it is, but it's a start. I'll let Clyde know we talked, and as soon as you're ready, the three of us will get together. We'll talk and keep talking. I think it's the safest way to move ahead. Maggie, you can't tell a soul. Not Issie, not Loretta, not Jo, not Jacques, not anyone. If you can't do that, you have to tell me now."

"Sam, love of my life, my devotion is to us—you, me and our child. I spent my life keeping secrets. I'm good at it."

"One more thing. Ben called me to his office on Friday and said he thought it would be a good idea for us to move to Livonia. I may have said something to Maxine or Skip in passing, but I don't remember telling anyone we decided on Livonia. In any event, Ben told me Jingo owns a small house on a one-acre lot on Six Mile. He gave me the address and I drove by Friday on my way home. Three mature willows, two large elms and a few lilac bushes surround the house. A white cape cod with green shutters, it's small, but there's an acre to build on. No cookie-cutter subdivision. Walking distance to the elementary school, a country block from a restaurant and riding stable, and in the opposite direction, a country block to a grocery, hardware store, hamburger joint and gas station. Ben said

Jingo would cover the mortgage. We can make mortgage payments through payroll deductions. You feel like a drive?"

Maggie looked hard at Sam. "Excuse me. This is Sunday and you didn't say word one about this house until now?"

"I know. I wanted to tell you about the mystery first, but I kept getting signals you were going into labor. Although I thought I knew how you'd react, I didn't want to freak you out. Today, it struck me that we could be waiting another week or more, and then you told me about Jacques' call. His call pushed me over the edge and I found the courage to begin a conversation about fears that haunted me for more than a year. Maggie, I don't want these fears to tear apart our marriage. Forgive me?"

Maggie loved Sam more than she'd ever loved anyone. He was far from perfect. Sometimes he skirted the truth. Even today. But, she heard a different tone. Today, Sam seemed to be reaching for a higher rung, more willing to expose his insecurities and vulnerabilities. This would take time. She, Sam, the baby—her family—deserved her best effort.

Sam wasn't aware he was tapping his fingers on the table until Maggie lifted his left hand with her right and stretched her open hand against his. She then weaved their fingers together to make a joint fist and looked at Sam. "I forgive you. I know it took courage to tell me and I'm not afraid. For some reason, I'm calm. And, as much as I'd love to see the house, I'll take a rain check. If Jingo's hooked to the mob, this might be a lair we avoid or use to our advantage. We need time to decide. Right now, I want to stay close to a toilet and catch Walter Cronkite's evening report. The moon! Sam, we're going to the moon!"

23

Moonlight

And the end of all our exploring will be to arrive where we started and know the place for the first time.

—T. S. Eliot

JULY 20, 1969 POST MERIDIEM—A fine breeze wound its way through the living room and kitchen screens, cooling itself as the Earth rotated on its axis toward darkness. For years, Maggie wondered why people insisted on talking about the sunrise and sunset, as if the sun moved. Poets were the worst offenders. Why was it so hard to understand the moon orbits our planet, waxing and waning, as the Earth spins on its twenty-four-hour axis during a twelve-month orbit around the sun? But the sun, the unmoving sun, only *appears* to rise in the east and set in the west. The truth is, we turn our back on the sun every day.

Earlier, during her now daily rocking-chair meditation in the nursery, Maggie caught the outline of the waxing crescent moon in the cloudy sky. Nearly invisible, Maggie imagined it peeking through the curtains, watching for the arrival of alien visitors. To say she was *jazzed* by the moon landing would be a gross understatement. Maggie felt as if she was taking flight.

After the rain, the world was delirious with sound. Field Crickets were reaching a fevered pitch, as Red-Winged Locusts and Meadow Katydids lusted in the warm, wet twilight, crying out in ecstasy, to once again, trigger the crickets in an orgy of noise. Birds of every feather and color called one another home—chasing one last insect, sipping nectar from wilted flowers on summer-weary vines, splashing in new puddles. Dogs barked at shadows and cats climbed screens to get a closer look. There was excitement in the air, as if something big was about to happen.

Yet, there was no sign of human life—no mowers, no walkers, no bikers, no drivers, no children playing kick-the-can, no neighbors shooting the breeze on porches. To Maggie, the contrast was surreal and eerie, as if an air-raid siren had sent humans tumbling for cover in bomb shelters while the rest of the world celebrated. No air raid, television sets were drawing people inside, feeding the fears of doomsday sayers who predicted humans would become slaves to technology.

Taking a just-in-case shower after dinner, Maggie did the best she could to reach the black stubble on the backs of her legs, before she thought *screw it!* With her hair wrapped in a towel, her body barely wrapped by Sam's old blue plaid cotton robe, Maggie sat down on the couch and tried to picture the millions of families across the world gathering around their flickering screens to watch a man walk on the moon.

"Hey, Sam, forgot to tell you, Maija called to see if I was in labor. She said if you get tired of grilled cheese while I'm in the hospital to let her know and she'll fix dinner."

"Tire of grilled cheese? Surely you jest! But, might be a good time to check on her. Farmington's a close drive and I, or we, could get to the hospital in time for evening visiting hours. You feel anything?"

"Just twinges, no labor pains. I'm going to turn on Cronkite. You about ready?"

"Go ahead. I'll get these dishes done. You need water, something to drink?"

"No way. My floodgates are on red alert."

After three short rings, Sam picked up the phone.

"Hello!"

"Hi daddy-to-be! How's Maggie?"

"Hey, Aunt Jo. Maggie's in the living room waiting for her water to break or see a man walk on the moon, whichever comes first." Sam looked into the living room, pointed to the phone and lifted his shoulders in a pantomime to Maggie. Maggie shook her head *no*.

As if she could see through the phone, Aunt Jo said, "I'm not going to ask you to put Maggie on. I'm sure she's tired of everyone calling to see if she's in labor. If you've got a minute, I want to pass something along."

"Sure. What's up?"

"I got a call from Jacques today. I can't remember the last time we talked, a decade or more. He told me he talked to Maggie. Did she say anything?"

"She did. Maggie said he called to see if she'd delivered and wanted to set up a time to visit once she got on her feet. That's about it."

"Okay. He basically said the same thing to me, about seeing the two of you and the baby. He also said he might bring Catherine with him. I think you met her in Toronto."

"We did. She tracked down Jacques and set up the lunch."

"Sam I've tried to stay out of this, and not sure I should say anything now, but there are things about Jacques and Maggie's parents she and Issie don't know. I'm not going to tell you what that is. Not now. Certainly not before the baby's born. So, I hope you'll keep this between us. Right now, I feel a responsibility to warn you about Jacques. He's very charming, but there's a dark side. This might sound like I've been nipping at the cooking sherry, but I can't help how it sounds. Please trust me here."

Sam turned his back to the living room and stretched the phone cord as far away from Maggie as he could before he said, "Jo, this is important. Some things have been happening to me that I'm not ready to talk about. Fact is I'm not sure I should even ask this, but my question is simple. Can I trust Clyde?"

There was a long silence. Sam said, "Jo, you there?"

"I'm here. Oh, Sam, it sounds like you're already in the soup."

"What soup?"

"Too risky to talk about over the phone. I've known Clyde since the day Angelo hired him. He's a good man. Listen to him. Trust him when your gut tells you to. Don't trust him if your gut tightens up."

"That's it? You can't say more?"

"That's it for Clyde and maybe everyone else in your life right now. Time to find your core and let it guide you. Listen carefully, pay attention and make decisions that make sense for you and Maggie. That's all I can say right now."

"What's at stake?"

"Besides sanity and well-being?"

"What about our behind the scenes push for civil rights? Does that put us at risk?"

"Maybe, I don't know. But, I think it's important, crucial, to keep your core. No matter what, keep your core, stick to what matters most to you."

"When can we talk?"

"You and Maggie might be fine. You may never have to deal with this craziness again. If that's the case, it's better you don't know more. I got lucky by staying under the radar. I can't impress how important it is for you to keep this from Maggie right now. I know it'll be hard, but not now. Please not now."

"I trust that. I'll call when the baby's born. Call me if you want to talk."

"Take care Sam, give Maggie my love."

Sam forced a lilt in his voice and said, "Sure, Aunt Jo!" After shaking himself from head to toe, Sam practiced a smile before he walked back to the handset and hung up the phone.

Walter Cronkite's formidable voice filled the living room. "Apollo 11. Everything going well for a moon landing . . . three hours, twenty-one minutes and fourteen seconds from now."

When Sam looked at his watch, it was 7:35 p.m., the same moment Maggie cried, "Oh god, my water just broke!" Maggie ripped Sam's robe off and began wiping the sofa.

Taking his robe from Maggie, Sam said, "Come on, babe," as he walked her to the bathroom. He then closed all the windows in the house, carried her suitcase to the back door, and called the hospital to let them know they were on their way.

Maggie ran a comb through her still damp, tangled hair, pulled it in a ponytail and put on some Hot Pink lipstick. Fighting her way into her now-tight gray dotted-Swiss maternity dress, Maggie didn't bother looking for her white flats. She kept her white beaded moccasins on, took a deep breath and whispered, "Hey, little one. It's time. We're heading to the hospital right now and there will be lots of bright lights and people in white. Don't be afraid. Sam and I will be there to greet you, hold you, take care of you always."

As she headed to the side door, Maggie said, "Sam, should I call the hospital to let them know we're on our way?"

"Done. You ready to boogie shoo? I'm supposed to avoid fainting and remind you to breathe. Much more exciting than a moon landing! You okay?"

Maggie placed her hand on her sinking mezzanine and smiled. "We're fine."

When Sam pulled up to the emergency room, he helped Maggie out of the car and walked her inside. No one was at the reception desk, but they heard Walter Cronkite's voice coming from a back room. Maggie sat down as Sam followed Cronkite's voice.

In the room, two nurses and a doctor were watching the moon shot on a small black and white portable television set.

Sam knocked on the door jam and said, "Hello, I'm here with my wife. Her water broke and she's waiting up front."

One of the nurses moved past Sam and headed to the front of the ER saying, "You shouldn't have left her alone. Why didn't you ring the bell?"

"Sorry. I didn't see a bell, but I could hear the TV."

The nurse gave Sam a *look* a lot like Maggie's *look*, forcing the question of whether *the look* has been plagiarized over the years or whether it's a natural feminine trait.

With one point of the nurse's index finger, Sam sat down to fill out the paperwork as Maggie was whisked into a wheel chair and carted to some unknown floor by a porter.

By the time Sam reached the maternity section on the third floor, Maggie was already set up in the delivery room. No husbands allowed. Sam asked a nurse if he could at least give Maggie a kiss before they began delivery. She curled her index finger and he followed her to the delivery room. It was packed. Three nurses and two doctors were standing in front of a nineteen-inch black and white television set watching Cronkite. Maggie was tipped up on the delivery table so she could see.

"Hey, Mag, what's up?"

"My cervix is only four centimeters and it needs to be ten before they deliver. So, I was given the choice to watch Cronkite or go home and come back."

"Why's the TV in the delivery room?"

"Sam, we're heading to the moon. This is a once in a lifetime chance to see the Swiss-cheese moon. We can't miss it. The moon I mean. Where was I?"

One of the nurses turned around and nodded to Sam, then turned back to the TV.

"Mag, you sound a little dreamy and you're slurring your words. Did they give you something for pain? You okay?"

"Fine, Papa Tervo. They gave me a little Twilight Sleep. Like moonlight, moon walking, flying through space. You okay?"

"I'm fine, Maggie. As long as you're fine, I'm fine. Baby sleeping?"

Maggie touched her rotunda, smiled, closed her eyes and was off in dreamland.

Before Sam turned to watch Cronkite, he noticed the lamb-skin-lined leather wrist and ankle restraints on the delivery table and the chill air in the room. There was so much he didn't know about childbirth. Would Maggie be conscious, restrained, exposed to non-medical TV watchers? Sam hoped the moon landing offered enough cover to let him watch the delivery. Scary as it was to be in the delivery room, Sam knew it would be scarier on the other side of the door. According to a black-handed white clock on a mint-green wall, it was 9:14 p.m., one hour and forty-two minutes before landing on the moon, NASA's *Sea of Tranquility*. The Apollo 11 crew and NASA had taken over the airwaves and it was hard to hear. Words crackled 240,000 miles from Earth, but the tension and excitement thrilled the listeners. The fuzzy photos being sent from the spacecraft to NASA told a story and transported TV goers to another world, another way of seeing this brilliant universe.

Walter Cronkite broke in and Sam heard him say something like 'a no go means abort the landing,' as Maggie cried, "Oh god, help me. I can't do this! No!" The nurse checked Maggie's pulse and the baby's heartbeat while keeping an eye on the TV. Dr. Stanley, Maggie's doctor, was away on vacation. Another doctor would cover his patients—a short, bushy-browed doctor. Sam didn't catch his name. The doc was a Southern European, maybe Italian, who placed a shoehorn shaped instrument in Maggie's vagina. The cold, hard steel of the instrument cut through Sam's solar plexus, but he was afraid to speak, afraid they'd ask him to leave. The doc said, "nine" and pointed to the restraints.

The nurse checked the slant of the bed and lowered it some, "Maggie, I want you to take deep breaths. Breathe in, breathe out. That's it. You're fine. Keep it up. Good girl. Another deep breath." The nurse repeated these demands and assurances as she slipped the leather shackles on Maggie's wrists and ankles and said, "The lambskin will keep you warm." Sam bit his bottom lip, pretended to watch TV and tried not to faint.

Maggie began kicking her legs against the restraints so hard the delivery table started to walk toward the TV. The doctor ordered the nurse to "up the dose a little and slow things down," then winked at Sam. *What the hell*, Sam thought, *does this space cadet think I'm on his team? That I'm fucking more interested in watching the moon landing than seeing my baby born?*

"Get me out of this fucking bed. NOW!" Maggie yelled, "the baby's coming!"

Dr. Space Cadet walked backwards to Maggie, put his hand on her thigh while keeping an eye on the TV, and said, "Mrs. Tervo, you have another centimeter to go. The baby is *not* coming. It's too soon. Do not push. Nurse is going to hold your hand and help you through the next contraction. You are not going to push until I tell you. Do you understand?"

The contraction must have passed because Maggie closed her eyes and fell asleep. The doc winked at him again and Sam thought *if he winks one more time I'm going to strangle him.*

Sam heard Cronkite saying, "About six minutes to go. Alarms are going off. At 27,000 feet now and more alarms. Eagle's computer is still sounding alarms." Sam looked up as the TV camera began to focus on the engineers at NASA.

— Eagle we've got you now, it's looking good. Over
— Rog GTC go
— Roger copy
— Eagle Houston—everything looking good here. Over
— Rog

Maggie tried to lift her head and said, "Who's Rog? Where is Rog?"

— Okay Control, let me know when he starts his yaw here

"Fuck this. The yaw has fucking started. The baby's coming."

Maggie's nurse walked backward to the bed and took Maggie's hand. "Listen to me, Mrs. Tervo, the pain might get a little stronger. I'm going to hold your hand. You aren't ready to deliver the baby, and I want you to breathe with me through this pain. Do not push. Do you hear me, do not push."

— Stand by. Looking good to us. You're still looking good at 3—coming up to 3 minutes
— We're going flight
— Okay. RETRO
— Go

"I can push?"

"No, Mrs. Tervo, don't push. Not now. I'll tell you when."

— It's going to stop and Eagle Houston we've got data drop-
out. You're still looking good
— Rog
— Standby
— That's affirmative
— Looks like it's converging

"The baby is converging? Is it time. Oh god, I can't take this
pain. It's too much!"

— Throttle down

"Now, I can push down now?"
"NO. DON'T PUSH NOW. Not until I tell you. Breathe.
Come'on. Let's breathe."

— Looks good now
— Ah, throttle down
— Throttle down on time

"Now? Push down now? PLEASE I have to push."
"NO. DON'T PUSH NOW. Not until I tell you. Breathe.
Come'on. Let's breathe."
"Fuck you. You breathe. I'm having this baby!"

— Roger
— Okay, looks like it's holding
— Yes, it looks beautiful

"Now? Push down now? PLEASE I have to push."

— Hang tight six and one-half minutes
— Going to go for the landing
— Go, go, go
— You're go

"I can push now?"

"NO, Mrs. Tervo. DO NOT PUSH."

— Altitude up AGS, looks good
— I think we better be quiet

"Oh god, the pain is gone. I'm going to sleep for a minute."

— Rog
— Rog
— Stay
— Thirty seconds
— Engine stopped, command override off Houston Tranquility

"The baby's coming! Oh god. I'm breaking in two. I have to push NOW!"

The nurse started to check Maggie's cervix to see if it had hit ten centimeters. "The baby's crowning. Doctor, the baby's crowning. We have to move, move, move!"

"Ready, set. Let's get this baby out," said the doc.

— Roger Tranquility. We copy you on the ground. You've got a group of guys about to turn blue! We're breathing again. Thanks a lot

Sam thought he never loved anyone as much as he loved this bushy-browed doctor. He reminded himself not to faint and grabbed Maggie's restrained hand and held tight.

— Very smooth touch down (Alarms still ringing!)
— Eagle is at Tranquility. Over
— Yes I heard the whole thing
— Good show
— Fantastic

The doctor caught and then hung the baby upside down and spanked it to draw his or her first breath. Sam couldn't tell yet. The cry was strong and belligerent. Sam thought he might faint until he looked at Maggie and saw the peacefulness and pride of a lioness. They squeezed each other's hands and communicated without words while the nurse cleaned the baby and wrapped her in a pink blanket.

"Mr. Tervo, congratulations, you have a beautiful baby girl. The doctor said it's okay for you to hold her and stay until the astronauts walk on the moon. Then, your wife and baby will need to rest."

Tekla's eyes were open and Sam got the sense she knew who he was. He kissed her cheek and felt love enter every cell of his body. The nurse removed Maggie's wrist restraints and she opened her arms to hold the baby.

"I'm sorry, Mrs. Tervo, but not now. You're under an anesthetic and it wouldn't be safe for you to hold her," said the nurse.

Sam held Tekla in his arms and rested her on the top of Maggie's chest so she could nuzzle Tekla's tiny, red, wrinkled neck, and touch and reassure her while everyone else's attention was fixed on the TV.

— See you coming down the ladder now
— Armstrong at the foot of the ladder. ". . . surface very fine grain, like a powder"

Cronkite held excitement in his voice, "There's a foot coming down on the moon—Armstrong is on the moon—Neil Armstrong a thirty-eight-year-old American standing on the surface of the moon."

— Armstrong stepping off the ladder. "One small step for man, one giant leap for mankind."

Cronkite repeated Armstrong's statement and Maggie heard someone say, "Ain't that something?"

Neil Armstrong and Buzz Aldrin, dressed in Jacques Cousteau adventure suits, placed a plaque on the moon. Cronkite read:

HERE MEN FROM THE PLANET EARTH
FIRST SET FOOT UPON THE MOON

JULY 1969, A.D. WE CAME IN PEACE FOR ALL MANKIND.

NEIL ARMSTRONG
MICHAEL COLLINS
BUZZ ALDRIN

Maggie smiled at the thought of men from outer space finding the plaque. Would they speak English? Would July or A.D. mean anything to them? What about the names—is that an Earth thing, unknown on other planets?

After two astronauts attempted to secure a framed U.S. Flag on the dusty surface of the windless moon, the camera shifted to the White House where President Nixon was ready with a prepared statement. Nixon *spoke* as if the entire world was listening—like some twentieth century Sermon on the Mount, he said, "The heavens have become a part of man's world."

Maggie looked up and said, "Screw you, Nixon, you sorry son-of-a-bitch. This is not a man's world!"

Dr. Space Cadet smiled at Sam and said, "Don't worry, it's the medication talking. It removes all inhibitions. She'll be back to normal in no time."

Sam thought if he hadn't been holding the baby, and if he wasn't concerned about Maggie's care for the next three days, he'd tell this dickhead Maggie was just getting started. Sam took it all in. He and Maggie holding Tekla while the nurse removed the ankle restraints. The porter lined up a gurney next to the delivery table to transfer Maggie to her room. In the corner, a small plastic bassinet was fitted with a pink card reading Tervo. Tekla would sleep in a strange bed, under bright lights, in an air-conditioned room. There was something so god-awful wrong with this plan that Sam considered putting Tekla in Maggie's arms on the gurney, then making their escape. But Maggie, under the influence of narcotics, and the imagined headlines in the paper, weakened his resolve.

Cronkite said, "Seems like a dream and it is a dream come true," before his usual closing, "and that's the way it is."

When Sam walked out of the hospital, he looked up at the moon and felt the beam like some kind of baptismal glow. After seeing the surface of the moon in communion with human beings, the godliness of the cosmos seemed more real. Sam resisted an impulse to drop to his knees, or lie on his back and bathe in moonshine, because he didn't want someone rushing out with a gurney thinking he was having a heart attack, or god forbid, fainting.

A slip of paper under the driver's side windshield wiper caught his eye. He pulled it off, started his car and turned on the interior lights. The paper was from a steno tablet. The note written in pencil:

> *I'm the last person you want to hear from. I get it. You must think I'm a total slut and crazy as a loon. You can't trust me. I get it. How do I know your car was here? Easy. Your side porch light was on and it's always off at 10. You are a good man. I will help when I can. You are being watched. Bore them to death but stop being so predictable. C.*

Sam tipped his head against the top of his steering wheel, amazed at how quickly his perspective moved from heaven to hell. Aunt Jo's plea for him to *keep his core* would become his battle cry. Whatever the threat, he gets to choose his thoughts, ideas and attitudes. Thanks to Carla, he'd become less predictable and more aware.

Before he turned off the overhead light, Sam noticed a small pink envelope on the passenger seat. He lifted it and recognized

Maggie's handwriting in ink on the front. *For Papa Sam.* Inside, Maggie wrote:

An Ode to Baby Tervo

*No quantum ripple signals a minute shift in awareness,
not this time. This time the cosmos collided and expanded
in shouts and waves. You showed up with new words to be
written, poems to be read, adventures to be salvaged from
memories so ancient we can only trace the outlines left
inside pyramid walls before they turn to sand. And, once
again, 'know this place for the first time.'*
—*Maggie Soulier Tervo, with thanks to T.S. Eliot*

On his drive home, Sam took Six Mile Road and stopped at the house, or lair, Ben wanted to sell them. Three willow trees were cast in moonlight.

END OF BOOK ONE

Acknowledgments

Heartfelt thanks to my *Unpaid but Illustrious Editorial Staff*, Sandra Whitener, Kirsten McLean, and Frank Cooley, who hung in there through multiple drafts for the past two and one-half years. Grateful appreciation to friends, colleagues and muses, including beta readers from the Vino Libra Book Club, who provided invaluable feedback. Many thanks to my ex-Detroiter peeps who generously shared their stories. Among them, Shirley Hosmer who inspired Maggie's adventure in Chapter One. Like Maggie, Shirley worked at a Detroit pizzeria and studied at Wayne State. A natural storyteller, Shirley's uncommon experiences brought life to the pulse of a city under siege.

A special shout out to Judith Helburn and Dianne Wesselhoft who held my hand, read, edited and gently prodded me to see my work in new ways. Cheers to Don Knight for his historical memory/ knowledge of Detroit sports and the *Hail Mary* editorial catches at the end zone. A rousing hallelujah to Randy Smith, *Mississippi*, who shared his genius of dialogue and cadence. And, *merci beaucoup*, dear poète Marcelle Kasprowicz, for editing my awkward French.

Once again, I had the remarkable good fortune to work with Danielle Hartman Acee, copy/content editing, social media consulting and publicity; and with Kenneth Benson for interior and cover design and printing/technology support. Wicked in their expertise, both are strong enough to stand up to me when I'm wrong-headed.

Like all stories, this one could not have been written without the love and coaching of friends and mentors who taught me about grace, acceptance, equality, oneness and otherness. Black, white, multi-racial friends and relatives, who had the audacity to speak their truth. Without doubt, each of them breathed life into my characters and helped me find my voice.

Then there's this man behind the scenes. The guy I live with. Loren. On-call editor, hugger, dog walker, cat groomer, hunter-gatherer, poet, psychotherapist, humorist, looks past the third-day-pajamas-and-crumbs-to-tell-me-I'm-beautiful kind of guy. Can't imagine life without him. My husband. Love of my life.

The Author

A native Michigander, Kathleen Hall co-authored the award-winning non-fiction *The Otherness Factor*. A writer, poet, lawyer, mediator, and workplace investigator, Kathleen's lifelong activism has been devoted to championing equal rights and promoting the power of diversity. She lives in Austin, Texas with her husband Loren, Emma Dog, Ms. Ming Cat and Sasha Cat. *If the Moon Had Willow Trees* is Kathleen's first novel.

The Preview

Turn the page for a preview of Book Two of this
exciting new series by

KATHLEEN HALL

featuring Maggie, Sam, Loretta, Stella

"What the hell Maggie? Really? You've got the chance to move to the burbs and see what the other side is all about. It's not like you have to hang there forever. Sam said you guys could afford a second set of wheels. I don't get it," said Stella.

"I'll move, just not now."

"Why not now? What's the hold up?" asked Loretta.

"Sanity, well-being, happiness."

Loretta threw her arms out and looked around before she said, "Girl, have you lost your mind? This train-wreck of a house is ready to collapse when the next eighteen-wheeler trundles down Grand River. I don't get the sanity, well-being or happiness angle."

"SistaHood, this is home. We rent it, but it's *our* home. All my friends are here. I know my neighbors; Buddy at the lunch counter at Cunningham's is like family." Maggie looked at Loretta then Stella. They weren't buying it. Maggie shook her hands like silent castanets to break the spell. With a raised and deliberate stage voice she said, "Okay, I get it. The house is decaying and the hood's about to explode in gang warfare, but this is where I feel safe. The burbs are like the other side of the friggin' moon. Another planet. They might as well speak a foreign language. I don't understand people who want to live in a place where everyone looks alike, talks alike, dresses alike, acts alike. It's death-by-sameness. Did I miss anything? What's so funny?"

Both Stella and Loretta were slapping their knees and cracking up.

Loretta said, "Oh my god, Maggie. You're one crazy, mixed-up white chick. Every black sister I know is looking through that invisible barb-wired fence at the city limits and thinking they *want* to be Donna Reed. But you, you've got your nose turned up, like this sorry ass little house is in high cotton. You are out of your mind!"

"Maybe. I don't know why you want to hog-tie me and throw me in the back of a moving van. If I had the will or energy to move to Livonia I would. I just don't. I'll spend time there to pick up the vibes. Shop at their crafty little malls; go to their barebones, make-believe library; play putt-putt; study dress styles, idioms and knock-knock jokes. How about that? When Tekla's ready for school, we'll move. When I have more time. As it is, I'm lucky to take a bath or wash a load of clothes. I confess to being a mess. But I can't move. Not now."

Loretta looked at Stella and nodded her head. Stella said, "Maggie, we're here for you. No one's going to put pressure on you to move until you're ready. We'll plan our coup d'état after I rock Tekla to sleep. That should give you enough time to reset the clock."

Which sent Loretta into her noiseless, bending at the waist laughter, and bombshell tears to Maggie's eyes. "Holy crap, Loretta, its not that funny."

"Hey, baby doll, what's going on? No one's gonna force you to move. You know that. The last thing we want is to make you sad. Stella was just jiving you."

No way was Maggie going to bring up Jingo's offer to sell them a house on Six Mile Road in Livonia. This was the major reason she was dragging her feet. A few days before Tekla was born, Ben Kabul, President of Jingo, tried to convince Sam that he and Maggie should buy this company-owned house from Jingo and cover the mortgage through payroll deductions. Sam had no idea how Jingo knew about their plan to move to Livonia, or how Jingo was involved in *The Puzzle*. An absurd, but somehow soothing pseudonym to describe the dread, demons and degradation of unseen, unknown, unimaginable forces aimed at Sam. Maggie played with the alliteration for a few minutes before she shook her head. *For crap sakes, this isn't material for a new poem.* Bottom line, she, Sam and Clyde needed time to decide if Jingo's house was a lair to avoid or a key to use to their advantage. Maggie thought time was on their side. *Teaching could wait. Civil rights could wait. The house in Livonia could wait. Or could it? Who warned us to keep enemies close? Machiavelli?*

Maggie heard Sam come in the side door. By now, Maggie knew Sam's routine. Careful not to wake Tekla, he left his penny loafers in the kitchen, padded across the cracked kitchen linoleum, creaked across the hardwood floors in the living room and hall. From their bed, Maggie could see Sam's shadow cast across the short hallway. She watched as his shadow leaned into Tekla's door to listen to her breathe, then disappeared in her room. Maggie pictured Sam's head resting on the crib rail, watching her sleep.

Almost three months had passed since they'd made love. Her ob/gyn had given her an *all clear* after her six-week check up, but Maggie's libido took a dive when Sam told her about his encounters with the dark side. According to Sam, the first time was the night before their wedding, almost two years ago. Sam said he was seduced at work by Carla, an administrative assistant. In his telling, Carla locked the conference room door and stripped off his pants before baring her gigantic knockers and pulling him down to the floor. After that, he lost all memory. Then, a year ago at the Auto Show, Sam described a sex scene in the hotel ballroom. A bunch of men in suits surrounded a half-naked, red-haired Cuban model, who was stretched across three bar stools. Sam said he didn't know if was real or drug induced, but he remembered feeling agitated, excited and caught up in the action. Images Maggie clung to; edited and re-edited. Like the truth and deceit of fiction finding its rhythm.

But today, after talking trash with Loretta and Stella, she felt invigorated—strong, healthy, human and sexy. Clean hair, shaved legs, a red satin slip, Maggie nixed wearing her long string of Gatsby-era pearls that drove Sam over the moon. Maggie was no saint when it came to raw sex, but tonight she wanted something different. Something she'd never experienced. Tonight, she found herself both thrilled and confused by a sense of *wellbeing*, a new kind of ecstasy. For reasons she couldn't fathom, the quiet tableau of infant, man, and woman excited her beyond any foreplay she'd ever known. Maggie waited for the shadow to move. In truth, she could barely contain the erotic anticipation of hearing Sam walk the few steps down the hall and fill the door. Lying still, Maggie watched as Sam undressed and slid into bed as if he were moving in slow motion. By the time he placed his hand on her hips, Maggie was somewhere else. A place where she watched herself arc her back, shudder and cry, "holy mother of god." Sam sat up and looked at Maggie as if she'd caught him in bed with another woman. Maggie smiled and whispered, "Do you by any chance live here?"

Sam started with her lips then moved down. Through muffled laugher he said, "You bet your beautiful ass I do." Then, with deliberate slowness, they began to move each other in the timeless dance of bamboo flutes, mandolins and tambourines.